harmony

harmony

a novel

CAROLYN PARKHURST

Pamela Dorman Books
VIKING

VIKING

An imprint of Penguin Random House LLC
375 Hudson Street
New York, New York 10014
penguin.com

A Pamela Dorman Book / Viking

LIBRARY OF CONGRESS CATALOGING-IN-PUBLICATION DATA

Names: Parkhurst, Carolyn, 1971- author.
Title: Harmony / Carolyn Parkhurst.
Description: New York : Pamela Dorman Books/Viking, [2016]
Identifiers: LCCN 2016017667 (print) | LCCN 2016024248 (ebook) |
ISBN 9780399562600 (hardcover) | ISBN 9780399562624 (ebook)
Subjects: LCSH: Families—Fiction. | Domestic fiction. |
Psychological fiction. | BISAC: FICTION / Family Life. |
FICTION / Psychological. | FICTION / Literary.
Classification: LCC PS3616.A754 H37 2016 (print) |
LCC PS3616.A754 (ebook) | DDC 813/.6—dc23
LC record available at https://lccn.loc.gov/2016017667

Printed in the United States of America
1   3   5   7   9   10   8   6   4   2

Set in Sabon LT Pro
Designed by Cassandra Garruzzo

To my grandmother Claire T. Carney, the strongest woman I know.

harmony

prologue

In another world, you make it work. In another world, you never even hear the name "Scott Bean." Or you do, and you maybe even subscribe to his newsletter, but on the night that he comes to speak at a library not far from your house, Iris is sent home from school with a stomach bug, or Josh is out of town and you don't want to hire a sitter. You figure you'll catch him next time. Later, when you hear his name on the news and it sounds familiar, you shake your head and think, "What a wacko." It doesn't even occur to you to say, "That could have been me." Because you know yourself, and it goes without saying. You would never get mixed up in something like that. End of story.

chapter 1

Iris

June 3, 2012: New Hampshire

The camp is in New Hampshire. We've been driving for two days now—well, not literally, because we stopped at a hotel overnight and we've taken breaks to eat and go to the bathroom, but you know what I mean. We've been driving for two days, *approximately*, and I can't decide if I want to be there already or not.

Tilly and I are both sitting in the middle row—she's behind our dad, and I'm behind our mom—because the way-back is all full of our bags and suitcases and everything. It looks like a lot, but it really isn't. Not for moving someplace completely new. For a while last week, Tilly got really obsessed with the idea that we could rent a U-Haul, and she was even looking up prices and showing my parents all of these websites and Yelp reviews and stuff, but she couldn't get them to say yes. They kept saying the whole point is to simplify, to figure out the bare minimum we need to live. I don't think that *is* the whole point, though, because we could have done that and stayed in DC.

Tilly was mad at me earlier this afternoon, but she's over it now. One good thing about her is that even though she gets mad pretty often, it doesn't last long. Okay, so: for practically the whole day,

she's been bugging my parents about stopping to see the place where
the Old Man of the Mountain used to be. Yes, *used to be*. Tilly has
this whole weird thing about big statues—or "big people," actually,
is what she calls them, because they don't have to be statues, and in
fact, this is an example of one that wasn't. The Old Man of the
Mountain was this piece of rock that used to be there on the side of
the mountain, jutting out, and it kind of looked like an old guy's
face. Tilly's shown me pictures of it, and it's on the New Hampshire
state quarter; it's cool, but not *that* cool. And then one night, it
fell off the mountain—it just collapsed and broke, and the pieces
rolled down onto the road below. It happened back in 2003, on
May 3, and I know the date because it was Tilly's fourth birthday.
Not that she would have known about it at the time, but she acts
like it's some big mystical thing instead of sort of an interesting
coincidence.

So now, nine years later, here we are in New Hampshire. And
the mountain is still there, but that's all it is: a mountain. No face on
it, no big person. But Tilly wanted to go look at it, and after a million hours of begging, my mom and dad finally agreed.

So we pulled off the road, and Tilly got out and walked up to the
fence and stared up at the empty space like it was amazing, like it was
a place where something holy and sacred had happened. "I can't believe
that it was there, and now it's gone," she said. "I can't believe I'm never
going to get to see it. It's like the Colossus of Rhodes and the Bamiyan
Buddhas." She looked like she might start crying.

And I mean, *this* is our one big stop on the way to the camp? We'd
been passing all these billboards for places that sounded amazing:
an alpine slide, Weirs Beach, and a Western ghost-town place where
you can get your face put on a wanted poster. And instead, Tilly gets
her way, and we stop to look at something that isn't even there. So
while she was going on and on with her random facts (". . . and
Nathaniel Hawthorne wrote this story about it, called 'The Great

Stone Face' . . ."), I just cleared my throat and said really loudly, "It was just a piece of rock."

It worked. Tilly got mad instantly ("zero to sixty" is what my mom calls it), and made a move like she was going to hit me as hard as she could. I shrank myself down and pressed into my mom's side, and my dad grabbed Tilly's hand.

"Guys," said my mom. "Come on. Tilly, you don't hit your sister, ever, no matter how mad you are. Iris, this is important to Tilly. Stop putting it down."

"Fucking fuck," Tilly said, enough under her breath that my parents let it go.

I just walked away like I was super-calm and totally above that kind of behavior, even though the whole time, I was continuing the conversation in my head. *This is the most boring tourist thing ever: let's go look at some air! You know those "Falling Rock" signs you see on the highway? That's the same exact thing—get your cameras out!* But after I stopped being angry, I felt bad for making fun of this thing she likes so much, so when I went into the visitors' center to use the bathroom, I bought her a postcard in the gift shop.

Now it's like a half hour later, and we're driving right through a forest, or at least that's what it seems like. I didn't even know there *were* roads that went through forests; I thought it was all like hiking trails and people camping. I can't decide if it feels cozy or spooky; everywhere you look, every window, nothing but pine trees. It feels like a fairy tale, but the beginning part that's a little bit scary, because you don't know what the characters are going to find. It feels like we're the only people on earth.

Tilly's all bored and fidgety. She starts humming something, a tune she made up. I know where this is going, and I turn and look out my window, so I can be outside it, kind of. Even though she's thirteen, and I'm only eleven, a lot of the time it seems like I'm the big sister.

"Daddy," sings Tilly, softly. "Gonna suck your cock." She draws the word "cock" out so that it's two syllables.

"Cut it out, Tilly," says Dad. He sounds a little annoyed, but not as angry or shocked as you might think if you were someone who wasn't in our family. Tilly says this kind of stuff all the time. We're all used to it. "No more, or you're jinxed."

"Jinxed" means she's not allowed to talk for five minutes, just like when you say something at the same time as someone else, except that she can't get out of it by someone saying her name. My mom and dad only do it when we're in the car; it's because they can't send her to her room or take away her computer or whatever. Taking away her computer has always been Tilly's biggest consequence. I wonder what they'll do at this camp, when there's no computer to take away.

"Hey," I say to her. Sometimes she just needs some other place for her mind to go. "Wanna play That Didn't Hurt?"

She grins, then leans over and pinches my arm.

"That didn't hurt," I say. I wriggle so my seat belt is a little looser, then whack Tilly on the back of her head.

"That didn't hurt," she says. We're both laughing.

"Guys," my mom calls from the front seat. She hates it when we do this. "This always ends with one of you crying."

"We don't care," I call back. Tilly punches me in the side, and I grab a handful of her hair and tug. Before I even pull my hand back, Tilly says, "That didn't hurt," and then scratches my arm hard enough that her fingernails leave white lines.

"That didn't hurt," I say, even though it did. I rub my arm. It is kind of a stupid game, when you think about it. "I don't feel like playing anymore."

"Hey, Mom," Tilly says. "Nobody's crying."

My mom doesn't answer.

For a little while, we're all quiet. Now that we're almost there, I'm starting to feel a little scared. This place we're going, Camp Harmony, doesn't sound like it's going to be much fun. The guy in charge is this friend of my parents' named Scott Bean. He's kind of famous for running parenting conferences (if that's something you can be famous for), which is how my mom met him. Eventually, she started helping him out, redoing his website for him, and sending out flyers and stuff.

And now she's helping him start up this camp. It's not a regular camp, though, like a place where kids go for a few weeks. It's something called a "family camp," and the idea is that whole families come and stay for a week, to learn how to get along better or something. But that's not what we're doing, the weeklong thing. We're actually moving here to help run the place, us and Scott Bean and two other families. And we're not going home after the summer's over, either, though my mom and dad haven't talked as much about that part.

"I need to pee," Tilly says suddenly. "It's an emergency."

Should've gone at the stupid rock place, I think.

My mom sighs. "We've only got maybe ten or fifteen more minutes until we get there. Can you wait?"

"No," Tilly says. "I told you, it's an emergency."

My dad looks at my mom. "Want me to pull over?" he asks.

"I guess," she says. "I think I have some tissues in my purse."

My dad pulls to the side of the road and stops the car. I don't have to go, but even if I did, I'd hold it. I wouldn't want to squat down and pee on the pine needles, in the middle of the woods.

"Okay," my mom says, opening her door. "Come with me."

"*Come* with you?" says Tilly. "Sorry, Mom, I'm not a lesbian."

I don't even really get that one, but I know it's something inappropriate.

"That's enough," says Dad, but Tilly's already closed the door.

I watch them walk away into the trees. Tilly's gotten really tall lately, like even just in the month since she turned thirteen. She's taller than my mom now, though even from the back, you can tell that my mom is the grown-up and Tilly is the kid, because Tilly walks in this all-over-the-place way, weaving around in all different directions, and she keeps her head down, not really looking where she's going. I'm prettier than Tilly, I think, but it's partly just because she never brushes her hair, and the medicines she takes have made her a little bit fat.

The car is quiet for a minute. Then my dad asks, "So, how you doing, kiddo?"

I shrug. "Okay, I guess."

"Nervous?"

"A little."

"Me, too," he says.

"You're nervous?" I say. I don't know why that surprises me, but it does. "So why are we going?"

He turns around and gives me a look like *We've already talked about this*, which we have a million times. All he says is, "Nervousness isn't a bad thing. It just means we're trying something new."

I don't really want to talk about it anymore, so I say, "I miss the motel," in this gloomy voice, because I know it'll make him laugh. It works, and I smile, too.

My parents hated the motel we stayed at last night, because they found a hair in the shower, and breakfast was just muffins wrapped in plastic. But Tilly and I liked it. Last night, we were going crazy, jumping from bed to bed and playing TV Bingo, which is where you click through the channels as fast as you can, and only stop when you see something that fits in a certain category, like animals or a commercial that shows a kitchen. Mom and Dad let us order pizza for dinner from a place that left ads in all the rooms, and no one even said anything about how this was the last pizza we were going to be eating for a long time.

This morning, though, neither of us talked very much. When we knew it was almost time to go—Mom was in the shower, and Dad was packing up, checking the room to make sure we weren't forgetting anything—we flopped down next to each other on one of the beds and turned on the TV. We didn't fight about what to watch; we just picked the first kids' show we found. It was *Blue's Clues*, which is way too young for either of us, but it made me feel kind of sentimental. Back when we used to watch *Blue's Clues*, we lived in our same house in Washington, the one my parents are trying to sell now, and life just seemed . . . solid, I guess. Like you didn't even have to wonder whether anything was going to change. I remember that for a while I thought that paw prints were some kind of universal symbol for "clue," and I liked to imagine what it would be like if there were tons of them out there in the world, just waiting for you to find them when you needed them.

In the episode we watched in the hotel room, the question that Steve and Blue were trying to answer was, "What does Blue want to build?"

"Probably a doggy door," Tilly said, "so she can finally escape from this madhouse," and we both laughed. But after that, we sat there quietly and watched like we were three years old again, and our parents didn't make us turn it off until Blue and Steve had found all the clues they needed to solve the puzzle.

It's almost four o'clock by the time we get to Camp Harmony. The sign where you turn in is wrong; it still says "Kozy Kabins," which I guess is what it used to be called here before Scott bought it. Tilly freaks out for a minute, thinking that we're lost, but then we see Scott walking toward the car, so we know we're in the right place.

Scott's a big guy, taller than my dad and sort of muscly, with dark hair that's always slicked into place, even if he's just wearing shorts and a T-shirt, like now. My parents have this joke about him being good-looking, like my dad will say, "Oh, he uses hair product—you think that's handsome?" and my mom will say, "You know your zip-per's down?" and my dad will say, "Oh, a zipped-up fly—you think that's handsome?" and they'll both laugh. I love times like that, when they're getting along and having fun together. (And honestly, I think my dad is better looking than Scott Bean, but whatever.)

Scott's pretty nice, I guess. We met him a bunch of times in DC, and he always had good ideas for games to play with us. He doesn't have any kids of his own, though, so I don't really get why people go to him for advice about being a parent.

My dad stops the car, and everything is suddenly quiet. Scott walks over and opens my mom's door, then leans in and puts a hand on the door frame.

"Welcome, Hammond family," he says, grinning. He has a deep voice, like a guy on a radio morning show.

"Hey," I say. Tilly doesn't say anything except, "Finally, we can get out."

"Are we the first ones here?" my mom asks.

"You are indeed," says Scott, stepping back so she can get out. "The Ruffins are arriving tomorrow; the Goughs were supposed to be here already, but I got a message from Rick that they had some car trouble in Connecticut, and they're running behind."

The rest of us have gotten out by now, and we're all just stretch-ing and looking around. We're standing in a circular driveway, made out of gray pebbles. Behind us, there's a row of little cottages, painted different colors, and in front of us there's a big patch of grass with a couple of buildings, and a path leading down to the lake. It's pretty, I guess, but everything feels sort of run-down and empty.

I think that when Tilly gets out of the car, it finally occurs to her what a big deal this is. "This is it?" she asks. "This is where we're actually going to be living?"

Scott's just finishing up hugging my mom and shaking my dad's hand, and now he crouches down between me and Tilly and puts an arm around each of us.

"Girls," he says, in a low voice. My mom and dad can probably hear what he's saying, but it's supposed to seem like it's just for us. "Don't worry, okay? I know this feels crazy and huge, but I promise: it's going to be great."

Then he just stays where he is, looking between the two of us, like he's waiting for an answer. I sort of nod and shrug; Tilly shakes him off and starts walking around in circles, tapping her cheeks really fast, like she does when she gets anxious.

"No," she says. She stops in front of my parents and grabs hold of Mom's shoulders. I can see my mom sag a little bit from the weight Tilly's putting on her. "I'm not going to live here. Take me home."

My mom doesn't answer, just gently disentangles herself. "So which one of these is ours?" she asks Scott, gesturing to the row of colorful cabins.

"None of them, actually," Scott says. "These are the visitor cabins. Come with me, and I'll show you the staff campground."

We follow him down a little dirt path that curves behind the dollhouse cabins and goes back into the woods. Tilly's still tapping her cheeks, but she comes along without saying anything. We walk a ways, and then a second group of buildings comes into view. They're the same size as the others, but less cute and more run-down. They're all painted the same color, a kind of dull green that makes them blend into the trees.

"You folks are in Number Five," Scott says, pointing to the one on the end. It's got a tiny front porch with two canvas chairs on it, and a white door right in the middle. I swear the whole thing is smaller than the jungle gym at my old school.

"Perfect," my mom says. "Do we need a key?"

"Nope," says Scott. "No keys here. We're an open-door community."

"Oh, of course," my mom says. "I'm still in city detox."

"I'll go get some of the bags," my dad says to my mom and turns back the way we came. My mom walks up onto the cabin porch and opens the door. Tilly stops in the doorway, and I stand behind her, waiting to get inside.

"You just get yourselves settled," Scott calls from outside. "I'm in Number One, if you need anything."

I nudge Tilly. "He's in Number One," I say quietly, nudging her into the cabin. "He lives in pee."

Tilly still looks upset, but her face twists almost into a smile. "I'm glad we're not in Number Two," she says.

Right inside the front door is a big room that's half kitchen and half living room. On one side, there's a white plastic table and chairs, and running along the wall, there's a refrigerator, a sink, and a counter with some stove burners built in. There are cupboards, but they don't have any doors, and neither does the space underneath the sink; they're just covered with dirty yellow-and-white-checked curtains.

On the other half of the room, there's a couch and two armchairs arranged around a coffee table. The furniture is old and ugly, and none of it matches. There are three doors, leading to a bathroom and two bedrooms. The whole place feels grungy, like it couldn't get clean no matter how hard we try.

"This sucks," I say. I'm getting really nervous all of a sudden, which is silly because nothing's happened, but maybe it's been building up. Like we were all so focused on getting here, and now we actually are. Here. So . . . now what?

"It really sucks," I say, louder. I feel like I'm filling up with some kind of thick, horrible substance. I picture it like the disgusting yellow goo my dad used one time to fill the spaces between the bathtub and the wall in our old house: it's called caulk, which Tilly would probably think is funny because it sounds like "cock," but right now, I'm not even thinking about that, I'm just picturing this gross, gluey stuff, ugly and poisonous, expanding to fit the inside-shape of my body, spreading through me and hardening as it seeps into every little crevice.

There's a thump as Tilly finally lets the screen door swing shut. She walks in, and I can tell by the look on her face that she's about to go over the edge. For some reason that makes me furious. I make a deep growling noise and punch the dirty, shiny sofa, to keep from punching her.

"I'm not living here," she says, her voice rising to a wail. She lunges at my mother, maybe to hit her, maybe to bite her, and my mom grabs her upper arms to keep her away. "I want my Xbox. I want my computer." She's screaming now. "I'll kill you if you don't give me my computer." I go into the bathroom and slam the door.

We're here for Tilly; she's the whole reason we gave up everything and moved here, even though nobody's saying it. But I can make a scene, too. "Fuck," I yell. Then louder, in case they didn't hear me: "Fuck!"

While I'm peeing, I check out the bathroom. There's no bathtub, just a nasty-looking shower stall. There are rust marks in the sink, and the blue plastic shower curtain is spattered with uneven white dots along its bottom edge. The toilet flushes with one of those sticks that you step on, like it's a public restroom. I wonder how many feet have stood on that dirty-white plastic shower platform, sending dirt and hair and who knows what else down the drain. How many mouths have spit into that sink? I feel like throwing up.

When I come out, my mom and Tilly are sitting on the couch. Tilly is crying in long soft moans, and my mom is trying to put an arm around her, but it's hard because Tilly keeps jerking her body around. My mom looks at me over Tilly's head and smiles in this sad way. She wants me to be more mature, to be the big sister even though I'm the little sister, but I'm not going to do it. I stand there hating them both for a minute, hating hating hating everything, and then it's like the hard yellow stuff melts back into liquid, and I'm crying like I'm never going to stop. My mom holds out her other arm, and I sink down next to her and press my face to her shoulder. I let her hold on to me and whisper soft things to both of us, as if it could make even the tiniest bit of difference.

chapter 2

Alexandra

March 2007: Washington, DC

You open the basement door, feeling as if you're setting out on an arctic expedition. It's your job to go down there and sort through the chaos. It's your job to find clothes for your family. All of your laundry is in garbage bags; you have bedbugs, and the first step in containing the infestation has been to seal up every item of clothing you own. Blankets, too, and stuffed animals—anything with a soft surface. Dirty items have to be washed and dried; clean ones just have to go through the dryer, where the heat is high enough to kill the bugs.

When the man from the pest control company came, he got down on the floor next to the couch and ripped open a side panel, pulling the fabric away from the board underneath. "Yeah," he said, pointing without touching. "See this, here?" You bent your head close and squinted until you saw a cluster of tiny brown specks. "That's their feces."

He was very well informed, this guy; he was a font of fascinating bedbug trivia. "White people tend to be sensitive to it, so we're able to catch it early," he told you; he was black, which somehow made it seem more okay for him to be saying these things. "Hispanics, it doesn't bother them till it gets really bad. I go in there, and I find the bugs in the wall sconces, in the closets, everywhere. By the time they call me, you can see the bugs with the naked eye." You glanced at Tilly, who was listening with interest, quiet for once, no doubt filing this away in some confusing, overstuffed "race" folder in her head.

Your best guess is that you brought the bugs home from a hotel where you stayed last Thanksgiving. A nice place, apparently clean. The kids loved the free breakfast buffet. It's like a metaphor come to life, your home polluted with invaders you can't even see. And what if—you suppose that this is the real source of anxiety for most people— what if the invasion goes even deeper than that? You've been to the fringe parenting websites and the homeopathy section at Whole Foods. You know that there are people out there who will tell you that it's too late, that our bodies are already tainted. That we're overrun with mucus or bacteria or spreading fungal growth. You picture a garden gone to seed: moss growing on the surface of our spleens, vines squeezing our kidneys. Tiny mushrooms spreading across the linings of our intestines. Kudzu, unstoppable, choking us from the inside. Has depression ever been this widespread, or autism or infertility or food allergies? Something's changed, even if it's just our own method of record-keeping. Impossible to say what might be causing what.

You've been thinking about this a lot during this dismal spring. So far, the year's key events—the ones you grimly imagine decorating with exclamation points and inserting into your next Christmas card letter—are the bedbug colonization and the new diagnosis you've received for Tilly. You've had a few false starts: OCD, ADHD, an autoimmune disorder called PANDAS (which you think about almost nostalgically every time you take the kids to see Mei Xiang and Tian Tian at the zoo). But in early February, you finally made it to the top of the waiting list of a highly recommended developmental pediatrician, and the diagnosis she bestowed on Tilly carries a weight that the others didn't. The new set of letters, the acronym you attach to your daughter like a degree she's earned, is PDD-NOS. It stands for "pervasive developmental disorder, not otherwise specified," and it doesn't actually mean a whole lot; it's a diagnosis of exclusion, nothing more than the doctors throwing up their hands and saying, "Something's going on here, but we can't say exactly what." But it's located firmly on the autism spectrum, and it has the effect of shifting all the pieces on the game-board, sliding Tilly into an entirely new position. And you're still trying to figure out what kind of endgame it might lead you to.

You tug at the knot on a bag of Iris's clothes—finally, it's occurred to you to use clear plastic bags, which makes it easier to find things. As you rummage, you're careful not to put any of the clean clothing down on any surface; the pest control people haven't done their second spray yet, and who knows where the parasites may still be lurking. "It's all safe for humans," the man had said about the chemicals, the man who seemed to know everything about bugs and their habits. "Humans and pets are fine." But you don't believe it for a minute.

When you were pregnant with Tilly, you subscribed to an online pregnancy calendar. Each morning, you'd turn on your computer and learn which organs were likely to be forming today, which cells might be fusing even as you sat there at your desk. You'd send Josh emails about it at work: "This week: the brain stem! What should I eat?" But it was a joke, because it was all going to be okay. You didn't actually believe it could matter much; women have been doing this forever, right, without this kind of second-by-second scrutiny?

May 3, 1999: Matilda Grace comes into the world at 7:25 p.m. Pregnancy and birth normal, although later you'll wonder whether that's true. You'll struggle to remember details that seemed inconsequential at the time: *Did you drink tap water? Did you eat any fish that might have contained high levels of mercury?* Having a baby is something that never changes, has never changed in the history of the world, and also something that changes all the time. The advice you got from doctors and baby-care manuals was cutting-edge and up-to-date; it was also completely different from the advice Josh's older sister had gotten five years earlier and the advice younger friends were given five years later.

You know that when you were a baby, you were put to sleep on your tummy, like most babies of your generation. It was thought to be safer, to prevent choking if you spit up while you were unattended. Your nephew, born in 1995, was placed to sleep on his side, an ungainly position for an infant and one that required a foam crib insert, to keep him from toppling one way or the other. By the time Tilly was born, it was imperative that you lay her down on her back. No pillows or blankets, though swaddling was encouraged; no soft toys that have button eyes or pom-pom noses. And you suppose it worked; neither of your babies died from SIDS. But who knows what they'll be told, Tilly and Iris, when it's their turn to bend over a cradle and place a wriggling baby down to sleep. (*Did you color your hair while you were pregnant? Did you take any over-the-counter medications?*)

By the time you were ready to get rid of the crib that held each of your babies safely for two years apiece, the mechanism that moved the side up and down had already been rejected as too dangerous. You couldn't get any charity to take it, or any pregnant friend; you were advised to break it into pieces before putting it out for bulk trash collection, so that it couldn't be appropriated by a passerby and used for some new baby who might not survive its outdated design. (*How well did you wash your fruits and vegetables? How much coffee did you drink?*)

If you look at the long history of women having babies, there is no right or wrong; there is no universal truth. You think about women in the nineteenth century, told that if they should happen to gaze upon anything gruesome or horrifying, their babies would be born deformed. Of course, that's ridiculous—right? (*Did you eat soft cheeses or sushi?*

Do you have lead fillings in your teeth?) Now, with more than a century of extra wisdom and confusion under your belt, you're not so sure anything can be ruled out. A crisis of faith doesn't have to be about God. You can have a crisis of faith about dust mites and food additives that cause behavioral changes. Pesticides in fruit salad and insect husks in peanut butter. Mysterious rashes caused by something you brought home in a suitcase.

There's a startling fact that you read somewhere: after airbags became standard in cars, statisticians noticed that the incidence of severe leg injuries increased dramatically. Think about it for a minute: Why should that be? Is there something about the way airbags inflate during collision that targets the passengers' legs, makes them more vulnerable?

No. It's a matter of checks and balances. Before airbags, there were certain accidents that would have killed you; you'd be a corpse in the morgue, and no one would be paying any attention to your legs. When we change the way we do things—the way we shop for groceries or take care of our children or protect ourselves from harm—we set other changes in motion, for good or for ill. And it may be years before we figure out what we've done.

You cried in the parking lot of the doctor's office, after that last meeting with the developmental pediatrician, the one where she broke her news so gently and so kindly. And you continued to cry off and on for weeks. You grieve; that's the conventional wisdom. You grieve for the child you thought you were going to have, though maybe it's also for the parent you thought you'd be. But soon—or so you keep hearing—you'll find that having an answer provides some measure of relief. Because now you understand why she acts the way she does. You understand that some problems are neither your fault nor hers.

You can begin to educate yourself; it's hard to use Google if you don't have the proper search terms. You can learn what kind of help your child needs, and you can find other people in the same boat.

Eventually, you'll feel less alone. A diagnosis, the conventional wisdom goes, is a beginning, rather than an end.

You're not quite there yet, though, to that place of clarity and relief. Now that you have the all-important label, the letters that will make your daughter eligible for the ominous-sounding set of benefits known as "services"—OT and PT and plain old T—now that you've gotten an answer that's supposed to be definitive, what are you supposed to do about it? There doesn't seem to be much of a consensus.

Just one more week until the pest control people come to finish their treatment, and then all this will be over. The day they come to spray, you'll stay in a hotel, just like you did the first time. It's money through your fingers and not fun for anyone—the four of you crammed into one room, waking up in strange beds on a school day. But it's better than putting your kids down for the night on mattresses still damp with pesticides. Better than bringing them home before you've had a chance to sweep up the white powder that settles on the floor as the toxic mist dries in the air.

You collect pieces of clothing, keeping track as you go: underwear for yourself, a shirt for Tilly. Denim legs twirled in the corners of bedsheets, spun tight by the movements of the dryer. You pull like you're playing tug-of-war at a picnic.

Josh's clothes are in here, too, mixed in with the rest, but you don't take any of them out for him. He can find his own. There was a time, you remember with some astonishment, when you used to do nice things for him on purpose. It's sad, and maybe you'll reach that point again someday, but it's not going to be now. You have a feeling of plague and panic, like you're living through the black death or the influenza epidemic of 1918. In plague days, you're learning, it's every man for himself.

"I am," you think, and "I want." And you have no idea how either sentence ends.

chapter 3

Iris

June 3, 2012: New Hampshire

We don't unpack right away, just drop our suitcases in the right rooms. We all sort of separate for a while, now that we're not stuck together in the car. Mom's doing something in the kitchen, making lots of busy noises, and across the room, Dad's lying down on the couch with his eyes closed, though I don't know if he's really asleep. Tilly is walking around, telling herself a story about giant statues coming to life; I can hear her whispering "Spring Temple Buddha," which is a really tall statue in China or someplace. And I'm sitting on my bed, wishing I was anywhere else in the whole world.

I'm in our new bedroom, mine and Tilly's, which I hate. The walls are brown wood, tall up-and-down planks with knotholes in them, and there's a thin blue rug that I'm not ever going to walk on barefoot. Our beds are probably the same size as our beds at home—all twin beds are the same, right, so you know the sheets will fit?—but they look skinny and lumpy and just kind of sad. The bedspreads are dirty white with little flowers on them, and the pillows are so thin they barely even puff up the covers. I can't believe that I'm going to sleep in here, not just tonight, but . . . and now I almost start crying again, because I don't know how long we're going to have to stay.

"Hey," says Tilly. "How tall do you think the Aluthgama Buddha would be if he stood up?"

"I have no idea," I say, as sarcastic and annoyed-sounding as I can. But she doesn't even notice.

I get up and walk to the window, which is between the two beds; I stare out until I can make my face stop crumpling up. I could probably go outside and walk around—that's part of why we're here, right, because we don't want to live in a place where you can't let your kids play outside by themselves? But I don't want to; I'm almost scared, like I might get lost in the trees. All the green that goes on forever like an ocean.

Around five, Mom calls out that she's going to go over to Scott's and see what he's got planned for dinner. "Anyone want to come with me?" she asks. Tilly and I both stare at her, like we're scared she's going to make us. Dad's finally awake, sitting up, rubbing his eyes.

"I'll stay here," he says, though I'm not sure Mom was really inviting him to go with her. Someone has to be with the kids. Or maybe not—maybe it's so safe here that none of the rules apply.

Mom sighs. "Okay," she says. "I'll be back in a few minutes. Just so you know, you're all probably going to need to pitch in to help with dinner."

I don't complain, because I know that's what she's expecting. Once she's out the door, the mood seems to change a little bit in the cabin, like we've all been holding our breath.

I go over to the couch and sit down next to Dad. "So," I say. "Why are we doing this, again?" I'm trying to make a lame joke, kind of.

Dad looks at me very seriously and says, "Because we don't like video games."

I crack up, so glad to have a reason to laugh, and Tilly comes over to join in. "That's right, Daddy," she says. "We don't like video games; we *love* them. We *adore* them. We *cherish* them."

"Hmm." Dad looks thoughtful. "So that can't be it. Is it because we hate TV? And delicious snack food? And using the computer?"

Tilly and I are both giggling. I'm leaning against his shoulder, and Tilly is climbing up on the arms of the couch to try to sit on his neck, like for a piggyback ride, even though she's way too big. "No, Dad," I say. "We love that stuff, remember?"

"That's right, we do." He turns to Tilly, who's practically climbing on top of him, like she'd stand right on his shoulders if she could. "Come on down, sweetie, okay?"

She does, and he hugs us both close to him, one on each side. "I don't know, then," he says. "Why *are* we doing this?"

He's going to make us say it.

"Because you only get one chance to raise us?" says Tilly.

"And you think this is going to be a better place for our family than Washington was?" I add.

"Oh, yeah," he says, like he's remembering something important. "That's right. Thanks for reminding me." He kisses each of us on the tops of our heads. I love my dad.

"You're welcome," says Tilly. She pats his head like he's a dog and adds, "We're always happy to help."

When my mom comes back, she's got Scott with her. He has to duck his head to get his shiny hair through the door.

"Get your shoes on," Mom says. "Let's go see the big kitchen."

"Or come barefoot," says Scott. "It's summertime. Gotta toughen up those feet."

Tilly goes barefoot, but I put my flip-flops on. Scott leads us out of the cabin and back down the path toward where we parked. He's a fast walker, and he keeps having to slow himself down so he doesn't get too far ahead of the rest of us. He's wearing a light blue "Camp Harmony" T-shirt, and I see now that it says on the back, "Be Who You Are." I wonder if he's still taking suggestions on slogans, because that one is so vague it barely means anything at all.

We come out of the trees and into the main part of camp. We walk past the cute visitor cabins, and already I feel jealous of the people who are going to get to stay in them. Past the main office and across a circle of green grass. Tilly and I stop for a minute when the lake comes into view, down a sloped hill that changes slowly from grass to beach. There's a pile of kayaks on the shore, and the water is dark, ruffling into gentle little waves. I feel something in me loosen, just for a second. I could like it here, maybe. That would make things easier.

Scott stands between us, puts a hand on each of our shoulders. "What do you think?" he asks softly.

"Nice," I say. I mean, it's a lake. Unless you're writing a poem or something, there's not a lot to say.

Tilly isn't even looking in the right direction. "Did you know," she asks nobody in particular, "that the Motherland Calls memorial in Russia is the world's biggest non-religious statue? It's almost five times as big as the guys on Mount Rushmore."

The grown-ups ignore her. "Pretty, huh?" says my mom, about the lake. I feel like any other time, it would be her standing between me and Tilly with her arms around us. But Scott's in the way. "Tomorrow, girls," she says. "We'll go swimming. I promise."

"I think we can fit that in," Scott says cheerfully. He pats my shoulder and moves away, to walk again with the adults. I hear him say to my mom, "Be careful about promises, though. We're going to be working in a very group-centered way; it may not always be possible for individual people to decide to go off in all directions."

"Yeah, of course," says my mom. Her voice is kind of tight; I don't think she likes feeling like she's being scolded. *Now you know how I feel*, Tilly would say, if she were paying any attention.

My dad, like always, breaks the weirdness. "And besides—swimming? I don't think anyone wants to do that. Yuck." That gets Tilly, and she and I run over to him, happy, yelling that he's wrong. "Who would ever think of going swimming on vacation?" he asks. "You don't go to a lake to swim."

We're all smiling and laughing now, relieved the tense part is over, but when I look at Scott, I stop. He seems strange to me, not mad but sort of blank. He's staring at the ground, instead of looking at any of us. I listen to the whole thing again in my head, to see if I can figure out what might have upset him, but none of it sounds bad.

Suddenly, he makes his face normal, putting on that same easy expression he usually has, like he's totally relaxed and just taking everything in.

"This way," he says, starting to walk again. He doesn't sound mad at all. I look at my mom and dad; I'm pretty sure they missed the whole thing. "Or the bears are going to hear our stomachs growling and think we're inviting them to dinner."

"Is that even a joke?" asks Tilly. "It's not funny at all."

Scott leads us toward a squat wooden building with a green roof. A sign out front with letters that look like they've been burned into the wood with fire says "Dining Hall." It reminds me of the signs you can put up in *Minecraft*; Tilly and I were really into that for a while this spring, and one of our jokes was that Tilly would put up signs with swearwords on them, and I'd take them back down. Or we'd build a jail and then do really crazy things, so the other one would put us inside; then we'd put up signs in our jail cell that said things like, "I'm sorry I put carpeting on the roof of your house." But I don't say anything, because it would probably just make Tilly miss the computer even more.

Scott opens the screen door for us, and we all pass through in a line. My dad is last, and as he goes inside, I hear Scott say, "Josh?" His voice is low and casual, like he's going to tell him he has food in his teeth or something.

"Yeah?" my dad says.

"We're not on vacation."

"Oh, yeah, I know. I was just . . ."

Scott cuts him off. "It's a small thing, but it's important. What are we always telling them? Words matter." Scott claps him hard on the back, and gestures us all forward into the darkening room. He raises his voice a little, to show that he's talking to all of us now. "Which is not to say there won't be swimming and sunshine and all kinds of fun. But we're not here for a holiday; we've got more important work to do."

He leads us through a set of swinging doors into an enormous kitchen. He flips the light switch. "And right now," he says, smiling at us and taking down a big metal bowl that's hanging on a rack, "that important work includes making spaghetti."

chapter 4

Tilly

Date and Location Unknown

At an unspecified moment in the future, in imaginary museums all across the country, the world tour of Hammond Family Artifacts is a wild success. Advance tickets are required; there are lines out the door in every city. Timelines are posted throughout the exhibit space, to help visitors place the display objects within the context of major Hammond family events: Josh and Alexandra Hammond meet in 1992, and are married in 1995; Matilda Grace (known as Tilly) arrives in 1999, and her sister Iris Victoria is born in 2001. In 2010, Alexandra makes the acquaintance of Scott Bean, founder of an organization called Harmonious Parenting; in June of 2012, the family leaves their home in Washington, DC, to help Scott Bean establish a "family camp" in Laconia, New Hampshire.

Some of the items on display are fanciful or beautiful, but many of them intrigue just by virtue of their ordinariness: Father's Day card, June 2006: washable Crayola markers on bright white twenty-pound paper. Fourth grade report on one of the thirteen colonies (Delaware) by Matilda Hammond, age ten. Signatures written by each family member with his or her non-dominant hand, autumn

2009. American Girl doll, "Samantha." (Nail polish on cheeks and lips added post-manufacture by Iris Hammond, age six.) Notes to a new babysitter, Alexandra Hammond, 2005. Reusable grocery bag filled with Tilly's drawings, 2006–2007 academic year. Primitive art, dating back to the dawn of the Hammonds as we know them.

A six-minute film entitled "Early Days: A Disaster in the Making" shows on a continuous loop; it includes footage from Josh and Alexandra's wedding and home movies of the girls singing songs and playing in an inflatable wading pool. Museum guests are invited to peer through the windows of the nonworking 1971 Ford Galaxie that Josh Hammond kept in the garage of the family's Washington, DC, home (and that the girls adopted as an unconventional playroom). They are led single-file through a full-sized re-creation of the cabin the family inhabited after moving to Scott Bean's compound.

When something cataclysmic has happened, an event that decimates an entire way of life, historians find it useful to look at what remains. These people we're trying to understand: How did they celebrate a marriage or the birth of a baby? How did they honor their dead? More prosaically, how did they prepare their meat for cooking? What methods did they use for washing their clothes or sharing news of recent events? What did they hold on to, and what did they throw away? We don't have much: pieces of their weapons, maybe, fragments of their dishes. But they tell us a story we wouldn't otherwise know.

Press a button to light me up like a museum diorama. *Here are her hands*, the plaque on the wall will say. *Here is her beating heart.*

chapter 5

Iris

I wake up to a clanging sound outside the cabin. It's barely light out, and the bedroom is chilly; I pull myself underneath the thin bedspread, but it doesn't block out the noise. When I finally get up and go to the window, I see Scott Bean walking up and down the dirt path, banging a metal spatula against a soup pot.

Next to me, Tilly moans. "Shut *up*," she says, sleepily, putting her pillow over her head. She's already got a bunch of her statue pictures and postcards hanging over her bed, including the one I bought yesterday. My favorite is the one of the guy cleaning out Abe Lincoln's gigantic marble ear.

We didn't get to bring much with us from home, but we did each have one suitcase, one backpack, and one medium-sized box. A lot of it got filled up with clothes, obviously, but I found some YouTube videos about how to pack things really small, like by rolling up your T-shirts and stuffing underwear into your shoes and things like that, so I could maximize my space.

I wanted to bring my iPad, but there are no electronic devices allowed, so I gave it to my friend Gabi, because she didn't have one.

I brought a lot of little things, like jewelry and nail polish and lip gloss, and this pretty flower-shaped pillow that I keep on my bed. I have two American Girl dolls that I decided not to bring, because I was kind of getting too old for them (although I feel a little sad when I think about it now). I was only going to bring two stuffed animals, but I ended up bringing four, because I couldn't narrow it down any more than that.

I packed a couple of my favorite books, and I got my mom to pack some board games in the boxes of family stuff, so I wouldn't have to use my own space for them. And I brought three journals: one that I used to write in when I was little (like in second and third grade), my password-protected one that I use now (which I got my mom to agree doesn't count as an electronic device, even though it takes batteries), and one blank one in case I run out of pages in the others.

And that's it; those are all my worldly possessions. The rest of my stuff—all my millions of art kits and birthday presents and Happy Meal prizes—either got thrown away or donated to A Wider Circle. And even though a lot of it was stuff I didn't care about anymore, and my parents talked a lot about how good it feels to "simplify" and "declutter" and whatever, I can't think about it for very long without feeling sad.

I pick up the flower pillow from my bed and hug it to my chest. Scott's still clanging away. Through the window, I see my dad stumble outside in boxers and a T-shirt. He looks annoyed.

"Okay," he yells over the noise. "We get it. We get it."

Scott grins and keeps right on clanging. "Just want to make sure we all get a jump on the day."

"We have an alarm clock," my dad shouts. "Are alarm clocks damaging our children in some way I'm not aware of?"

"Yes, actually," Scott says, banging out a steady rhythm. "Alarm clocks train us to rely on external forces instead of our own instincts."

I can't see my dad's face, but whatever expression he's wearing makes Scott laugh. "I'm kidding," he says. "This is just more fun. Be at the dining hall in twenty minutes."

He turns and walks away, still beating the spatula against the pot. As he passes the middle cabin, two down from us, the door opens, and a woman in a pink terry cloth robe steps out onto the porch. She has red hair, so red that I think it must be dyed that color, and she's barefoot. She leans forward to talk to Scott, and I jerk back and sit down on the edge of Tilly's bed.

"Tilly," I say, shaking her arm. I feel panicky; I had just enough time to get a little bit used to things, and now it's already changing. "There's someone else here. One of the other families."

"Really?" she asks, sitting up. She's suddenly wide awake. "Which one?"

"I don't know," I say. "I just saw the mom in her bathrobe."

The front door of our cabin opens and closes, and my dad calls out, "Hey, guys, time to get up."

"One of the other families is here," Tilly yells back. "Iris saw the mom out the window."

"I'm sure we'll meet them at breakfast," says my mom, sticking her head into our bedroom from the hallway. "Five-minute showers, please, and then get dressed."

"I'm not taking a shower," says Tilly. Her voice is very matter-of-fact, like she's not challenging my mom or anything, just correcting a misunderstanding.

"Yes, you are," says Mom. She uses the same voice as Tilly, casual, like this isn't a big deal, like this isn't something they have huge fights about all the time.

"Why?" says Tilly. "We went swimming yesterday morning, remember? In the hotel pool."

My mom gives her this look that she's been working on lately, kind of calm and amused, but still in charge. "And did you use soap and shampoo in the hotel pool?"

Tilly sort of half-smiles, and I can see her following the idea in her head. "Yeah, we did," she says. "Remember? The whole pool got filled up with bubbles, and the hotel people were really mad at us, and they said we had to pay nine hundred dollars to fix it, and we could never stay in that hotel again." She laughs. "Ha, ha. I'm being sarcastic, in case you didn't know."

"I knew," says my mom, smiling back at her. "Go get in the shower."

And amazingly, Tilly does. "No deodorant, though," she yells from the hallway.

"That's fine," says my mom. She closes her eyes for a minute and shakes her head, and I'm not sure if it's for me or for both of us, or maybe just for herself.

Once we're all dressed—which takes a while, because even though Tilly never wants to get into the shower, she also never wants to get out—my mom herds us out the front door, toward the path to the dining hall. I know we're not going to run into the new people, because I heard them leaving ten minutes before we did, which makes me nervous in a different way, like now we're late. I know it's not like we're in some kind of contest with the other Camp Harmony families, but it feels like we are, and I'm not sure who's ahead now: us, because we got here first, or the new people, because they got to breakfast on time. I think about the other family that hasn't even arrived yet; whoever they are, their kids still don't have any idea what their bedrooms are like, or how early Scott wakes us up, or how the lake looks as you walk to the dining hall. We're definitely ahead of *them*; even though we just got here yesterday, we're already way more settled in. But then I think about how they're probably listening to CDs in the car and having breakfast at McDonald's, and how it's still just *them*, just their own family, the kids and their parents, a little unit all wrapped up together inside their car, and I have to concentrate on breathing slowly in and out through my mouth so I don't start crying.

My dad holds the swinging screen door open, and we walk into the building. The dining hall is divided into two rooms: in front, there's an area with a bunch of long tables, where you sit and eat, and in the back is a swinging door with a little window that leads to the kitchen. There's also a long counter at the back of the actual dining part, where you put the food out so people can take it. Or at least, that's what we did last night. I always liked buffets and being able to choose which food you want, but I don't know if I'm going to like having one for every meal.

There's no one at the tables yet, but I can hear voices from the kitchen, and I slow down, sticking close to my mom. Tilly jumps right in, announcing herself loudly as soon as she's inside: "Hey, new people," she calls, making herself heard over the sounds of talking and clanging spoons. She pushes the swinging door open and then stops in the doorway to run her fingers down each side of the doorjamb, before continuing through. "Which family are you?" she asks.

I follow, peering in cautiously to see what we're dealing with. Scott, cooking bacon on the giant stovetop, and the redheaded woman I saw from the window, dressed now and mixing something in a bowl. A big guy wearing a muscle shirt and a baseball cap, lining up glasses next to a pitcher of juice. And three kids—a teenage girl, a boy about my age, and a little girl who might be four or five (she's wearing a tutu, if that tells you anything)—are busy gathering plates and silverware, or at least it seems like that's what they were doing before they stopped to look at Tilly.

I'm not sure what they're going to think of her, partly because I know that we're in a place where every family has at least one kid like Tilly. Or not *like* Tilly, but not like anyone else, either, in the same kind of way. If that makes sense.

"Good morning," says Scott cheerfully; he picks up a pair of tongs and begins to remove slices of bacon from the pan, setting them on paper towels. "Just let me finish this up, and then . . ." He trails off, and we all stand and watch him until he turns off the burner and wipes his hands on his apron.

"Introductions," he says. "Hammond family: Josh, Alexandra, Tilly, and Iris"—he points to each of us in order of age—"meet the Gough family: parents Rick and Diane and kids Candy, Ryan, and Charlotte."

The grown-ups move forward to shake each other's hands; I stick by my mom's side and politely introduce myself after she's done. The other kids all just stand there, staring at each other. Ryan seems like he might be annoying; he's got one of those faux-hawk haircuts, and it looks really stupid. The older girl, Candy, seems like she might be nice, though. She's tall and tomboyish, with chin-length hair and glasses. I like her T-shirt, which shows a cookie jumping off a diving board into a glass of milk.

"I didn't think it was going to be 'Goff,'" says Tilly. I guess she's talking about the pronunciation of their last name. "I saw it on my mom's list. I thought it was going to be 'Gow,' or maybe 'Gowg.'"

"You're pretty stupid if you think anyone's named 'Gowg,'" says the boy.

"Ryan," says his mom, warningly.

"That's interesting, isn't it?" says Scott, cutting her off. "How you can see a word in print and imagine that it's pronounced completely differently, and you never know until someone says it out loud. I remember once when I was about ten, I was talking to a bunch of grown-ups, and I used the word 'horizon,' only I pronounced it 'hor-i-ZON,' like 'horizontal.' They all laughed, and I was really embarrassed, but my mom said that it just showed that I liked to read a lot."

It's a stupid story, more teacher-like than he usually is, and I can tell that Tilly and Ryan aren't paying any attention to him.

"Gowg," says Tilly. "Hi there, Ryan Gowg."

"Tilly," says my mom.

"Shut up!" yells Ryan. "It's 'Goff'!"

"This is Tilly Hammond," says Tilly, pretending to speak into a microphone, "reporting live from the kitchen. Some kid named Ryan Gowg is getting really upset, probably because he has such a stupid name."

The moms are still hovering like nervous birds, chirping quiet little words that get lost under the bigger sounds. When Ryan lunges at Tilly, the dads step in, holding the kids apart, so they can't get to each other.

"Come on, Tilly," says my dad. "Pull yourself together."

"Game face," says Ryan's dad. "Come on, buddy, game face."

And that's when Scott moves into the middle of everything and sinks down to his knees on the floor.

"Okay, guys," he says. He puts one hand on Ryan's shoulder and the other on Tilly's. "Let's calm down a little, so we can talk. You can do it. Take a breath." He demonstrates, sucking in air and then blowing it out.

Tilly resists, like always. "You could change your name to Ryan Fuck," she says. "That's a nice name."

The older girl, Candy, starts laughing, and her dad puts his hands on her shoulders and leans down to whisper something in her ear. She covers her mouth and tries to stop, but then I accidentally meet her eyes and smile, and she starts laughing harder and has to turn away for a minute. I look down at the brown tiles on the floor and try not to start laughing, too.

Meanwhile, Ryan lets out this noise, this wordless howl of frustration, and tries to hit Tilly, and my mom says, "Tilly, stop it!" in her extra-firm and on-the-verge-of-being-mad voice, which is usually her last resort before she starts losing her temper herself. But Scott just stays there on the floor, calmly holding the two kids apart. He watches Tilly with a serious expression, staring at her closely. He has these strange eyes, dark gray and really intense, and I can see Tilly's face getting a little less angry as she looks into them.

"You can do it," he says again. "I know you can." He breathes in and out, showing them what he wants them to do. Ryan starts following the same rhythm, breathing deeply in this exaggerated way, and then I guess Tilly wants to show that she's as good as he is, so she starts doing it, too. The whole kitchen is silent for what seems like a long time, listening to the three of them breathe together.

"Okay," Scott says, after a minute. "I want you both to listen to me, because I'm going to tell you something important: no matter how hard you try, you're never going to be able to control how anyone else acts. All you can control is yourself. Tilly, you know you're not stupid, and Ryan, you know the right way to pronounce your name. When someone teases you and you get upset, you're giving power to that person. You're showing them that they have the power to make you mad and unhappy. Ryan, are you going to let Tilly ruin your whole morning?"

He stops and turns to Ryan. "Yes," says Ryan, though he's not yelling anymore. His face is all red, though, and he's gotten kind of sweaty.

"Really?" asks Scott. "This is up to you. Your first morning here. Are you going to let her ruin it?"

There's a long pause. "I guess not," says Ryan.

"Okay," says Scott. "Good job." He takes his arm from around Ryan's shoulders for a moment and holds it out for Ryan to shake. It's the wrong hand, the left one, which makes the whole thing look strange, like he and Ryan are just holding hands instead of shaking them, but I guess Scott's not sure yet if he can let go of Tilly.

Scott puts his arm back over Ryan's shoulders, but more loosely this time. He turns to the other side. "And, Tilly, are you going to let Ryan provoke you into losing control?"

Tilly's still got her fiercest angry look going, which makes me feel nervous, because it means anything can happen, no matter what Scott does. But I also feel like: Okay, good. This is Tilly; here she is. What does Scott think he's going to do about it?

"Fucking bitch," Tilly says, though her voice is a little quieter than before. Ryan lets out a sharp, high laugh. "Fucking cocksucker motherfucker."

This is the point at which my mom or dad usually sends Tilly upstairs to cool down (if we were still at home and there was still an upstairs) or else starts handing out consequences. But Scott just smiles at her and gives her shoulder a little squeeze.

"Are you done now?" he asks.

"No," she says. "Goddamn fucking fuck . . ." and then she just starts crying.

"Okay," Scott says. "Okay." He squeezes her to him, just for a minute, and everyone stays quiet while she sobs herself down into silence.

"Good job," he says. He looks back and forth between Tilly and Ryan, smiling like they've done something amazing. I feel kind of jealous and annoyed; what about those of us who didn't start acting like two-year-olds in the first place?

"I don't think either of you wanted to be in that place you were in a few minutes ago," Scott says, "but once you got in, you weren't sure how to get out again by yourself. But you did it. You did it. Try to remember, guys: everyone here at Camp Harmony wants to help you. You don't have to do it by yourself."

Ryan's looking at the ground, and I think Tilly might start crying again. Scott gathers them into a group hug before standing up and brushing off his pants.

"Okay," he says. "Let's try this again. Who wants some breakfast?"

We all do. We're hungry, and we want to get to the next part. We gather around Scott, grown-ups and kids together. "Me!" we all shout. "Me! Me!"

After breakfast, Scott divides us up into two groups: one to work in the garden, and the other to start cleaning out the guest cabins. My mom and I both get put on cabin duty; I don't really want to do either one, but I guess this is a little better, since at least the cabins have ceiling fans. Scott gives us pails and gloves and rags and a whole bunch of organic cleaning supplies. Mom and I start with the cabin closest to the lake, while the Gough dad and Ryan start at the other end.

It's not so bad; I always kind of liked helping my mom around the house, and we take turns picking out songs to sing. It's so dirty inside the cabins that it feels like we're in a TV commercial for Windex or something: when you wipe a counter, your rag comes away completely black, and the place where you rubbed has made a new, clean stripe in the dust.

In the second cabin, while I'm cleaning the bathroom, I pull back the shower curtain, and there's something horrible lying right near the drain. It's some kind of animal, gray and furry, except for its long naked tail, and it's completely, totally dead. I scream and leap out of the room in two big jumps.

My mom comes running, all concerned, and I just point and say, "Shower." I'm shaking and crying, which is silly because I know it can't hurt me, but I don't think I've ever seen anything dead before, except a bug. My mind keeps showing me how it looked, and my arms and legs feel tickly all over, like maybe there's something crawling on me.

I'm far enough away from the bathroom door that I can't see my mom when she finds it, but I'm surprised that she doesn't make any kind of noise. I'm sort of expecting her to freak out; she's usually a coward about yucky stuff. But she comes back out, after a minute, looking completely calm. She walks over and gives me a hug, holding on until I quiet down. Then she walks me outside with her arm still around me and says, "Why don't you go and take a break? I'll ask Scott where I can find a shovel."

I sit in the grass underneath a tree, and my mom walks in the direction of the garden, retying the bandanna she's been using to keep her hair out of her face. I feel calmer now and almost happy with relief, happy to be out of the cabin and happy to have my mom making things safe. I'm kind of impressed by how calm she is, how brave and casual, like she does this all the time. "I love you, Mommy," I call after her, and she turns her head and blows me a kiss as she walks away.

By lunchtime, everyone's here. The new family is the Ruffins; they're from Philadelphia, and they're black, the only black family here. The parents are named Tom and Janelle, and they just have one little boy. His name is Hayden, he's four years old, and he doesn't talk.

My mom gives Janelle a big hug when they see each other, and they sit next to each other at lunch, chattering away. I know that they met a couple of times before, at different Scott Bean events, and that sometimes they used to talk on the phone, but I'm surprised to see that they seem to be such good friends. It hits me that I haven't seen my mom with friends very often; I don't think she had very many in DC.

There's a lot to remember; I keep running through the names in my head, trying to get them all down. Ryan and Hayden are the only boys. Charlotte's five, and her dad calls her Princess. Candy's the oldest; her birthday's two months earlier than Tilly's.

The afternoon is more chores, but Scott has told us that we should all wear our bathing suits to dinner, so at least we know there's something to look forward to. Now that there are more of us working, Scott divides us up into new groups; I end up painting the walls of the office with my dad, Candy, and her mom, Diane.

The office is its own little building, just one room. It's also the only place in the camp that has an air conditioner; Scott points out the big ancient-looking thing propped in the window while he's giving us our work instructions.

"Not my idea," he says, grinning. "It was here when I bought it. I guess the Johnsons—that's the couple that used to run the place— I guess they liked to have a cool place to work. But since we've got it, we may as well use it." He clicks one of the knobs, and the machine starts making a loud wheezy noise and blowing out puffs of dust.

"Whoa, there," says Scott, waving his hand in the air to spread out the particles. "That should stop in a second, but I'd better let Tom and Janelle know that they should keep Hayden out of here until I've had a chance to change the filters. Poor little guy has asthma, in addition to everything else. Are all of you okay with a little dust?"

"Okay with me," says Diane. She grabs a handful of her red hair, lifts it up like she's going to put it in a ponytail. I've decided I like her hairstyle. "As long as it makes it a little cooler in here." We've only been in here a couple of minutes, but our faces are all wet with sweat.

"No problem," says my dad, knocking on his chest like a door. "We've got strong Hammond lungs. And if *you* don't have any ideological problems with . . . you know, CO2 emissions and hydrochlorofluorocarbons and what have you, then neither do I." I tense up a little. He's teasing Scott, and I'm not sure Scott's going to find it funny.

But Scott just gives him an ordinary smile. "I don't think one little AC unit is going to bring about the downfall of the planet anytime soon. Or were you talking about something other than the environmental impact?"

"I'm not really talking about anything," says my dad. "Just trying to 'be consistent about eliminating the unhealthy effects of modern society.'" I recognize that phrase from the Camp Harmony brochures; we had enough of them lying around our house, back in DC. "It all adds up, right? Genetically modified foods and video game violence and light pollution and so on. You know, I've seen some interesting research that suggests that the rise of air-conditioning may be partly responsible for the increase in obesity in the last few decades."

"Dad," I say. I don't like it when he gets like this. And I know he doesn't really have anything against air-conditioning; we had it in our house in DC. He's just trying to make Scott mad. I look over at Candy and Diane, wondering what they're going to think of us.

Scott laughs and shakes his head a little. He's looking at my dad like he finds him genuinely funny, but also like he doesn't quite understand him and wants to figure him out. "Lighten up, Josh," he says. "You want to go find an Amish camp, be my guest."

"Nah," my dad says. "I'm just messing with you. I'll gladly accept twenty square feet of cool air."

"All right, then," Scott says, turning to leave. "You all can get started. I'll see you at dinner. And don't forget . . ." He pauses and points to me, waiting for me to fill in the blank.

"To wear our bathing suits?" I ask.

"Ding, ding, ding," says Scott. "Give that girl a prize." The screen door creaks as he pushes it open and steps out into the sun.

The four of us stand and look at each other for a moment.

"I don't get it," Candy says. She's already holding a paintbrush and a tiny drop of paint has fallen onto her T-shirt, right on the picture of the glass of milk. "How can air-conditioning make you fat?"

We paint for a while without saying very much, and slowly, the room gets a tiny bit cooler. I don't have a watch or a cell phone, so I don't know what time it is, but it feels like this day has been going on for a very long time. It's weird: things that happened this morning, like Tilly arguing with Ryan Gough, or finding the dead rodent-thing in the shower, seem further away in the past than going swimming with Tilly and my mom and dad in the hotel pool yesterday. I start to freak out a little every time I think too much about being here—so is this what our life is like now? Is every day going to feel this long? So instead, I make up an email in my head to send to my friend Ana. *There's no TV and no DVDs and no iPhones and no computers. I bet if there was a blackout, nobody would even notice . . . Scott thinks he's like that* Man vs. Wild *guy or something. If he tries to make us drink pee, I'm calling you to get your butt up here and rescue me . . . Tilly's on the dinner crew tonight, so if you don't hear from me, it probably means I've been poisoned.* And then I mentally erase that last part, almost before I'm done making it up. It's hard to know how to talk about Tilly to my friends; *I* can make fun of her and complain about her, but I don't want anyone else to.

I keep glancing over at Candy, trying to figure out if we're going to be friends. She's skinny and mostly pretty, with the type of straight hair that looks like it probably always stays in the right place, even though people with that kind of hair always say that there's nothing they can do with it. She has pierced ears, and she's wearing little yellow emoji earrings—one smiling, the other sticking out its tongue.

At first, I can't tell if she's friendly or not, but she smiles when I say I like her earrings, and then when her mom leaves to go to the bathroom, and my dad's not looking, she gives me a piece of gum from a pack that she snuck in. "Enjoy it while it lasts," she whispers. We both chew slowly and quietly, but after a couple of minutes, the room smells like fake watermelon, and there's not much we can do about that. My dad gives me a look like he knows exactly what I'm up to, but he doesn't say anything, and he doesn't make us spit it out.

Candy's thirteen, so you'd think she'd be more likely to be Tilly's friend than mine, but things don't always work right with Tilly and making friends. So maybe she'll be my friend instead. Or both of us, or neither, though there aren't enough kids here for anyone to be too picky about who they get along with.

Finally, after painting for about ten hours, I tell Ana in my head, *my dad finally said it was time to stop, so we're going back to our gross cabin to put on our bathing suits. I hope Tilly remembered to shave her legs in the shower this morning, but I wouldn't bet on it.* And then I erase that part, too.

chapter 6

Alexandra

September 2007: Washington, DC

The first time you hear the name "Scott Bean," you are sitting in a booth at Bamboo Garden, and your daughter is knocking her head gently against the floor. A moment ago, you were all seated more or less normally, though Tilly was fidgeting wildly and Iris was banging a spoon against her glass. Then, like she's been zapped by an electric prod, Tilly's out of her seat and kneeling on the ground. She moves through the motions quickly, twisting to touch the necessary parts to the tiles: first the left side, just above the temple, then the same spot on the right. Then she stands and bends herself double, like she's about to do a somersault, and touches the ground with the top of her skull, looking at the world upside down and through her legs. The whole thing takes maybe four seconds. Then she slides back into the booth and starts teasing her sister about having been born in the Year of the Snake.

You and Josh sip at your water resolutely, not checking to see if any of the other customers are looking at you; Iris doodles on her place mat, apparently oblivious. The waitress approaches, smiling brightly, and Tilly launches into a well-argued critique of the menu.

She's been reading about different Chinese regional cuisines, and she has a lot of points to make about the dishes the restaurant could be offering.

"Tilly," you say, trying to rein her in, but it's more so that you don't appear to be condoning the steamroller monologue. You know there isn't much chance you're going to get her to stop. The waitress listens, smiles indulgently, and then—when it becomes clear that Tilly is not about to stop talking anytime soon—she just raises her voice and talks over her to ask if you'd like anything to drink.

You've been wavering about whether or not to order a beer, noting that there are still several hours to go until the girls' bedtime, and knowing that you're more likely to stay on an even keel if you keep your head clear. But you've just watched your daughter rub her head on the floor of a Chinese restaurant, and the question is no longer really a question. You order a Tsingtao.

Your reach for your phone in your pocket, before remembering that it's out of power. You feel unaccountably lost; there's no possibility of escape, no chance to set it glowing in your lap, so you can check your email or look in for a few minutes on Facebook. You're stuck in the here and now, nowhere to go but the present. Enforced Zen.

You'd like to make eye contact with Josh, share a moment of harried-parent commiseration, but you're feeling a little disconnected from him today. It happens; you figure it's normal in a marriage. It reminds you of a *Sesame Street* skit, one from when you were a kid, the one where Grover illustrates the concepts of "near" and "far" by running back and forth between the camera and a distant spot in the pleasant mauve background. Sometimes you feel like you and Josh are standing together, firmly united; other times (like today) you feel like you're shouting across an empty purple space.

He's a better dad than you are a mom. You don't know for sure that this is true from any objective standpoint, but it's one of your fundamental beliefs about your marriage. He's more patient, more willing to get down on the floor and follow any flight of fancy the kids might come up with. More secure, too, more confident that he's taking the right path. Even now, in your eighth year of parenting, you often feel completely at sea. You learn a lot from watching him, though you bristle when he makes suggestions about your interactions with the kids. You may not always feel like you know what you're doing, but you don't want to be told that you're doing it wrong.

Iris has slipped under the table now, and Tilly is talking quietly to herself and chewing on a thick hank of hair. This is behavior that emerges every time her hair grows below the length of her chin; you've thought about keeping it shorter, but she desperately hates haircuts. The last time your mother visited, she made a number of attempts to curb the habit: gum, she thought, might take care of the need for oral input. That ended predictably, with a pink blob swinging back and forth in a tuft of hair. Tilly sobbed, panic-stricken, for forty-five minutes while you rubbed her back and searched the Internet for tips about freezing the gum with ice cubes and lifting it off with peanut butter. After that, your mother gave up the crusade.

"Come on, Iris," you say, reaching under the table and finding an arm. "Restaurant behavior."

You reach for your phone again, automatically, then remember again. You've recently discovered in yourself a vast capacity for hiding. You know a million ways to avoid being here, sitting in a restaurant with your husband and children. (Here comes your beer, dripping with condensation; that's one of them.)

At home on your laptop or in the car-pool line with your phone, you're desperate to find something to fix your attention on. You want to be absorbed, in an almost literal sense. You're thinking about paper towels here—or no, you're thinking about commercials for paper towels. You're thinking about that mysterious blue fluid that people are always spilling and pouring on counters in paper towel commercials. You start with a puddle, an unnameable shape with ever-changing edges. But once the towel hits it—dropped flat on top, in a way no human being has ever actually used a paper towel—it becomes something new. A fixed stain. The towel has put a stop to its unpredictable movements, constrained its messy edges. Made everything flat and manageable and neat.

You find yourself idly staring at a bulletin board hanging by the door, covered with all the usual neighborhood flyers. You can't read much of the fine print from here, but it looks like someone's offering guitar lessons, someone else is selling a bed. And toward the bottom, there's a pale green sheet of paper with the heading "Do You Have a Challenging Kid?"

Back here at the table, Iris is trying to get your attention to show you a picture of a puppy that she's drawn, while Tilly continues her monologue about Chinese food. "Did you know," she asks, "that 'dim sum' literally means 'touch your heart'?"

You do know this, and so do Josh and Iris; Tilly mentions the fact at least twenty times a day. "Proud annoyance" might be a good description for your current emotional state. It tugs at you, the way she phrases it as a question; she knows that conversation is supposed to contain both give-and-take, and she's trying so hard to get it right, even as she talks right over any answer that a listener might give.

So *yes*, you silently answer the flyer on the wall. *Yes, I do have a challenging kid.* You squint, trying to make out the rest of the text, but the only words you can see clearly are a bulleted list of symptoms (*emotional lability, repetitive behaviors, tics, attention-related issues*) and a jumble of acronyms (*ADHD, OCD, ASDs, SID, PDD-NOS*).

It seems like it should interest you—what are they trying to sell, anyway? A parenting seminar? A self-published book? A behavioral consultant? But you've hit some kind of informational overload, and you don't want any more input. It's everywhere, this talk about special-needs kids. Earlier this week, Jenny McCarthy was on *Oprah*, spouting her particular version of the vaccine hypothesis. The whole thing annoys you, partly because it seems like sloppy science—the study that first raised the question has been revealed to be deeply flawed, and a number of more recent investigations into the matter have shown no connection—but you can see why it strikes a chord with parents. *We were just trying to do what we were supposed to*, they seem to be saying. *We followed all the advice, and this happened anyway.*

Something you've discovered over the past few months is that there seem to be two groups of autistic kids; sometimes you even wonder if they might be suffering from two completely separate disorders. There are kids like Tilly who seemed a little quirky, a little off-center, right from the beginning. Her development hasn't been smooth the way Iris's has; Iris is your "typically developing" child, your yardstick for normalcy. You can take her for haircuts without worrying that she'll scream the minute anyone touches her ears. You can expect her to make charming mistakes, like counting "one, two, three, nine, eight," and to learn to read at the ancient age of six. But Tilly has always been wildly ahead of her peers in some areas and behind in others: she could read and do simple multiplication at the age of three, for example, but now, at eight, she still can't ride a bike or tie her shoes. Essentially, from the moment she was born, Tilly has always been *Tilly*. She met most of her milestones and had all her shots, and there's never been a moment you can pinpoint as the instant she went off the developmental rails.

So maybe you're not in the right subset to comment on the vaccination question. Because there's also that second group of autistic kids, the ones whose stories aren't anything like Tilly's. The ones who seemed normal, perfectly fine, until the day after their fifteen-month checkup, or their eighteen-month, or their twenty-four. You can see why parents can't help but draw a connection. If you can trace it back to that day in the exam room, your little one chattering away on your lap in his diaper, if you locate that as the last time that he really seemed like himself, then it's impossible not to wonder if all these losses might be traced to the moment when the nurse knocked on the door and walked in with her bouquet of needles. To the way she was both gentle and steely as she held your baby down and made him cry. To the soft words of reassurance as she pasted *Bob the Builder* Band-Aids on both his thighs.

There are too many people with the same story for it not to mean anything, although it may not have anything to do with mercury or thimerosal or the MMR vaccine. It may be years before anyone finally figures out what's going on, but there's something there. It's going to come to light eventually.

And who knows what it'll be? Medicine is ever-evolving, like anything else. There was that thing about stomach ulcers, remember? Everything you ever heard about stomach ulcers suggested two things: one, there's almost nothing anyone can do about them, and two, if you have them, it's probably your own fault. Stress at work? Too much coffee and whiskey and spicy foods? Guess what? It's caught up with you. It was like gout, almost Dantesque in its perfect irony. Then, a million years later, but still within the span of your lifetime, this comes to light: most stomach ulcers are caused by a particular strain of bacteria. Give the patient a couple of rounds of antibiotics, treat the infection, and he recovers completely.

So maybe a cure for autism isn't so far off. Autism isn't exactly what Tilly has, but "autism spectrum" is close enough that you can use it as shorthand. Asperger's is almost right, but it doesn't describe her completely; you also suspect that Tourette's may play a role, though you haven't really explored it. Labels oversimplify (and contain criteria that are subject to change whenever the next DSM comes out), but they also serve a purpose. "She's on the autism spectrum" gets you understood; when you say PDD-NOS, all you get are blank stares.

It's not even clear that a "cure" is the right thing to be hoping for. But you know this much: you need help, and for now you're on your own. So you do what you can to make things easier for her and for yourself. Don't assume anything: if you tell her not to pick up her food with her fingers, she may lean forward and put her mouth directly on the plate. Make her feel safe. Don't let your own anxiety about her behavior get in the way of giving her what she needs. Remember that there's a larger picture here: we're all scorned and admired, celebrated and pitied. Today you may be the mom whose child seems too old to be having a tantrum in the post office (or the one whose child is touching her head to the floor of a Chinese restaurant—right there, she's doing it again), but tomorrow you may be the mom whose child holds forth on the difference between "time" and "thyme" in the produce aisle of the grocery store.

When she's having trouble with something—like now, as she begins to lose patience with how long it's taking for the food to arrive—try to look at things from her point of view. (Isn't that what we keep saying she lacks? Okay, then; you try it first.) Imagine that your fingers fumble and don't always do what you want them to. Imagine that you feel like you're wearing a pair of thick gloves while trying to zip zippers and button buttons. Imagine that public restrooms are so loud that you're genuinely frightened to go inside them, and that the fresh-ground coffee smell at Starbucks is so strong that it makes you want to gag.

Imagine that everything is loud and hard and overwhelming. Imagine that you can't always tell when you have to go to the bathroom. Imagine that sometimes you become so involved in your own thoughts, the electrifying beauty of your own plans and ideas, that you can't pay attention to what the rest of your body is doing, whether you're stepping on someone's foot or about to knock a glass of juice off the table.

Josh is telling the kids knock-knock jokes, delaying Tilly's meltdown, even if you can sense the desperation in his forced cheerfulness. Better this way, though, you think, even as you make another aborted reach for your pocket. Better not to remove yourself from your life. Try to *be here*, at dinner, with your family. Pay attention to the colors of the fish in the tank by the door, the scent of soy and garlic in the air. The spot on your place mat where your beer has made a damp circle around the Year of the Ox. Nothing's wrong, not at this moment. No reason to wish you were anyplace else. Iris tries to stand on the seat to look at the people behind you; as you pull her down, you press a kiss to the back of her head.

They're beautiful kids. You think so, at least. They get their hair color from you, dirty blond—a phrase given new meaning by this new tic of Tilly's—but it's wavy like Josh's, which you think makes it prettier than your own straight (and often limp) head of hair. Brown eyes, big and expressive. Smart and funny and brave, both of them. And they're yours. They're yours.

The food arrives, trailing banners of steam. You're relieved to see that they remembered to leave the onions out of the lo mein; that's a meltdown forestalled. You bat away the girls' hands as they reach for the hot dishes, and begin spooning food onto everyone's plates. There are complaints and comparisons about who has more of what, but there's enough here for all of you. Your little corner of the restaurant falls quiet. You pick up forks and spoons and bow your heads in anticipation of the first bite.

On the way out, you stop briefly by the bulletin board, turn your eyes toward the green piece of paper. You don't have time to absorb very much of it, but the words "parenting" and "help" capture your attention. You rip off one of the tabs at the bottom, the phrase "Scott Bean, Harmonious Parenting" written sideways with a phone number and website, and jam it in your purse. Later, when you look for it, it will be gone. It will be three more years before you hear the name "Scott Bean" again. That time, you'll pay more attention.

chapter 7

Iris

June 4, 2012: New Hampshire

Tonight's dinner is a cookout: something special to celebrate our first night all together. When my dad and I walk to the dining hall, I see that the grills are set up outside, in a big grassy space without trees. My mom is one of the ones doing the grilling. She's wearing her black bathing suit, with a pair of shorts over it. She always wears one-piece bathing suits—I think she thinks she's too fat for a bikini—but she looks pretty in this one. It kind of shows off her boobs, but not in a gross way. Her boobs are on the big side, and I always wonder if mine will be, too. Tilly's are getting big, I guess, but they always look kind of floppy because she doesn't like wearing a bra.

When my mom sees me, she smiles and raises a big two-pronged fork like she's making a toast. Tilly's going back and forth between the dining hall and the food table, carrying out trays and bowls. It's weird: it feels like a long time since I've seen my mom and Tilly, like it's been long enough for me to miss them, even though I actually just saw them around lunchtime. I wonder if time is ever going to feel regular here, or if it just seems weird because it's still the first day.

There are a bunch of little tables set up with folding chairs, and after a minute I notice that there are name cards on them, telling people where they should sit. I can tell right away that Scott's playing some get-to-know-each-other game with the tables. Families don't get to sit together; everyone's all split up and mingled. I'm sitting with Diane (who I've started thinking of as Candy's mom, even though she's also the mom of both Ryan and Charlotte), and Hayden, the little boy who doesn't talk. I feel annoyed; I just want to sit with my mom and dad and Tilly and act like things are normal for five minutes.

Scott's all over the place, getting everything ready. He's wearing a chef's hat, which somehow doesn't look dorky on him; he just looks like a guy in a barbecue sauce commercial. He walks over to the serving table and sets down a big bowl of fruit salad, then pauses, peering around with his forehead wrinkled, doing a head count or something. Then he whistles through his teeth, loud and shrill, to get our attention. Hayden starts crying.

"Good evening, troops," Scott says in his talking-to-a-crowd voice, louder than usual to cover the noise of Hayden shrieking. (Hayden's mom, Janelle, is bent down next to him now, trying to shush him, but it isn't working.) "Grub's almost ready, but before we start, why don't you all take a minute to look around and see where you're sitting. Big kids help the little ones."

When the food's ready, we all take plates—real ones, not paper ones like at most cookouts—and walk past the food table. There are hamburgers and hot dogs, but I can tell the hot dogs are the weird ones with no nitrites or nitrates or whatever, no preservatives or artificial colors. Veggie burgers and fake hot dogs, too, and skewers of grilled vegetables. No chips or anything like that. Big pitchers of water. Nothing else to drink.

I let my mom put a hamburger on my plate, from a big platter she's carried over from the grill. "It's regular meat, right?" I ask.

She smiles. "What—you don't like kangaroo burgers?"

"Mom, come on." I sound whiny, but it's been a long day.

"It's fine, honey. Regular beef. You'll like it."

I go sit down at my table and start eating, even though no one else is sitting there yet. A couple of minutes later, Hayden and his mom, Janelle, come over. Janelle's short and skinny, with black hair cut close to her head. She smiles at me and says hi, puts a hand on my shoulder like she knows me already. But she's looking at the cards, and when she sees how things are set up, she makes a little noise under her breath. She helps Hayden settle down into the chair next to mine and gives him a plate of food, then she calls Scott to come over.

"Hey, Janelle," he says cheerfully. "What's up?"

"I'm sorry, but one of us has to sit with Hayden, either me or Tom. He'd rather have me, though."

Scott nods and listens to her with a serious expression on his face. "I understand what you're saying, Janelle," he says. "There have already been a lot of changes for one day. But you know that we have to begin the way we plan to continue. And there are a whole lot of people besides you and Tom that Hayden's going to have to learn to trust."

Janelle laughs softly and shakes her head. "Yeah, that all sounds great. But I'm not talking about preferences here: 'Oh, gosh, Hayden would really *prefer* to sit with his parents.' I'm saying, no way is he going to sit here and eat with a bunch of people he doesn't know, unless you're planning to tie him to the chair."

Scott turns to watch Hayden, who's holding a chunk of watermelon to his mouth, sucking out the juice; it's already white around the edges. "He looks like he's doing all right."

"That's because I'm standing right here. I walk away, he's going to be following right behind me. You try to stop him, he's going to melt down completely, and I don't see how that's going to be constructive for anyone."

"Janelle, Hayden was in day care back in Philadelphia, right?"

"Until they couldn't handle him anymore."

"And did you drop him off and leave every morning, or did you stay all day, so he wouldn't get upset?"

Janelle rolls her eyes. "No. That is not what's going on here. I'm not being overprotective, I'm not saying I can't let Hayden ever get upset. He gets upset about twenty times a day, as I think you've seen. I'm just trying to figure out a way that we can all take part in your nice little get-to-know-you barbecue, without me having to carry out a screaming child."

Scott says, "Let's just give it a try, okay? Not for the whole meal, even, but for a few minutes. Leap of faith."

Janelle's quiet for a minute. She looks doubtful, but she says, "Yeah, okay."

She crouches down to talk to Hayden. "Listen, buddy, Mommy's going to be right nearby. You just sit here and eat your dinner with"—she glances around at our place cards—"Diane and Iris, and afterward, we'll go for a swim, and you and Daddy can play Speedboat, okay?"

Hayden just stares at her. He's really kind of cute; he's got these gigantic brown eyes, and he's wearing a plaid shirt that looks like someone took a grown-up shirt and shrunk it down. I can't tell if he understands what his mom just told him, but as soon as she starts walking away, he makes a noise that sounds like "mm mm mm" and tries to get up from his seat. He can't, though, because Scott's got his hands on his shoulders, keeping him in place.

Hayden starts to howl. He starts hitting his own head with his hands, and his face is all crumpled up, like he's terrified or completely miserable. I get this feeling that I have with Tilly: half sympathetic because he's so upset, and half annoyed because, honestly, his mom's only five feet from him, and it shouldn't be this big a deal. But he's just a little kid, and Tilly is older than I am, so with him, I'm leaning more toward the sympathy side.

Janelle's standing with her back to us. She's got a hand covering her face, and I can tell she really wants to just come back and fix the problem. Scott's talking to Hayden in a low voice, trying to calm him down, but it's not working, and then I have an idea. I reach in my pocket and pull out my key ring. I've had it in my pocket since we left DC; all the keys are for our old house, so they're not much use anymore, but I like feeling them there, this reminder of our old life (which wasn't our "old life" until yesterday). Anyway, there's a little flashlight on the key chain that turns on when you squeeze it, and I hold it up in front of Hayden and make it blink a few times.

He doesn't stop crying completely, but I can tell he's interested. He stops hitting himself and reaches out toward the key chain. I let him grab it from me, but of course the light turns off, because he hasn't figured out the squeezing part yet.

"You have to do this," I say. I put my fingers gently on his and show him, and when I take my hand away, he's doing it by himself. He's not yelling anymore, though his breath is still catching sometimes that way it does when you've been crying. "Yeah," I say. "Good job."

Scott slowly takes his hands away, and Hayden stays put. "Nice work, Iris," Scott whispers to me, and I take a bite of my hamburger, feeling kind of proud and embarrassed at the same time.

After dinner (which is pretty good, except for the burger buns, which are gluten-free and fall apart almost immediately), Scott gets our attention by raising his water glass over his head and clinking it with a spoon. He waits for everyone to quiet down, and then he stays quiet for a minute longer, turning to look at each person individually. He's smiling like he's going to burst with happiness.

"I cannot tell you," he begins, "how good it is to see all of you here. The birth of Camp Harmony is a triumph, not just for me, but for all of us."

He pauses, looks down, and swallows. A couple of the parents take it as a suggestion to clap.

"When I first met each of you, each of these beautiful families I see before me, you were people in trouble. Each of you had traveled a painful path, and each of you was struggling to find a way to make things better."

"No, we weren't," someone interrupts, and I don't have to look around to know that it's Tilly. She never seems to get it that when someone's talking to a whole group of people, it's not a personal conversation between her and them.

I hear my dad call Tilly's name from whatever table he's sitting at, and I know he's going to quiet her down, even if it means taking her somewhere else. I'm mad, suddenly. Furious. He'll take Tilly to a different part of the woods, and she'll be free to wander around and talk about giant statues, and she'll have all his attention, and she'll never even get that it's almost like a punishment. That he's taking her away because she can't act like a normal human being.

But Scott holds up a hand to stop my dad. "My turn to talk, Tilly," he says. "Please wait till I'm done." He takes a breath, tries to remember where he was. "I guess I'm talking to the grown-ups here, more than the kids. I'm glad, Tilly—and the rest of you kids—if it didn't seem like your family was having a hard time. That means your parents were doing their jobs, protecting you from the bad things in the world."

I look over at Tilly. My dad's crouched down next to her, whispering in her ear, probably reminding her not to talk. But he's not letting her out of the situation, out of sitting here and listening like the rest of us are doing, and I'm glad in a way that feels a little bit mean.

"But let me tell you something, kids: I've talked to your parents, at great length. I've talked to them for hours, and I've hugged them and held their hands and sat with them while they cried."

That sounds wrong to me, and I wonder if it's supposed to be a joke. But when I look around at the grown-ups, they're not laughing or objecting or acting like Scott is saying anything crazy. They're dead serious, every last one of them, and some of them are nodding their heads. Some of them look like they might start crying right now.

"And I can tell you two things: one, your parents love you very much, and two, they weren't happy with the way things were going."

Now *I* almost feel like crying. I try to catch my mom's eye, so she can send me a secret smile and let me know that he's being kind of ridiculous. But she's got her eyes on Scott, and I can't get her attention.

"Anyway," Scott says. "I didn't get up here to talk about the way things were. I'm here to talk about the way things are going to be. Because now, none of you are alone. As of tonight, you're not just the Ruffin family and the Hammond family and the Gough family. From this moment on, you're part of the Camp Harmony family, and let me tell you, that's a pretty special place to be."

There's clapping from everywhere, all of the grown-ups and some of the kids. I put my hands together once, softly, so they don't make any sound.

"Now, you're all wearing your bathing suits, am I right?" Scott asks. Everyone yells "Yeah!" or something like it. I say it, too, but not very loud.

"Okay, then. If you're wearing anything else—shoes, socks, T-shirt—take them off now, or they're going to get wet with the rest of you." He pulls his own T-shirt off and waves it over his head. His chest is tan, and it's hairier than my dad's.

"All right, now. I think we're ready. Everybody join hands—grab on to whoever's closest to you, it doesn't matter who."

The only one near me is Diane; Hayden left to sit with his mom a while ago. She smiles at me, and I let her hold my hand. A minute later, Hayden's dad, Tom, takes my other hand, and soon the whole group of us is joined together.

"As we go down to the water," Scott says, "we're going to sing the Camp Harmony song. I know you all know it—your folks have told me you've been practicing."

He's right; Mom and Dad made us sing it a bunch of times in the car on the ride up here. I guess it's based on an old song that was used in a Coke commercial (which my dad seems to think is really funny), but Scott's changed some of the words. As we begin to sing, Scott pulls forward from the front of the line, and we're walking down the hill to the lake, all in a line like we're one long creature.

I'd like to build the world a camp
And furnish it with hope
With stars aglow and room to grow
A perfect antidote

The sun is setting over the water, and I feel happy and sad at the same time, the way you do sometimes when you're singing. I've been keeping my voice quiet, but when we get to the next verse, with the part about harmony, I let it take me over, and I shout it as loud as anyone.

Scott snakes the line of us down to the edge of the water, and then we step into the lake, one by one, all joined together. The water's chillier than I'm expecting, and the bottom feels different on my feet from the sand at an ocean beach; instead of being firm, it's kind of soft and muddy. But Scott keeps singing, as he leads us further in, as we step down a sudden drop that brings the grown-ups into the water up to their waists and the littlest kids up to their chests. He's still singing when he stops and looks around and nods, then he gets us into a circle and jerks downward with his hands, causing a chain reaction that drags each of us under the surface of the water and then back up again. And as we all pop our heads back out, wet and sort of shocked, it's like we all make a decision, together in a split second, to keep singing, right where we left off.

I'm shivering a little, but I'm smiling and almost laughing, happy for no reason at all. I squeeze the hands of the two people on either side of me, and I know before it happens that they'll continue the pattern. I know without any question that those squeezes will make their way around the circle, to my mom and my dad and Tilly and everyone else, and come right back to me.

chapter 8

Inside the Coal Mine

From Scott Bean's Parenting Blog
October 2011

You are cruel to your children every day, whether you mean to be or not. You are cruel by treating them better than anyone else ever will. You are cruel by giving in to their demands sometimes, but not others. You are cruel by making them the center of your lives.

Children, especially those children who are a little bit out of step, need firm, clear boundaries. They need limits and consequences. They need to learn to meet the world on the world's terms.

The world around us has become toxic so gradually that we barely even notice. We think, "I watched a lot of TV as a child, and it didn't harm me." But children's programming was on for a few hours in the mornings and a few hours in the afternoons; in between, you either went to play outside, or you were subjected to endless soap operas and game shows. Seeing a movie meant going to a movie theater—a specific outing, a rare treat—not buying a DVD and watching it as many times as you liked. We all have stories of finding a *Playboy*, or something a bit raunchier, in our parents' closets or in a trash pile somewhere, but it wasn't possible for any child in any house to find a hundred varieties of pornography, just by pressing a few buttons.

We breathe tainted air, and we eat tainted food. Is it any wonder that your children are having trouble?

Who knows how much we've damaged these children already, without being aware that we're doing anything wrong? Not so long ago, doctors used to recommend that pregnant women take up smoking to curb anxiety. Who's to say that in thirty years, people won't be shaking their heads over the foolishness of prenatal ultrasounds and plastic sippy cups?

Your kids are sensitive; that's one of the things that sets them apart. It may be that most American kids are ingesting artificial colors that are illegal in Europe, and sleeping on mattresses treated with flame retardants. And not all of them show ill effects, at least not as far as we can tell. But your kids' systems can't handle it, and the results are devastating.

Difficulty regulating emotions, repetitive behaviors, tics and OCD-like symptoms, inability to process social cues: these are warnings. They are indications that something needs to change. These kids are coal-mine canaries, and we can't even see how hard they're struggling to stay upright on their perches.

That's where I come in. My question for you is: are you going to let me help?

chapter 9

Alexandra

March 2008: Washington, DC

Some days you're an idiot, and some days you're a fucking idiot. It's the winter of 2008, and you've developed a habit of berating yourself while you drive. You wait until you're alone in the car, the girls dropped safely at school: no one here but you and your wretched brain. It's not hard to find material; you've got thirty-nine years' worth of evidence to draw from, and it's all up for scrutiny. You said something stupid (maybe last week, maybe in the third grade). You failed to say something smart (to your first boyfriend or to a random woman in line at Safeway). You missed an opportunity. You raised your voice. You made the wrong choice. You behaved in a way that was morally ambiguous. You were rude to a stranger. You were cruel to someone you love.

"Idiot" is not quite right—it's not that you think of yourself as stupid, exactly—but it's a good enough placeholder. "Bitch" could be satisfying, if it weren't sunk so deep in cultural muck, buried under alternating layers of misogyny and saucy reclamation. ("You say I'm a bitch like it's a bad thing!" You've seen it in catalogs: you can have it embroidered on pillows. Perfect for Mother's Day.)

Were you ever a good person? Some part of you knows that you were, maybe even are. But the bad stuff is so much more prominent. When you were a kid, you never once stuck up for someone who was being teased; instead, you'd watch, relieved, glad that no one was examining you with such focus. You screamed at your parents, too many times to count. You let a longtime friendship lapse, out of awkwardness. You spanked Tilly once, in fury: four hard swats across her bottom.

So many offenses, and so many car trips. It's a ritual, your own private sacrament; you're zealous enough that you've become your own church. You take yourself to confession; you whisper your own private gospel: the Idiot's Prayer. Penance, penance, penance, but that's where it stops. This is a church that has no use for forgiveness.

Luckily, it's time-limited: you're done the moment you pull up in front of your house, the moment you step out of the car. Go in peace; pause button pressed. Because you know you're on your way to fill up your mind with something else.

When you sit down with your computer, you feel both anticipatory pleasure and anticipatory guilt. Your role as a stay-at-home mom has changed in recent years, now that the girls are in school, and it's less obvious what you're supposed to spend your days doing. But it almost certainly isn't this. Come on, though; ease up already. Give yourself a break. We're done with this, remember? Save it for the car.

You open your laptop, and there is your city. You've built it up from nothing, a stretch of worthless brown dirt, a primitive population still working on their farming skills. Now it contains a city hall, sixteen restaurants, and a sports arena. You're saving up to build a world-class art museum.

This is the latest in a series of video games you've played over the last several months. Before this, you ran a cartoon diner, selling burgers and milk shakes to customers in a number of different historic settings. If you took too long with their orders, they'd fume and storm out. You sold chili dogs to Napoleon and apple pie to Shakespeare. Cleopatra had a particular fondness for your french fries.

Now you're building a city that you call Dizzantium. You grow crops, run factories, design parks, all to keep your tiny inhabitants happy. They're an adorable but fickle bunch, these masses you command. If your "civic balances" get low, they stalk through the town in gangs, causing riots and defacing your monuments with graffiti. Fights break out in the streets. But if you give them what they want— a new grocery store, a naval victory over a rival city-state—they throw tiny parades in your honor.

You see what you're doing, channeling your social and emotional needs into this predictable artificial environment. An hour before Tilly's third birthday party, Josh found you sitting in the middle of a messy playroom, organizing the furniture in a dollhouse. It may not be terribly fruitful to rearrange deck chairs on the *Titanic*, but that doesn't mean it isn't satisfying.

You keep your phone next to you while you play. Because one of the things you're not thinking about while you're strategizing battles and civic upkeep is the fact that Tilly is coming very close to being too much for her school to handle.

Matching up Tilly with a school that works for her has never been an easy task, although it took a while before you really understood that you needed to start worrying. The two years she spent at her second preschool—she'd had to leave the first because of a potty-training deadline that the two of you couldn't seem to meet—were happy ones, for the most part. She didn't connect with many of the kids, but she was still young enough that you didn't think it was necessarily a problem. (The going theory, even among the parents of some of her classmates, was that she was simply too smart to find other three-year-olds interesting.) And the teachers seemed to like her, which made every difference.

It was already clear, though, that your local public elementary school—a good one, one of the reasons you bought the house you did—wasn't going to be the best place for her. She was quiet and dreamy, often locked inside her own head. Spinning out elaborate fantasies when you wanted her to listen to directions, pacing the room when you wanted her to sit still. But she could also be alarmingly rigid, tantrums bursting out of nowhere if (for example) you added the cheese powder to the macaroni before you poured the milk, when last time you did it the other way round.

You and Josh did your research, and you figured out what you could afford, and you applied to a private school whose website said all the right things about nurturing. And you sent your child into a situation she was not the least bit prepared to handle.

She started in September, and by Thanksgiving, she was in the middle of what might be, without too much exaggeration, called a breakdown. Here is what a breakdown looks like in a five-year-old: She has nightmares. She wets her pants. She kicks and she bites. She does every single thing she's ever been asked not to do.

The school tried to help, during the early part of the trouble, before things got too intense. They called you in for conferences with the teachers and the school counselor. They gave you books to read; they suggested, of all things, that you buy her a trampoline.

The trampoline thing seemed to come out of nowhere, even after the teachers tried to connect the dots for you, with lots of phrases like "sensory input" and "motor planning." But it didn't take a lot to convince you. *It doesn't have to be big*, they told you. *They have these little round ones, three feet in diameter; try a toy store or a sporting goods store.* And yes, you told them, of course. Of course, you would buy her a trampoline. Of course, you would drive out to the suburban mall; of course, you would find a place for it in your house and encourage her to jump for ten minutes before school each morning. You remember how hopeful this felt: *I will buy this for my little girl. I will do this because I want to help her.*

And maybe it did help, but not enough. You can say that she was expelled, or you can say that she was asked to leave. You can say, if you're in a particularly bad mood, that those assholes kicked her out. What you can't say, will never be able to say, is that you couldn't have prevented it from happening.

The thing is: she was still so little. You can hardly believe it when you look at pictures now, how little she was. There was so much about her that was big: the force of her tremendous will; the astonishing vastness of her intellect, still emerging; the outsized chaos she brought to your household. But this is all she was: a little girl. God, the picture of her on her first day of school, standing on the porch in her little purple jumper. Will you ever be able to look at that picture without wondering if that was the day you made all the wrong choices?

You walk through your city, keeping an eye out for tasks that need to be done. A rival army has burned down your armory—bad for morale. Once you finish repairing it, you should have enough points to advance to the next level, which will mean a cache of gold coins and a new set of goals to unlock. You gather materials and begin the painstaking task of reconstruction.

You remember reading once, in a college psychology class, about a process called "thought-stopping." It's a component of mind control, used by cults to gain control over new inductees. You give people a task that occupies their minds fully, and they'll pay less attention to any nagging questions that might occur to them. Chanting works, and singing, and speaking in tongues. Backbreaking labor is always a popular choice: work until you're exhausted, then fill up your brain until it's time to sleep. If you're chanting with a group for hours every morning, you're not wondering if this is where you really want to be. If you're going purposefully blank so that you can speak in tongues, you're not asking whether you chose this life or it chose you. And the thing is, you're complicit in it. You've agreed to every step.

After Tilly's diagnosis, you got in touch with the special-education team of the local public school system and requested an evaluation. Their placement suggestion—an autism classroom inside a mainstream elementary school—has not been ideal. Most of the kids in her class are more severely disabled; some of them are nonverbal. The teachers and aides are overstretched, and none of the kids seem to be getting what they need. The environment is chaotic and not particularly stimulating, and Tilly's behavior is becoming more and more out of control.

You have the feeling, lately, that your days are made of tempered glass, the kind they use in making car windows. Safety glass, as you learned in college on a drunken December evening when one of Josh's friends held a cigarette lighter to the frosty back window of his Toyota Camry, is not actually shatterproof. It's "safe" because when it does break, it crazes itself into a thousand small, dull pieces. The glass is designed so that when it suffers an injury it can't withstand—a massive impact, most often, though it can also be something as random and momentary as an impulse in the head of a nineteen-year-old boy who's going to have a hard time explaining this to his parents—it breaks in such a way that no single piece can hurt you. You'll end up with glass in your hair and on the seats; you'll find it months later in the pockets of the coat you were wearing that evening. The pieces are harmless: blunt little jigsaw fragments, not a sharp edge in sight. But inarguably broken beyond repair.

When you wake up in the morning lately, you have a sense that the day ahead of you is shaky, but still solid. You know what you need to do: get the girls up, pack lunches, get everyone dressed and fed and into the car. Drive them to their separate schools. Every morning, you give Tilly a kiss, and you have a little talk about what's going to be expected of her, and how she might act to meet those expectations. And then you go home and wait for the phone call, hoping that today might prove to be made of sturdier stuff than yesterday was.

You play your video games and control what you can. Build your society, a tidy little microcosm. Keep your residents well fed, keep their landmarks clean. Plant your crops and wait for time to pass.

You're trying to make things better for Tilly: you've had multiple conferences with her teacher, and you have a call in to the district special-education office, but it's been hard to connect with a real person. Now the situation is coming to a head, and you don't know what you can do to fix it. And you have no idea at all what's going to come next.

Right before the phone rings, a little box pops up on your screen. Congratulations: your citizens have acquired the ability to manufacture rubber. Welcome to the modern world.

chapter 10

Iris

June 5, 2012: New Hampshire

The next morning, Scott gives us a talk after breakfast. We're sitting in the dining hall, with our empty plates still in front of us. The grown-ups have moved the picnic tables around, so they're set up like three sides of a square. Scott's at the top table, right in the middle.

"So," he says. "Listen up." He stops to take a sip of his coffee, while we all scrape our chairs so we're facing him. He waits for it to get quiet, then he puts his cup down and sits up a little straighter.

"Okay," he says. "We've got five more days until our first batch of Guest Campers arrives, and we've got a lot to do in that time. It's not all going to be fun, and it's not all going to be easy, but we're in it together, and that counts for something. You, me, all of us . . ." He makes a circular motion with his finger. "The thirteen people in this room, we're the Core Family of Camp Harmony. The CF, that's us. And not one of us ended up here by accident. I chose you guys because I saw something special in each of you. And you were the people I wanted by my side on this journey."

I look down at my plate. It's always kind of embarrassing when grown-ups get all sincere and touchy-feely.

"So," Scott says, after a pause. "Let's get started. What we're trying to do here, we're basically trying to build our own little city. We've already got the houses, and the paths that lead from one place to another. What else do you think our city might need?"

"Cars," says Ryan. He's wearing a shirt with *The Simpsons'* Duff Beer logo on it.

"Yeah, okay, good," says Scott. "But we've already got cars, and it's not going to be *that* big a city."

"A castle," says Charlotte. Still wearing the tutu from yesterday.

Scott nods and pretends like he's considering it. "Interesting," he says. "Good idea." And then he looks straight at me and gives a tiny nod. "Anyone else?"

He's smiling a little, like there's a joke that nobody else is in on, like we both know these are stupid answers and he knows that I have it in me to say something smart. "Food," I call out. "Like a grocery store, or you know, not a *store* exactly . . ."

"Bingo!" he says, pointing at me. "We've got to be able to eat, right? Most important thing." My mom turns and smiles at me, and some of the other grown-ups are looking my way, too. "So if we want to be our *own* city and not always relying on other cities for our food, what are some things we can do?"

I wait, but it doesn't seem like anyone else is going to answer, so I speak up again. "Plant a garden," I say.

"Absolutely," says Scott. "First order of business, plant a garden."

He stands up and goes to get an old art easel that's folded up in the corner. He sets it up where everyone can see it and puts a big pad of paper on it. "Candy," he says. "Come on up and be our note-taker."

Candy walks up to the front of the room, and Scott hands her a thick black marker. Candy runs her hands across the top and side of the pad of paper, with a big flourish, like she's one of those girls on *The Price Is Right*.

"Garden," Scott tells her. "Write that at the top. And underneath, we'll list the smaller tasks we need to do to get our garden going."

"Hey," Tilly says suddenly. "I know."

Everyone turns to look at her, and I get that nervous feeling in my stomach, because this isn't group-conversation time, and anyway, who knows what she's going to say? I doubt she has any helpful gardening tips. She might start talking about statues or make a joke about how Scott's name rhymes with "snot" or something.

"Yes, Tilly?" Scott says. He looks kind of amused, not all annoyed that she interrupted him in the middle of his speech. And down the table, my mom and dad seem totally fine. They're not like sitting up extra-straight, getting ready to grab her arm if she says something embarrassing. And I realize: it's okay for Tilly to be *Tilly* here. No one's going to care; no one's going to think we're weird for having her in our family.

"We can call it Beantown," Tilly says. "Our little city. Either that or Scottsdale."

Some of the grown-ups laugh, but it's not mean or anything. My mom's even smiling at her.

"I like the way you think, Tilly," says Scott. "Always looking at the big picture. But the problem with those names is that they're all about me, and that's not really right, I don't think. What do you guys think about calling it Harmony?"

"Harmony, New Hampshire," Tilly says. I can tell she likes it, because she gets up out of her chair and does this thing she does when she's excited where she taps all of her fingers on her cheeks, in order (pinky to pointer), a couple of times really fast. "That can be our address. Camp Harmony, Harmony, New Hampshire."

Even I know it's not as simple as that; you can't just decide to call yourself a town and expect it to be all official, like with the post office or whatever. But as Scott moves the conversation back to gardening, I reach over and put my arm around her and give her a hug from the side. She's my sister, and she drives me crazy, but I love her more than anything. And sometimes—not always but sometimes— I like the way she thinks, too.

We spend most of the morning brainstorming our "city-building tasks" (which is a phrase that Tilly came up with, in case you couldn't tell). There are four main categories of things we have to do to get everything up and running:

- Food cultivation (which includes gardening, and a whole bunch of other related stuff, like composting and collecting rainwater for irrigation);
- Animal keeping (we're getting a chicken and we're going to hatch baby chicks! And we might eventually get bees for honey, but I don't want anything to do with that);
- Daily maintenance (boring stuff like cooking and cleaning, laundry, shopping for anything we can't make ourselves);
- And "camp growing," which is a bunch of random but sort of fun things, like building a play structure and making a new sign that says "Camp Harmony," so we can finally take down the "Kozy Kabins" one.

I'm kind of hoping that I can help with that one, maybe even come up with the design. I'm really good at art, and I don't think I'm bragging by saying it, just "identifying my strengths," as Scott says. But that's the last thing on the list. The first project I'm working on is setting up an irrigation system for the garden. I'm on a team with Scott and Ryan, and right after lunch, Scott takes us over to the planting area, which is a big flat rectangle of land by the edge of the woods. I thought we were going to have to start totally from scratch, which I was kind of excited about, because I already know how to do that a little bit. At my school in DC, there was a garden in one corner of the playground, and all the classes helped out with it. But this already looks like an actual garden: the dirt's all in rows, with green leaves starting to poke up here and there, and in some places there are poles stuck in the ground (for beans, I bet) and little signs saying what's planted where.

"Are those all weeds?" asks Ryan, pointing to the plants. I sigh, but quietly, so he won't hear me. But I mean, duh. Even if you're a city kid (which, by the way, so am I) or someone who's never planted anything before, do you really think that weeds would be spread out in perfectly spaced intervals? Or, for that matter, that they'd be marked with signs?

"Nope," says Scott, and I have to give him credit, he doesn't sound like he thinks Ryan's an idiot for asking, or even nervous like he's afraid Ryan's going to pull up all his good plants. I'm kind of comparing Scott to my parents, in the way they deal with Tilly when she says things like this. They're pretty good at not sounding like she's an idiot, but the nervous part is usually there, especially with my mom.

"These are actual vegetables," Scott says. "Or at least, they're going to be. See, you guys just got here, but I've been here for a month already. And actually, I started working on this even earlier than that. I came up in March, right after the snow melted, and I laid out a bunch of newspapers and mulch to get rid of the grass. Then when I came back up last month, I was able to get started pretty quickly on planting."

"That makes sense," I say. I'm showing off maybe, but I want Scott to know that I'm not a total idiot about this stuff. "Because if you want any of them to be ready to pick over the summer, you have to get the seeds down early."

"Exactly," he says. "Sounds like you know a little bit about growing plants."

So I start telling him about the school garden at my old school in DC, and we're having this whole conversation, while Ryan just kind of meanders around the edges of the plots with his head down. Then all of a sudden, he comes back over to us and interrupts me right in the middle of a sentence. "Webster's dictionary," he says, "describes a wedding as 'the process of removing weeds from one's garden.'" And then he wanders away again.

I raise my eyebrows and try to throw Scott a look like *that was odd*, but Scott's grinning like it was a great joke and totally fit the context of the discussion.

"Hey, Ryan," he calls out. "Get back here."

It takes him a minute, but Ryan eventually weaves his way back to us.

"*Simpsons* quote, I'm guessing?" asks Scott.

Ryan looks up like *huh?*, like he's already forgotten the whole thing and he's on to something else entirely. "She's always so deep in her own head," my mom says about Tilly.

"Wedding and weeding," prompts Scott. Still not annoyed, not bothered that our conversation got interrupted or that we still haven't started whatever this irrigation project is. Just interested in what's going on in Ryan's mind.

Ryan smiles. "Yeah. Isn't that hilarious? It's when Homer's teaching a class about how to have a successful marriage."

Scott turns to me. "Ryan is a walking *Simpsons* encyclopedia," he says. "It's pretty impressive. Now listen up, both of you. In that shed . . ." He points at a little white building with a slanted roof on the far side of the garden. "I've got a whole bunch of plastic milk cartons that need to have holes poked in them. Any idea why they need to have holes poked in them?"

I start to say something, but Scott holds up a finger to stop me. He smiles at me the same way he did in the dining hall this morning: like he knows I know the answer. He wants to hear what Ryan says.

"Ryan?" he says. "Any idea why we'd be poking holes in milk cartons? For a reason that has something to do with our garden?"

I can see in Ryan's face that it's hard for him to drag himself back from wherever he is in his mind. But then there's a moment when I think he plays back Scott's question in his mind, and everything clicks into place.

"To water the plants," he says. "So the water will drip in there a little at a time." Which is even more than I'd figured out, actually. I knew we'd put water in the jugs, but I hadn't really thought about why.

"High five," says Scott, and he holds a hand up to each of us. "And here's how we're going to make this fun. While we work, Iris is going to tell us things about her life in DC—little stories, random facts—and Ryan is going to see if he can come up with a *Simpsons* quote that fits the situation. Got it?"

And the thing is, I *know* this is one of those things where grown-ups think they can fool kids into getting along or doing chores by making it into a game—but it actually does sound fun. And once we get going, it becomes a kind of friendly contest; I try to come up with stories that will stump Ryan, and every single time, he manages to find a *Simpsons* quote to match. And it's not like I've never watched *The Simpsons*. Sometimes I throw him an easy one, or surprise him by coming up with a quote of my own. By the time we're done with the milk cartons, we've gotten into songs. Like I tell them about this really cute white fake-fur vest that my grandma bought me, and Ryan sings "See My Vest." As we're putting everything back in the shed, I talk about my favorite Mexican restaurant, and how I really liked their gazpacho, and I say along with him, "It's tomato soup, served ice cold!" And the two of us walk back along the path with Scott, singing, "You don't win friends with salad," and doing our own goofy little conga line all the way to the cabins.

chapter 11

Tilly

Date and Location Unknown

There's a sculpture that stands in an imaginary square, a memorial to those whose lives were changed by the events of July 14, 2012. This is where the Hammond Living History Society holds its meetings.

The society was formed in 2017, with the goal of uniting several different existing groups of Hammond history reenactors; the society aims to provide a common network for interested hobbyists, regardless of their level of commitment to authenticity of historical detail.

Every year, the society sponsors the Hammond Days festival in Laconia, New Hampshire, on a plot of privately owned land about a mile from the former site of Scott Bean's Camp Harmony. Concession stands sell items from a list of family member favorites published by the American Hammond Association: cucumber spears served with a cup of ranch dressing; *Dora the Explorer* Popsicles in any color except green; slices of chicken cordon bleu from the recipe in *The Joy of Cooking*, which Alexandra made on request for birthdays and other special occasions. Popcorn sprinkled with garlic salt. Fresh plums. Chocolate chip cookies baked from rolls of refrigerated dough.

While more serious reenactors give meticulous consideration to each element of their attire (taking care, for example, to know which patterns of Hanna Andersson pajamas Tilly and Iris wore in the winter of 2007 and which patterns the company did not introduce until 2008), plenty of festival attendees take a more casual approach. Most visitors make an effort to reproduce the general style of the family's clothes within a given period, without worrying too much about whether Tilly wore the fuchsia-and-teal-striped long johns that Christmas, or the lavender-and-ocean-blue ones.

The climax of the weekend-long festival is a show entitled "The Other Hammonds," presented at the bonfire on Saturday night. One by one, festivalgoers stand up, against the backdrop of night hush and fire crackle, and present a story of how things might have gone a different way for the family. How one different decision or divergent circumstance might have changed everything. Picking apart the seams of the story and finding a new way to stitch it back together.

chapter 12

Iris

June 6, 2012: New Hampshire

It's the night of our fourth day here (which is Wednesday, I think), and I'm hanging out with Tilly, Candy, and Ryan in Town Square, which is what we call the grassy area between the guest cabins and the dining hall. It's after dinner, around seven thirty or eight, and the little kids—Charlotte and Hayden—have already gone inside to go to bed, but the rest of us are allowed to stay out until nine thirty.

This is our basic daily schedule: every day, we have a meeting after breakfast and make up a project list and job chart for the day. Then we have Morning Block (where we work on our projects), lunch, and free time, and then Afternoon Block until dinner. At night, there's more free time, or sometimes something like Moonlight Swim or a sing-along.

Ryan and Tilly are playing some game—not really a game, more like they're acting out a story—where the Simpsons go to visit the biggest statues in the world. Candy and I are both sitting on the ground, and we both have books on our laps so we can write. I'm making a map of the camp, and she's writing a letter to her dad (who it turns out isn't really Rick).

I've already done a rough pencil sketch of the different areas, and now I'm starting to fill in the names that we've come up with. The staff cabins are called Springfield, and the guest cabins are Shelbyville (those were both Ryan). For the little office building, we used Tilly's idea of Beantown. The dining hall is the Great Hall, after *Harry Potter*; Candy and I both picked that out. The beach is Rehoboth, because that's a place we've all been on vacation, and Tilly and I named the lake the Sea of Knowledge, after *The Phantom Tollbooth*.

I pick up a purple marker and start coloring in a big block-letter *H* at the top of the page, the first letter in Harmony. Candy looks over from her paper and watches.

"So what are you saying to your dad?" I ask her.

She shrugs. "I told him about baking bread and putting together the incubator for the baby chicks." The eggs are supposed to arrive tomorrow. We're also getting a full-grown chicken, which Scott is picking up on Saturday. "He didn't really think we should come here," she says. "So I'm just telling him some of the cool stuff we're doing."

"Why didn't he think you should come?" I ask. Tilly's pacing around us in big lopsided circles, and when she gets close, she brushes my arm and my hand veers off course. I start widening the *H*, to cover up the stray marks.

Candy watches me draw. She's wearing a necklace, a silver chain with a *C* on it, and she's holding on to the letter, fiddling with it. "I think mainly just because he wouldn't get to see me as much," she says. "Plus, Ryan's not his kid, so you know. He doesn't care as much whether he ever . . . gets better or whatever." She picks up her letter and shakes it in the air, brushing off a few pieces of grass. Then she laughs. "He also thought Scott sounded kind of creepy. He said the whole thing sounded like a cult."

I laugh, too. "Well, he *is* kind of creepy. But in a good way, mostly."

Tilly's back near us again and joins in our conversation, even though I didn't think she'd been listening. "Why did your parents divorce?" she asks Candy.

I sort of cringe, because I know you're not supposed to ask questions like that, and also because of the weird phrasing. Tilly does that with certain words, like "marry" and "divorce" (and there are probably others, too, though I can't think of them right now): instead of saying "get married" or "get divorced," she just uses the plain form of the verb. It's one of those things that's not grammatically wrong, but it makes it sound like English isn't her first language.

Anyway, Candy doesn't seem offended. She shrugs again. "I don't know. I was pretty little, like still a baby. If you ask my mom, she says they were just too young, but I don't really know what that means."

"Do you like your dad better than Rick?" I ask. Now that the topic's open, I'm sort of curious, too. I mean, I've had friends who have divorced parents, but I've never really discussed it with any of them.

"Yeah, of course," she says. "I love my dad. He's awesome."

She goes back to her writing, and I start coloring in the A. Tilly wanders back over to talk to Ryan. But a few minutes later, when Candy's folding up her letter so that it will fit in the envelope, she says, "But I guess it's kind of hard to say." It takes me a second to remember what we were talking about. "'Cause I've never really lived with my dad, you know?"

"Uh-huh," I say, because I can't think of anything else.

She takes off her glasses and cleans them off on her T-shirt. For a minute, her dark hair falls forward so that I can't really see her face. "I mean I did," she says, "but I was too young to remember it. And my mom's been with Rick since I was like two, so he's the one who's always been around." She runs her fingers along the crease in the folded page, making it firm and crisp. "Sometimes when I'm pissed off at Rick or my mom or Ryan, I think about how cool it would be to go live with my dad instead, but I can't really imagine it. He lives in this little apartment, and I always have to sleep on a pullout couch when I'm there. And I'd have to go to a new school and everything. So."

She stops talking. I guess that's the end of what she was going to say. She puts her letter down on the grass and picks up the envelope, resting it against the book on her lap. "Hey, can I borrow your markers?" she says. "I want to decorate this before I mail it."

"Sure."

We sit there for a while, coloring silently. Ryan and Tilly are both talking at the same time, and neither one of them seems to be paying much attention to the other, but somehow it's working for them.

"So Mr. Burns is raising money for the Burns Monument," says Tilly, "because he doesn't want to pay for it himself, even though he could . . ."

"Yeah, and he starts taking money out of everyone's paycheck," says Ryan, "but Homer doesn't mind because they start giving the employees free beer. Did you ever see the one . . ."

". . . he's like, 'No! If the tallest statue in the world is 420 feet tall, then this one has to be 421 feet tall!' But he forgets to add a base to the bottom . . ."

"'Dental plan! Lisa needs braces! Dental plan!'"

"What are they even talking about?" I say, looking up. I notice a mosquito on my arm and accidentally draw a purple line on my skin as I swat it away.

Candy laughs and says, "Nice." She reaches over with her marker like she's going to draw something else on my arm, but I push her away.

"That looks really pretty," I say. Candy's covered the envelope with a design of flowers and curlicues, except for a space in the front where she's drawn a black box around her dad's name and address. I read, "Michael McNeil. So is your last name Gough or McNeil?"

"McNeil," she says. She lowers her voice. "Which is fine with me. Don't tell Ryan, but I was dying the other day when Tilly called him Ryan Gowg."

"R.I.P. Candy," I say, grinning. "Candy Gowg."

Candy grabs my arm and tries to write on it again, but I jump up, dumping the book and the paper off my lap, and start running away. As Candy chases me across the lawn, I run past Tilly, who's saying, ". . . pure gold, and he'll have his arm raised up like the Statue of Liberty, but holding a nuclear atom," and loop around Ryan who's saying, "Twenty dollars can buy many peanuts!" I lead Candy in a big circle around the dining hall, laughing and screaming whenever she gets too close. And when I pass by Ryan and Tilly again, the two of them are cracking each other up, even though I'm not even sure they're having the same conversation.

The next morning, my dad and I are on breakfast crew with Tom and Hayden. I like Tom; he kind of reminds me of my third grade teacher, Mr. Pagano. Well, not exactly, because Mr. Pagano was a short white guy, and Tom is a tall black guy, but they're both Philadelphia Eagles fans, and they both have a similar sense of humor when joking around with kids.

Scott made a Costco run last night, so we've got lots of good food to eat. My dad's making French toast, and Tom is taking the pits out of cherries with this thing that looks like a hole punch, and it all looks really yummy.

I'm setting out plates and silverware. Hayden's sitting on the floor, lining up spoons on the linoleum. My dad and Tom are chatting about nothing in particular, and I'm hearing about half of it as I move back and forth between the kitchen area and the dining area.

". . . suits our needs," Tom is saying. "It's not like I was expecting a five-star hotel."

"Yeah, no," Dad says. "Could've been a lot worse."

I carry a pile of napkins out to the serving table. We use cloth napkins here, for the environment. I tried to get my mom to do that once when I was in like kindergarten and we were learning about ecology or whatever. I remember that she got that stressed-out look she always had, and she said we could try it, but that it would mean a lot of extra laundry. My mom hates laundry, maybe because she's not very good at it; back at home, we always had to go down to the basement to look for clean clothes in the morning, because there was always a mountain of things she hadn't gotten around to folding yet. Here, though, there's a laundry room with a couple of big industrial-sized washers and dryers, like they have in hotels and Laundromats, and one person is assigned to laundry duty every couple of days.

I fold the napkins into squares and make a neat pile next to the forks. The napkins are all sorts of different patterns. Ryan and Candy's mom, Diane, has a sewing machine, and she made them out of whatever fabric she had around: clothes, pillowcases, dish towels. Tilly wouldn't use any of them until Diane assured her that none of them were made with Ryan's old underwear.

Back in the kitchen, my dad and Tom are laughing about something I didn't hear. Tom is saying, ". . . crazy? My brother was like, 'Black people do not go off the grid. Off the grid is a white people thing.'"

"What's off the grid?" I say.

My dad says, "It's . . ." and then he stops like he's not really sure how to explain it. "I'll tell you later. It's just . . . it's kind of like what we're doing here, but not really."

"It's like what we're doing, but crazy," says Tom.

"Come on, Daddy, tell me."

"Seriously, honey, it is so boring and complicated that it's really not worth going into right now. Finish the setup, okay?"

I let it go. Tilly wouldn't let it go, if she were here; she'd get more and more upset, and then she'd start making up reasons why he didn't want to tell her about it. Like it's something inappropriate, maybe about sex, or else maybe *he* doesn't know what it is. But I've been around long enough to know that I should take Dad at his word on this one. If he says it's complicated and boring, it's probably complicated and boring.

I open up the giant dishwasher and take out a handful of clean silverware. As I walk out of the room, I hear Tom picking up the conversation again with my dad. "Of course, there are people in my family who'll tell you that autism is a white people thing, too . . ."

I take the silverware over to the serving table and start sorting it into these baskets we use at mealtimes. I don't entirely get what autism is, because it seems like whatever's wrong with Hayden can't possibly be the same thing as whatever's wrong with Tilly. But I know that's what people say Tilly has. The weird thing is, I don't know if *Tilly* knows that. I don't think I've ever heard her say the word, but you can never tell what she hears and what she doesn't hear.

I do a quick count—first forks, then knives, then spoons—and make sure there are a few extra of each, in case someone drops one or something. Behind me, the screen door opens from outside and Scott comes in. "Good morning, Iris," he says.

"Hey, Scott." I neaten the utensil baskets so that they're in a straight line, then turn around and smile at him.

"Are you responsible for any of the great things I'm smelling?" he asks. He knows I like to cook; we were talking about it yesterday while we were setting up the chick incubator.

"No, but you're going to love it. My dad is the French toast master."

"Awesome. I can't wait."

I gather up the extra silverware and head back to the kitchen, with Scott behind me. Dad's flipping a slice of bread in the pan; next to him, he's got a platter with a pretty big pile of finished pieces. He looks up when we come in.

"Hey, Scott," he says. "You got my keys for me?" It was our car that Scott took to Costco last night. Kind of funny to think of him driving it when none of us were there. Even stranger: the fact that I haven't been in a car in almost a week.

"That's exactly what I'm here to talk about," says Scott. "I'm actually going to hold on to them, if that's okay with you. I'll take yours, too, Tom, if you've got 'em with you."

"Why, what's up?" asks Dad.

"I figured we could keep them all in the office. Just good to have them all in one place, you know?"

My dad keeps his eyes on the stove, but his expression changes a little. He doesn't look mad, but his eyebrows go up, and he looks . . . skeptical, maybe. Or annoyed.

"This isn't just because you want to make sure we can't leave the camp, is it?" he asks.

When Scott doesn't answer or laugh or anything, I look up. Everybody's doing the same things they were a minute ago: my dad's still making French toast, and Tom is wiping up cherry juice from the counter, looking like he's really absorbed in it. Scott's leaning against the doorway, his eyes on my dad. He's not mad, I don't think. He looks unhappy, but not too surprised.

"So why are you here, Josh?" Scott asks, after a long, quiet minute.

My dad watches him but doesn't answer. He's still annoyed.

"Because your wife talked you into it? Or because I'm some kind of mind-control genius, and I robbed you of your free will? Or are you here because you want to be here?"

"Obviously," my dad says, "I'm here because I want to be here. But I don't think I ever agreed to relinquish all my personal property, for the good of the collective."

"How about working together to create a new community? Did you agree to that?"

My dad shakes his head. "This just feels like a power grab.

You're in charge, and you're going to prove it by taking away our car keys, so we have to—"

"Oh, come on. You're acting like I'm just here—"

". . . ask for permission before we can drive our own goddamn cars."

". . . to take advantage of you, and you don't—"

"We've given up a hell of a lot to be here, and—"

". . . watch me like a hawk at every turn—"

Their voices have been getting steadily louder, and now they're pretty much yelling. For the past minute or two, Hayden's been making these little groaning noises, hitting the floor with his hands, and now he starts straight-up screaming.

I'm closest to him, so I sink down onto the floor and reach out toward him, without actually touching him, because I don't know if that'd freak him out more. "Hey, there," I say softly. I don't know what'll calm him down; I don't have that little flashlight with me today. He puts his hands onto his head and starts pulling on his own hair, so I take hold of his hand and try gently to pull it away.

But then Tom is there, and Hayden reaches up his arms for him.

"Thanks, Iris," says Tom, as he picks him up. He just holds on to him for a minute, jiggling him up and down, and then he walks toward the door. "Guys," he says, turning his head toward my dad and Scott. "You're acting like kids. Pull it together."

I listen to Hayden's yell getting softer as they walk through the dining room and out the screen door. I watch them walk past the kitchen window, on their way back to the cabins. Tom's holding Hayden against his chest like a baby, rocking him from side to side as they walk.

My dad and Scott are still standing where they were, sort of frozen in place, but I think the thing with Hayden took the wind out of their sails.

Finally, my dad takes a deep breath and exhales slowly. "Hey, look," he says. "I'm sorry. I was sort of making a joke, but . . ." He shrugs. "Yeah, it was inappropriate. I'm sorry, man."

Scott nods. "Yeah, I'm sorry, too." He sighs and runs a hand through his hair. "Okay, here's my thinking about the car thing. There are going to be times when someone needs to take one of the vehicles, and the owner of said vehicle might not be easily available. You know, we're out in the woods, and we're walking around without cell phones. I just thought it would be simpler—and safer—if we made sure that the cars were available to any adult who might need them."

"Yeah," says my dad. "I get it. That's fine. It makes a lot of sense."

"Good," says Scott. "Look, this is hard, this whole thing, and we knew it would be. We're all out of our element. But . . . you know. It's not going to work unless we trust each other. Right? I've gotta be able to look at you and say, 'I trust this guy with my life.' And I don't know if I'm there yet, either, but I'm working on it."

"Yeah," says Dad. "You know what, though? I can do you one better. Never mind about trusting you with my life . . ." He picks up the platter of French toast, and starts walking toward the dining room. As he walks past me, he swoops down and kisses me on top of my head, then sends a smile to Scott over his shoulder. "It's more than that, dude. I trust you with my kids."

As he walks out to the serving table, I'm right there next to him. My dad with the French toast, and me with the maple syrup.

chapter 13

Alexandra

October 2009: Washington, DC

Sometimes, it seems, you and Josh make dates so you can fight. Not consciously; it's not like you decide to put on makeup and weather the children's complaints about having a babysitter (whose presence will cost you eighteen dollars each hour you're out, in addition to any other expenses you may accrue during the evening), so that you can sit in a restaurant and try not to cry. But more often than not, that's the way it turns out.

It makes sense; there aren't a lot of other times when the two of you get to talk, without being interrupted. You've forgotten the layout of the field, maybe, the map of where the land mines are. Or you've been carrying something heavy without even realizing it, waiting for the moment of relief when you can simply drop it on his head.

Tonight, you're at a bar in a neighborhood far from your own; it's a fairly crappy area that's supposed to be moving up: not the next hip place to be, but maybe the one after that, or at least that's what one of you read somewhere. You came because there was a noodle place you wanted to try, two doors down from where you are now, but you ended up leaving because there was an hour wait and nowhere to sit down. You feel tired and old. It's just before Halloween, and all of the staff are dressed in costume. Your waitress has impressive cleavage and a bloody third eye on her forehead. It's hard to know where to look.

You're on the downhill side of the fight now, though you're still pissed off, and it would be easy to bring it back to life. "About" is a deceptive word when it comes to marital arguments, but it's probably fair to say that this one was about money, or perhaps about lack of communication about money. He's the one who has more of a sense of the big financial picture—how much money you have, and how long it will last, and how much more you need—but you're the one who takes care of paying the bills and handling the everyday expenses, and this lack of coordination sometimes leads to conflicts. Like tonight, when you passed him a handful of cash and an ATM receipt, and he was surprised to see how low the checking account balance had gotten.

Money is nobody's favorite topic these days. Tilly has just started at a new school: private, special-ed, and very, very expensive. And the question of who's going to pay for it is still up in the air.

The language of the law is important here; that's the key to getting the city to pay her tuition, fingers crossed. Every child is entitled to a "free and appropriate" education, and if the local public school system can't provide a classroom that makes sense for Tilly, then they have to arrange for her to attend a school that does. Even if that means paying full tuition at a private institution.

They don't make it easy, though. You've hired a lawyer and an educational consultant, and you've shown up for all of the required meetings, which manage, somehow, to be both boring and emotionally fraught. You're prepared to go to court to fight, though you're hoping it won't go that far. And you understand the opposing side of it, really you do; it sounds outrageous, on the face of it. But you're so tired of the way that it's set up to make you feel like you're trying to pull a scam. As if all of *this*—having your child observed and evaluated, finding experts who can testify to all the ways your child isn't normal and can't just go to the school down the street, like everyone else—was something you'd been planning since she was born.

I don't actually want this, you'd like to say. *Nobody actually wants this.* You look at them across the table, these tired, skeptical women who work for the city (who are certainly decent people, fundamentally, and who probably never thought their jobs would entail denying therapeutic services to children who need them), and imagine telling them, *This is a last resort—you know that, right?* You imagine cutting through the bullshit and just saying out loud what all of you know: *You don't want to pay for my kid to go to a special-ed school? Well, too bad for both of us. It wasn't our first choice, either.*

But that's not the way it's done. And until the matter is settled, one way or another, you and Josh are responsible for paying the tuition, with all its built-in services. It's not cheap; you've had to remortgage your house and dip into your retirement savings. But the school itself is a lovely place. They *like* Tilly, which is a refreshing change; more than that, they seem to *get* her. There's a whole team of people working together to help her make her way through the battlefield of fifth grade. And when things don't go smoothly, they know how to handle it. You can—*finally, finally*—leave your daughter at school in the morning and be reasonably certain that if you get a call at 10 a.m., it'll be because Tilly has a sore throat or forgot her lunch, not because she had a meltdown *again* and the teachers are even closer to the ends of their ropes than you are.

The waitress drops off your drinks, and you smile at her forehead. There's a big screen showing '80s videos, probably ironically, but you don't care. It's good music. You're watching the video for "Dance Hall Days" by Wang Chung, and it's totally ridiculous—there's a disco ball and a snake, and the lead singer is wearing something that wouldn't look out of place on your grandmother in Boca—but it's also your life, your past. For a minute, you have the ability to be in two places at once: you're forty and pissed at your husband and too old to be in this bar, but you're also twelve and sitting in your child-hood living room, watching MTV like you're going to be tested on it. Like it might actually teach you something. You're practically taking notes. The way they're dancing, the way the women have applied their lipstick: this is one way a life can be. In a few minutes, Van Halen or Cyndi Lauper will show you another way, and you'll see what you think of that one.

"Take your baby by the wrist," the guy sings, and then, without warning, the screen goes black. Whoever's in charge—someone younger than you, certainly—has had enough.

"Hey," you complain. "I was enjoying that." And that's some-thing, you saying that. The words cost you a little something. Your voice is still faintly acid, but you're including Josh in what you're thinking. You're willing to let him move back into your orbit. He shrugs, without meeting your eyes; it's kind of half a gesture.

After a minute, the music jerks to life again on the screen, and now it's Bryan Adams's "Summer of '69." You look at Josh, smiling without quite meaning to, and you know exactly what he's going to say. "Well," you begin, and you wait for him to catch up. You speak together: "Mr. Bryan Adams, you got no complaints." And you're laughing helplessly, both of you together, because it's funny, and because the fight has to end sometime, and because you've been together for more than half your lives.

It's from *Fargo*, the line you just quoted; Steve Buscemi says it, and the actual line is "José Feliciano, you got no complaints." (No telling how you both misremembered the "mister" part, because you've checked on YouTube and it's not there.) But it's also not from *Fargo*; it also belongs to the two of you. It's part of your pop-culture patois, the rag rug of song lyrics and catchphrases and *Simpsons* references that you've laid out together to stand on. It's a type of shorthand, a way of marking up the map. Whatever's happening right now? It isn't new. We've seen it before, and we'll most likely see it again.

Someday, you imagine, when Josh is dead and the kids are elsewhere and you're living in some old-age home, the staff will talk about you, the crazy woman with all the non sequiturs. No one who's young at that time will know any of the references; they'll think you're making it all up as you go along. You'll be entertaining, at least. You'll tell the woman who brushes the knots out of your hair that you're not going to pay a lot for this muffler. You'll tell the man who helps you from bed to wheelchair and back again that it's time to make the donuts. There will be no one there to understand you, to catch your eye and speak the well-frayed words along with you. "I'm all lost in the supermarket" might mean "Thank you" or it might mean "I don't understand how I got here." "My name is Inigo Montoya" might mean "My legs hurt" or "Please, can I hear some music?" or "Pay attention: it happens faster than you think."

There's a story you used to tell, a funny little anecdote from your courtship: one night, when you and Josh had been dating for about three years, you went out to dinner together. You'd been talking about marriage; you both knew it was an inevitability, but you'd made it clear that you wanted there to be some kind of proposal. (You ruined it, basically; that's your take on it now. You were impatient and you cajoled and you gave him no freedom to take his time and plan something on his own. But that's a different story.)

Anyway, you'd gone out to dinner, and there was a period of comfortable silence after you ordered. During that time, you created a little fantasy that this was going to be *it*, that he was going to pull a ring out of his pocket and say something sweet to you. You were ready; you sat up straighter, you ran a hand through your hair. You imagined all the phone calls you'd be making later, all the people you'd need to tell. And then, when Josh finally opened his mouth, what he said was: "I think I might be allergic to dust."

Hilarious, you thought later: a Dave Barry column brought to life, illustrating the way that men's brains work differently from women's. But here's the thing: it turned out that he actually *was* allergic to dust, and he coughed every morning for the next eleven years, until you bought a foam mattress. The conversation in the restaurant was a marriage moment, not a proposal moment. And you were still too young and untested to recognize the difference.

You know this by now, right? Life is never what you expect it to be. Sex has more to do with salt than with sweetness. The sky is white as often as it's blue.

"Fried pickles," Josh says, looking at the menu. "Is that good, do you think?" His voice is carefully casual, and you take the question for what it is: a promise, a tiny gift. A hand reaching out, an offer of a small-but-tangible happiness that the two of you can share.

You have an answer immediately, as easy as "Mr. Bryan Adams," but this one is yours alone. "What's life without risk?" you ask. It's the first part of a call-and-response that dates back to your college days.

He's ready with the next part: "How bad could it be?"

And you bring it home: "You've gotta do *something*."

This is the man you married: for the first two months that Tilly was at her new school, Josh worked every night to create a "mystery dessert" to put in her lunch. Tilly would give him vague yet terribly specific instructions—"something with green apple frosting" was one—and he'd figure the rest out from there. At least two or three times a week, he'd end up going out to the supermarket at ten o'clock at night, hunting down specialized ingredients. For the green apple frosting, he ended up buying flavored syrup from the cocktail mixers aisle. But he was fully prepared to melt down Jolly Ranchers, if necessary.

By the time the waitress returns to take your order, the two of you are chatting easily. Nothing has changed, nothing's been settled, but you know now that the rest of the night will be okay. You'll drink your beers and eat some greasy bar food, and you'll talk about Bananarama. ("Did you know that one of them is married to Andrew Ridgeley from Wham!?") When you've had enough, and you're sure the kids will be asleep, you'll go back home and pay the sitter and sit together for a while on the couch. Sex is a possibility, though not a certainty. Eventually, you'll lie down together in a bed that keeps you both safe from allergens, and you'll rest your aging bodies together.

chapter 14

Iris

June 8, 2012: New Hampshire

I'm sitting at a table in the empty dining hall with Janelle, who's helping me sketch out the new Camp Harmony logo for the sign. It's Friday morning, two days before the first group of Guest Campers (also known as GCs) arrive; they'll be getting here around lunchtime on Sunday.

The logo is really good, if I do say so myself, since I'm the one who designed it. Well, mostly. I mean, Janelle was technically in charge of the project, because she knows about graphic design, but she pretty much left it up to me.

So here's what it looks like: it's a pine tree, surrounded by a circle of stars, and there are thirteen stars total, to represent the thirteen members of our Core Family. I don't know, it probably sounds cheesy when I try to describe it, but I think it's going to look awesome when we're done. And Scott said it was exactly what he wanted.

"So, okay," says Janelle. "Let's talk about colors. We're thinking about white lettering, and sort of a medium blue for the background, right?"

"Yeah, I want it to look like it's nighttime. But Scott doesn't want it to be *too* dark, or it'll be less visible to people driving by."

"Right. Same thing goes for the green, I think—we want to make it brighter than the color of a real pine tree."

"That sounds good," I say. Janelle has a good eye for colors. I've noticed that her clothes are brighter than any of the other adults' at camp. Today, she's wearing a halter top with a red and pink pattern; I wouldn't expect those shades to go well together, but they do.

"Okay, cool," she says, making a note on a piece of paper. "And yellow for the stars. Scott's going to go to the paint store after lunch, so let's plan to get started later this afternoon."

"Can I go with him?" That would be really fun, I think, getting to pick out the colors myself.

She shakes her head. "Sorry, baby. The rule is that kids stay at camp, at least for the time being. Adults, too, as much as possible."

I stare at her. I've never heard that rule before. "You mean we're not allowed to leave?"

She laughs. "Well, don't say it like that. Nobody's keeping you prisoner. It's just . . . well, okay. You know, the reason we're all here is because we want to create a different kind of environment for you guys, right? So we figure it's best if we give you time to get used to it."

"Like for . . . therapeutic reasons?" I ask. My mom and dad and Scott are always throwing around phrases like that when they talk to each other. But I never know: are they talking about me, too? What about the kids who don't need therapeutic reasons for stuff?

Janelle tilts her head and sits back a little. For a minute, she just looks at me, thinking. "You know, sweetie," she says finally, "your parents didn't come here just because they thought it would be good for Tilly. You know that, right?"

I just shrug and look down at the piece of plywood we've been sketching on. Because actually, no. No one's ever said that to me. I thought that Tilly was the whole reason we were here.

"Iris?" says Janelle. She reaches out and gently pushes my chin upward so she can see my face. "You must feel pretty left out, huh?"

I sort of shake my head, because that's not exactly . . . well, I don't know. Maybe it is. Up until we came here, it was always Tilly who seemed to get left out of stuff. She was the one who had to go to a weird school and had to go home and lose all her privileges if she acted up somewhere. But here, I'm realizing, everything's a little bit upside down.

"Listen, sweetie," Janelle says. "It's true that the reason this particular group of people got together is that we've all got kids who have issues. But every single plan we've made, every single conversation we've had, has been about what's going to work out best for *all* our kids. So this is not just, Iris can't go to the paint store because we don't want the kids with issues to feel left out. You know? This is all of us saying, for right now, the kids stay at camp, because that's what we think is best."

I nod. I have a lump in my throat, just out of nowhere.

"Good. But listen, I'll tell you what. The store's not that far; I bet Scott would be willing to make two trips. How about I ask him to go and get some color swatches and bring them back here, so you can pick?"

"Yes! Thank you. That'd be great." I'm almost laughing, I feel so much better.

"Okay, then," she says. She's smiling. "See? Every problem has a solution."

While we're putting away our supplies, my mom comes in with Hayden. Different grown-ups have been taking care of him for a little while each day, so that he gets more comfortable being away from his parents.

"Hey, sweetness," says Janelle. She kneels down on the floor, so that she's on Hayden's level. He makes a big squawking noise when he sees her and runs over. He doesn't hug, I've noticed, not with his arms. But when he gets to Janelle, he rests his forehead on her cheek, which is really kind of sweet.

"He do okay?" she asks my mom.

"Oh, yeah—we had a good time. I let him organize all my pens by size and color."

Janelle laughs. "Now that is a party. I bet he loved that."

"Oh, he was thrilled." Mom puts her hand on my shoulder. "So how are the sketches going?"

"Really good!" I say. I hold up the plywood so she can see it better.

"Oh, wow," she says. She squints and leans a little closer, taking a good look. "That's amazing."

Hayden wanders over to me. "Da," he says, pointing at the picture. "Da." I have no idea if he's trying to say something specific, or if he's just making any sound he can.

"Da," I say back, because I've noticed that his parents do that and Scott, too: repeat back whatever he says. He smiles a big smile and reaches out to grab my arm, which is a little gross because his fingers are wet from being in his mouth. But I let him do it.

"I may be crazy," says Janelle, "but I swear he's been vocalizing more since we got here."

"You know, I was thinking that, too," says my mom.

"Is that good?" I ask.

"I think so," says Janelle. "I mean, it must be, right? But really, who knows? A hopeful mom can talk herself into anything."

After dinner, Scott gets up to make announcements, like he always does. "Great work today, everybody," he says. "Our salad tonight was made from the very first lettuce we harvested from our garden."

The grown-ups all clap and make little cheering noises. Ryan calls out, "When we got married, you promised me my harvesting days were over." Everyone ignores him. Is that a *Simpsons* quote? I don't even know.

Scott continues. "We also made good progress today on the

camp sign—which is turning out great, by the way, thanks to Iris and Janelle . . ."

I smile and duck my head down, hoping I look humble, while the adults clap again.

". . . and thanks to Rick, for taking care of the plumbing problem in Guest Cabin B."

While he's talking, I gather up my utensils and place them carefully across my plate, so I'll be ready to get up and clear my dishes when he's finished. Free time after dinner is my favorite part of the day, so I want to be ready to go.

"Now I'll let you all go in a minute," Scott says, and I look up quickly, wondering if he saw me neatening up my stuff. "But there is one more thing I want to talk to you guys about first. The adults know about this already. It's about the topic of consequences and discipline."

The kids all start groaning and complaining, and Ryan wails, "Oh, why do my actions have consequences?" I join in with everybody, even though I'm not the kind of kid who gets a lot of consequences for my behavior.

"Yeah, I know," says Scott. "Nobody's favorite topic. Not even parents and caregivers, despite what you may think. And up till now, we've been doing fine just handling problems as they come up— which, by the way, has not been often. But we wanted to get something official in place before the first group of GCs gets here. So starting tomorrow, we'll be instituting something called After Dinner Block, or AD Block for short."

"Let me guess," says Tilly. "You're going to make us eat dinner again, but this time it'll be poisoned."

Most of the grown-ups laugh, including Scott. The thing is, she's not really being sarcastic. Some part of her is actually worried that this is what they're going to do.

"That would be a little extreme, don't you think?" asks Scott.

"I guess so," says Tilly, even though it was probably a rhetorical question. Also, she doesn't sound convinced.

"All it will be is a little extra work—cleaning up the dining hall and whatever small tasks need to be done—plus a chance to talk about whatever happened to get you there."

"What *does* get you there?" asks Candy.

"Good question. And I'm sure you'll all be happy to know that I've made a lame little acronym to help you remember what rules you're supposed to follow."

He drags over the easel with the big pad of paper on it and turns to a new sheet. Then he writes the word "SPARK" in big letters, going down the page.

"Spark!" says Charlotte. She always gets all excited when she can read a word.

"Yep," says Scott. "SPARK. I can tell you all that I spent the better part of last night trying out combinations, and I'm sorry to say that this is the best I could come up with. I tried for 'camp,' I tried for 'harmony,' but these things are harder than they look. So here's what we've got."

He goes down the list, pointing at each letter as it comes.

S is for safety, which always comes first.
P is for participating and following directions.
A is for acting and speaking appropriately.
R is for responsibility, as in taking responsibility for your actions. And
K is for kindness and respect.

I lean over to Tilly. "I think he means 'kindness and kespect,'" I whisper. She giggles, and my mom looks over at us and puts a finger to her lips. Scott looks around the group. "Any questions? Pretty basic stuff, right? It's really just about making good decisions."

I can feel Tilly straightening up next to me, her body getting tense. By the time she raises her hand, she's already in mid-sentence.

"If you hit somebody, does that count as not being safe or not being respectful? Or maybe it's not acting appropriately."

I feel like rolling my eyes (but I don't, because I *know* what it means to be respectful). Tilly's always weird about rules. She immediately starts looking for loopholes and asking what happens if you take everything to the most insane extreme. It's like how she asked if they were going to punish us by making us eat poisoned food; she wants to figure out if there's some type of circumstance where the consequences would be to kill her or to put her in prison forever or something.

She starts to say, "Or maybe it's not following directions, because—" but Scott cuts her off.

"Tilly, it doesn't matter what category it falls under. You know it's wrong, right?"

"Yeah, but . . ."

Scott puts up his hand like he's saying "halt" and he raises his voice to talk over her. "So don't do it. That's what I mean about making good decisions."

"But what if there's something that doesn't fit into any of the categories, like . . ." She stops talking while she tries to think of an example.

Scott takes the opportunity to try to get things back on track. "Tilly, if there's anyone who can find a way to work around the rules, it's you. But we've just got to work together on this and trust each other to be fair, okay? These SPARK things are just guidelines."

"Okay, well, what if you do something that breaks one of the SPARK guidelines, but it's for a reason that's good? Like if you hit someone because their clothes are on fire and you're putting them out?"

Scott's laughing and shaking his head by this point. My dad says Tilly would make a good lawyer, because she's so good at this kind of nitpicking. I think he's wrong, though. I think she nitpicks because she doesn't really understand why we have rules at all. And because she doesn't understand them, she worries she won't be able to follow them.

Finally, Scott puts his hand up again and says, "Tilly, if we keep going like this, we're never going to get to the candy bars."

That gets Tilly's attention, and everyone else's.

"Candy bars?" she asks.

"Yeah, I said candy bars." Scott's grinning. "Anyone who gets to the end of the summer without ever being assigned to AD Block will receive three candy bars of their choosing. And I'm not talking about gluten-free, low-fat, no artificial flavors and colors candy bars. I will personally go out to CVS and buy you any three regular old, rot-your-teeth, bad-for-you candy bars that you want."

Tilly can't even leave this alone. As we all clear our dishes and walk out of the dining hall, she's hovering around Scott, asking, "What if we want a kind of candy that doesn't come in a bar?" and "Isn't giving us candy totally the opposite of what all your goals are?" He's letting her chatter and answering her questions when there's a pause. I walk a little faster to catch up with my parents.

My mom takes one of my hands, and my dad takes the other. I remember when I was little, I used to have them swing me back and forth when we were walking like this. I'm way too big for it now, but back then it seemed like the most fun thing ever.

"So have you got your candy bars picked out?" my mom asks me.

"I'd probably get a Twix and a Reese's, and I don't know what the third one would be."

"If it were me," Dad says, "I'd get all PayDays."

"You're weird," I say.

Tilly comes running up and takes my dad's other hand.

"This is so awesome," she says. "I can't even decide. There are so many that I like."

If you can make it through the summer without AD Block, I think but don't say. But then she says it herself.

"I mean, I probably won't get the prize," she says. "Let's be realistic here."

"Hey," I say, leaning forward so I can see her around my dad. "You can do it."

And who knows? Maybe I'm not even lying.

chapter 15

Alexandra

November 2010: Washington, DC

The second time you hear the name "Scott Bean," it's from the mom of one of Tilly's classmates. At a parents' potluck at the start of the fall semester, you speak to a woman whose son (Asperger's, anxiety, various food allergies, and celiac disease) is in Tilly's class, and she mentions a parenting newsletter she's recently signed up for, something called "Harmonious Parenting."

"It's just really commonsense and down-to-earth," she says. "I almost always find something useful in it." She takes out her phone and emails you a link, there and then. Which is how, two months later, you find yourself standing in a meeting room at a public library, waiting to introduce yourself to Scott Bean himself.

It's still a few minutes before seven, and he's got you all engaged in some forced mingling. It's a good-sized group, maybe a dozen people, more moms than dads. Small enough to feel relatively intimate, but big enough that you don't have to say much if you don't want to, though it's already looking like Scott Bean is the kind of guy who encourages participation.

He's good-looking, in a character-actor-but-not-quite-leading-man way. Dark hair, sculpted into place with some type of guy-product, intense gray eyes, and a supremely sympathetic and welcoming aura. But whatever. You're not here to find a boyfriend.

You've done some Googling, naturally. He's from Montana, originally, went to a Big Ten school. He has training in education and speech pathology. Your age, but he doesn't seem to be married or have kids of his own. Which raises a couple of question marks for you, but you've met enough good childless teachers (and enough bad parents) to know that raising kids isn't necessarily a prerequisite for understanding how they work.

Tilly's eleven now, and in fifth grade. She's having kind of a tough year, despite the excellent staff at her new school. She's been using violent language, giggling when she gets in trouble—all the usual stuff, pushing limits to find out what happens if she goes too far, with a few new elements thrown in. Most horrifyingly, she's been teasing a boy in her class who uses a wheelchair. You suspect that (like most things with Tilly) it stems from anxiety: it scares her to imagine living in a body that doesn't work in the usual ways, so she fixates on it. Or tries to distance herself from it, maybe? You're not sure, but you're shocked at some of the cruel things you've heard coming out of her mouth lately.

So here you are. You don't enjoy forced social situations like this one—you're a little like Tilly that way, it's not as though you don't see the connection—but you have some hopes about this evening. Not just about Scott Bean and whatever he might say, but about the other parents who have come here looking for help. You are hopeful, as juvenile as it sounds, that you might make some friends.

You're talking to a woman named Janelle, who's driven all the way from Philadelphia to be here. "Well, kind of," she says. "I have an aunt who lives here, so you know, two birds with one stone. But really, I planned it around coming here tonight."

She seems nice. From the brief exchange you've had, it sounds like her son is more severely impaired than Tilly, but you've still found a number of things to connect you.

Right now, she's talking about Facebook. "I can't even look at it anymore," she says. "For a while last summer, Hayden had to have a feeding tube. And whenever I'd look at Facebook, I'd see these posts about normal kids, you know? I have a girlfriend from high school, and she has a little boy who's three weeks older than Hayden. And every time I sat down at the computer, there's just picture after picture of him up there learning how to ride a tricycle." She pauses, shrugs. "It's not that I'm not happy for them, you know? It's just . . . my days are so different from theirs."

"Yeah," you say. "I know." And you do, even though you take a moment to be silently grateful that a feeding tube has never been on the list of things you've had to deal with. It's taken you a long time to understand how lonely you are, but it's one of the main reasons you're here. A couple of months ago, you had a phone conversation with a woman you know slightly from your neighborhood. She was looking at special-ed schools for her son, and she wanted to hear a little bit about Tilly's experiences. It turned out that your kids had totally different issues; her son seemed to fall pretty clearly into the "learning disabilities" category, which is an entirely different type of profile. But talking to her was like talking to a cousin or a childhood friend: you understood each other, without having to explain. You felt almost giddy, and it wasn't just because the kids were finally asleep and you were sipping wine while you talked.

"So here's an example," you'd told her, this neighborhood mom, in an effort to explain Tilly. "Earlier tonight, I found her writing swearwords on her bedroom wall with sidewalk chalk."

This is the kind of story that usually brings down a wall between you and everyone else. You can share funny mom stories with the best of them, build an easy camaraderie, add your own well-worn snapshots (minor tantrums, car sickness) to the communal slide show. But the moment you load up Tilly on the screen—Tilly bright and jagged, Tilly angry and hurting, Tilly in such clear focus that you almost have to look away—something changes. Shock or concern or pity, you're not always sure which. And usually, you perceive judgment, whether it's there or not. Autism is one thing, but bad manners? Whose fault do you suppose that is?

But the woman you were talking to that evening just said, "Hmm." She sounded thoughtful. And then, genuinely curious: "Well, was she spelling them correctly?"

Talking to this other mom now, Janelle, and glancing at the other parents in the room, you feel the same sort of kinship and relief. Recognition. You came close to skipping this thing tonight—long day, everyone tired, and so on. But you're already glad you talked yourself into it.

"Janelle and Alexandra," says a male voice behind you. You swing around and see that it's your turn to meet Scott Bean.

"Hi there," you say, shaking his hand. This is the part you weren't looking forward to; you feel desperate a lot of the time, and you would give almost anything to find someone to help you (in whatever vague form that might take). But there's also a part of you that's wondering who this guy thinks he is. So you're deconstructing his approach—calling you by name, which makes him seem warm, even though you know he got it from the sticky tag on your sweater; making eye contact like a politician and patting you on the shoulder before moving on to Janelle—even as you watch yourself making the first tentative gestures toward shifting your hope in his direction.

"Glad you could be here," he says. "Go ahead and find a seat. We're almost ready to get started."

You sit down at the round table in the center of the room and make yourself busy taking out a pen and some paper. You've got a new purse-sized, spiral-bound notebook, purchased expressly for this evening. A dollar nineteen offered up to the gods of please-let-this-work.

"Hi there," Scott says, once everyone is settled. "And welcome. I think I've met you all, but let me just begin by saying that my name is Scott Bean. I don't know you yet, and you don't know me, but I think it's fair to say at least this much: you're here because you've been having a hard time. And I'm here because I think maybe I can help."

Hokey, you think. But your throat feels tight. You're not so starved for whatever it is he's offering—attention, compassion, understanding—that you're going to burst into tears after a single sentence. But you know yourself enough to recognize that this is exactly what you hoped he'd say.

"To admit that your kids aren't 'typical,'" Scott continues, "is hard. There's no one who hears that euphemism and doesn't know it's standing in for 'normal.' But until you recognize your child for exactly who she is, you're never going to get anywhere."

Well, yeah. This isn't news. This is every parenting book you've ever bought and never found the time to read. *Yes, and they also need limits and consequences, right? Fascinating. Tell us more.* You're playing a kind of game, trying to figure out how much of your faith you're going to put in this man. You're waiting for him to win you over.

Scott smiles suddenly. "Okay, now, I'm going to show you all something, and I'm interested in seeing how you all respond." He slides something out of a folder in front of him on the table and holds it up: it's a photo, a head shot of the actor Denis Leary. You groan audibly, without really meaning to, and you're not the only one who does.

Scott laughs. "Yeah, okay. So this guy got into some trouble a few months ago, for saying that most of the kids diagnosed as autistic are actually just brats. I'll bet that pissed you off, and rightly so. You may have posted a nasty comment on Facebook; you may have composed a strongly worded letter in your head, on a night when you couldn't get to sleep."

He pauses, looks around the table. His face is serious. "But maybe—tell me honestly, now—in the back of your mind, was there just a tiny part of you that was wondering if he was right? No, not that there's no such thing as autism; we all know that's a load of crap. But did any of you think, in some small, hidden place in your mind, that maybe these kids—and by 'these kids,' let's be clear that I mean *your* kids—shouldn't be acting this way? That they *don't need* to be acting this way, and that maybe you're contributing to their bad behavior?"

You look down at the pad of paper you've brought, squeeze your pen, and then carefully put it down. The room is perfectly silent.

"Think about the last time you went out to dinner and your child acted out. Let's say, for the sake of argument, that you took your kids out to the Cheesecake Factory last weekend, and things didn't go as well as you'd hoped. Your kid raised his voice, or tilted his chair until he fell over backward. He spilled things and ate with his fingers and melted down when the waitress forgot that he asked her to leave the onions off of his sandwich."

Scott's voice is clear and strong. He can fill up a room in a way you've never quite learned to. A few people are nodding. You're with them, even though you're keeping your gestures neutral for the moment.

"You know why it happened: it's hard for him to sit still, he gets cranky when he's hungry, there were unfamiliar smells that bothered him, and he was anxious about whether he'd like his food."

By chance, his eyes meet yours directly as he speaks, and a faint shiver travels the skin of your arms. His voice is louder now, forceful and confident, but there's a note of compassion in it that nullifies any sense that you're being lectured. You can tell, hearing him talk, that he cares about what's happening to these kids. He cares about Tilly, without ever having heard her name. It's going to be hard for you to explain this later, to Josh or to anybody else, but it's the soft note of concern in his voice that undoes all of your careful defense-building. How to explain that you feel safer in his presence, knowing that he's on your side? How to explain that you came here tonight because sometimes you feel like you're being mummified, and that you didn't even realize it until Scott Bean offered you a pair of scissors?

Scott pauses here and nods, like whatever expression you've got on your face has confirmed something for him. You glance around at the other parents. You can see that some of them aren't with him yet, aren't with *you*. Blank expression or pursed lips. But you get it, you get them. It's okay if you're not exactly on the same page; what you share is more important than what divides you. You all want the same things here. You all love your kids.

Scott takes a sip from his water bottle, then goes on. "But do you suppose that anyone observing your family last week at the Cheesecake Factory was thinking, 'That child with special needs is having trouble behaving appropriately in this environment'? Or is it more likely that all those people observing you were thinking, 'Hey, if you can't control your kid, then go home so I can enjoy my Tuscan layered salad in peace'?"

There's some laughter, but it's subdued. It hurts to talk about this. It *hurts*.

But something tiny and indefinable has changed. You're with him now. You're with him all the way. Even after so short a time, you trust that Scott Bean will not inflict pain on you without following it up with something that soothes. There's work to be done here, important work, but it's going to be messy. And you already know that you're going to sit through it without flinching.

Because the other thing he's here to do is to remind you of this: you are lucky to have this child. You wouldn't trade her for anything, and that's not just a platitude, an easy greeting-card sound bite; it's a position you question and revisit with some frequency. She's yours and you're hers, and you don't have endless time. If you can't find a way to help your daughter, your lovely fire-bright girl who thrills and confounds you, who spells every swearword perfectly . . . well. If you can't do that, then you've failed at the most important task you've ever been given.

chapter 16

Iris

June 9, 2012: New Hampshire

It's Saturday, the night before the first batch of Guest Campers arrives, and Scott is leading us all out into the woods for something called Saturday Campfire. Scott's been working out here for a couple of days with the help of the dads, fixing up a clearing for us, and this morning, Candy and Diane and I made these special fire-starters by collecting pinecones and dipping them in melted wax.

We've been walking for a while, maybe five or ten minutes, which isn't that long when you're playing a game or watching a movie or something, but it feels pretty long when you're walking on bumpy ground, tripping over tree roots and ducking down so the branches don't hit you in the face. We all have flashlights, but we haven't turned them on, because it isn't dark yet. It's shadowy, though, because of the tall trees, and . . . well, it's not quiet exactly, but everything sounds a little softer than usual: grown-ups talking, and birds making noise here and there, and our feet crunching along on the pine needles. Even though I know it's not true, I could almost believe that we were walking someplace where no humans had ever gone.

I'm creeping myself out, so I slow down until Tilly catches up with me.

"It's weird out here," I say.

"Yeah, kind of," she says, but I can tell she's not really paying attention. She's deep inside her head, as always.

"Did you know," she asks, "that the Motherland Calls memorial is sinking into the earth?"

She's talking about this giant statue she likes in Russia. It's a humongous woman with a sword sticking up in the air; it's got something to do with World War II. I don't really like it. Actually, it kind of scares me.

"Yeah, I know," I say. "You told me."

"It's shorter than it used to be, and it's because it's so heavy that the ground can't completely support it. And no one's doing anything to fix it."

"Yeah, I know."

"What if it sank down so far that it was completely inside the earth? Like first her legs would disappear, and the bottom of her dress, and she'd be sticking up out of the ground halfway. She'd look like she was buried and she was climbing out, like the Statue of Liberty in *Planet of the Apes*." Not that either of us has ever seen *Planet of the Apes*, but our dad found a picture online, back when Tilly was first getting into all this monument stuff.

"That wouldn't happen. You said that they think it'll just fall over someday."

"I know, but what if it *did* sink that far down? In the end, you'd only be able to see the tip of her sword sticking up out of the dirt. And hundreds of years in the future, people would wonder what it was. And if they ever dug it up, maybe they'd think that God put it there, instead of people, and they'd make up a whole religion about it."

I sigh. Obviously, that's completely stupid, because in this future place, wouldn't they still have history books and the Internet, and wouldn't they know that there used to be a huge statue in exactly this spot? Or wouldn't there be a big hole in the ground or something? But she's busy thinking about it now, getting deeper and deeper into the idea, and there's not really any point in arguing with her.

This is what Tilly's mind is like. You know how teachers are always saying that the imagination is this great thing, because it lets you go anywhere and do anything? It's not really true for everyone, though, the way it is for Tilly. It's like the rest of us have our brains cooped up in a little box, and we're always bumping into the walls whenever we try to think about anything too big, like *Is it possible for a statue that big to sink completely into the earth?* Or *But wouldn't the future people know that the statue used to be there?* But somehow Tilly never hits those walls. It's like she flies right through.

Sometimes I wish I could be inside her head, just to see what it's like. But I guess that being inside her head would also mean all the other stuff, like forgetting to eat with a fork sometimes and freaking out when you lose a pen, because maybe you'll never find it, maybe it's not under the couch or in some other room that you carried it into when you weren't paying attention. Maybe nothing is the way it's supposed to be, and maybe the pen is just freaking *gone.*

Up ahead of us, there are two trees that are leaning toward each other, with a path between them, like a gateway, and just beyond that there's a big empty area. We've all been walking in groups, but everyone sort of narrows down into a line to go through the trees. And then suddenly everything's brighter, because there aren't any branches above us, and we're in a big clear space, with a bunch of firewood piled in the middle.

Everyone crowds around the woodpile in a circle. Tilly and I are standing together, with our mom and dad behind us. The four of us squeeze in tight, till we're all touching, which is nice, sort of like a family hug.

Scott waits until everyone's there and has found a place, and then he says, "Welcome, Core Family. Welcome to the Harmony Circle."

I want to giggle because he sounds so formal, but I know he's trying to be serious and solemn, so I don't.

"This is a space," he says, "that's just for us, the Core Family, the CF. Once the Guest Campers start arriving, there are going to be a lot of other people moving in and out of Camp Harmony. But every Saturday night, in between one group of GCs leaving and the next one arriving, we'll gather here, and for that little slice of time, it'll be just us again."

Next to me, I can feel Tilly starting to get twitchy; her arm jerks against mine, and she starts moving her shoulders up and down. She doesn't like to stay in one place for very long; it's almost like she can't, like her body starts bothering her if it goes too long without moving. I wonder how long Scott is going to talk.

"The Harmony Circle is a place of renewal and purification," Scott says. "It's a weekly chance to clarify our purpose, to check in with each other, to remember why we're here. So let's get started, okay?"

He picks up the cardboard box that has the fire-starters in it. "Kids, come on up here," he says.

"Oh, good," I hear my dad whisper to my mom. "Let's give them open flames." Mom laughs quietly.

Tilly and I and the rest of the kids move away from our parents and gather around Scott. Ryan ends up next to me, and I hear him repeating something quietly, under his breath: "Arson for the parson, arson for the parson." I'm assuming it's some *Simpsons* thing, and that he really wants to say it, but he doesn't want to get in trouble with Scott for making a joke about the fire. No one's gotten AD Block yet, and nobody wants to be the first one.

Scott passes around the box of fire-starters, and we each take one. I grab one for Hayden, too, and put it into his hand for him. I overheard the grown-ups having a talk about this, about whether it was safe to let Charlotte and Hayden use one of these, especially Hayden since he doesn't really understand what's going on most of the time. Janelle wanted to skip it, and maybe give him something else to throw in the fire, but Scott convinced her that it was important for all the kids to be treated equally. He said, "We'll practice with him before dinner, we'll make sure he knows what he's supposed to do. How do you know whether he can rise to the occasion if you don't give him a chance?" And Janelle shook her head and was quiet for a minute but finally said okay.

"Here we go, guys," says Scott. He has a big long lighter, like the kind you use to light a barbecue grill, and he moves down the line of us, touching the flame to the tips of our pinecones.

I watch mine for a second after he lights it; I'm interested in the way that the fire starts just at the top tip and works its way downward along the rows of scales as if it were a living thing. For a second, everyone's quiet and the air smells like Christmas, and we just stand there, holding the glow in our hands.

Then, really quick, I feel heat on my fingers and I toss the pinecone onto the firewood. Mine hits first, and then there are others flying through the air to land on the pile, and everything crackles as all the little fires join into one.

"Scott," someone yells. It's Janelle. "Scott, get it from him."

I look over at Hayden, who's still holding his pinecone in his hand, eyes wide and dark as he watches the flame travel down toward his hands. Then Scott pushes past me, knocking me and Tilly over into the dirt. He lunges at Hayden, and I don't see what happens, but then Hayden starts yelling big angry noises, and Scott's howling because his hand is on fire. The pinecone sails through the air in the wrong direction, flying over my head and into the trees. All the adults are around Scott, pouring bottles of water and yelling, and I'm the only one who thinks to follow the pinecone into the woods to stomp the fire out. I'm the only one who thinks to put my arms around Hayden and give him a hug as he cries and yells for the bright, pretty thing that Scott gave him and then took away.

chapter 17

Alexandra

December 2010: New York

You're sitting at a table at a banquet facility in Poughkeepsie, New York: the wedding of one of Josh's cousins. It's a sit-down meal, and your table has been waiting for salad for a while. The girls are getting fidgety.

"I spy . . ." you say. You've just got to keep them going till you can get some food in them. You're thinking you'll say *D*, for Daddy; you can see Josh across the room, making conversation with an uncle.

"No, wait, I've got one," Tilly cuts in. "I spy, with my little eye, something that begins with the letter *F*."

"Flowers," Iris says.

"No, but close."

You have a bad feeling. "Is it flower *girl*?" you ask, giving her a look.

"Yep." Tilly laughs; Iris makes a frustrated noise in her throat and punches her sister in the arm. She turns and stomps away toward her dad. The flower girl—five-year-old niece of the groom, currently twirling adorably on the dance floor—is a touchy subject. Iris is nine now, beyond standard flower-girl age, and not close enough to the couple to have been considered. But she's never been a flower girl, and she always wanted to be one, so she's been grumpy for the whole trip. And Tilly's more than happy to needle her about it. "Not really necessary, Till," you say.

"No, but fun," she says, taking another roll from the basket on the table. She looks pretty tonight; she's wearing a purple silk dress and low heels, though you weren't able to talk her into panty hose. Relatives who haven't seen her for a while have been commenting on how much darker her hair has gotten in the last couple of years; you're with her every day, yet you can't quite say when it changed from dark blond to light brown. Iris's hair still has that baby-gold sheen, but you can really only see it in sunlight. So easy to miss your children changing before your eyes.

It's been almost two months since you went to Scott Bean's seminar, and you think maybe you can say that things are getting a little better. Not that there's a direct correlation, necessarily—you've also been working with Tilly's doctor to fine-tune her medication, and it's hard to say what's causing what. But you think the Scott Bean stuff is helping. You ended up ordering his set of CDs, and you've been listening to them in the car. None of it is particularly revolutionary—limits and consequences, rewarding and redirecting, staying calm and encouraging responsibility. But there's something comforting about his voice, in the air, surrounding you. He sounds sympathetic. He sounds like he believes you can do it. It's probably a better use of your driving time than beating yourself up.

"I need to pee," says Tilly suddenly, jumping up.

You catch her arm before she goes, tug her closer so you can lower your voice. "Need any help?"

She groans and rolls her eyes, like any tween girl, like every picture of a daughter you ever imagined. "No, Mother," she says and walks away, leaving you smiling.

She has her period, first time ever. It arrived this past Tuesday, while she was at school. She didn't notice it right away; she doesn't like the school restrooms and tries to avoid using them if she can help it. The school nurse called you to come pick her up at lunchtime, because the blood had soaked through her pants.

Tilly seems to be taking the whole thing in stride; mostly she's annoyed by it. She doesn't like the imprecision, the fact that she doesn't know for sure when it's coming or how long it will last. She's freaked out by the way she inevitably gets blood on her hands, and she's horrified (almost morally outraged, it seems) by the existence of menstrual cramps. She's made a few awkward jokes about sexual activity and pregnancy. Fairly average stuff, really; probably not so different from the responses of her neurotypical peers. You've been dreading this moment for a while, but it's not nearly as bad as you'd feared. You underestimate her sometimes, you think.

Big family events, like this wedding, can be hard for you. You're seeing other kids Tilly's age and comparing; you're wondering how she appears to people who don't know her very well. On the car ride from the church to the reception, you listened to your girls pick apart the ceremony, enumerating which aspects they would or would not like to include in their own weddings. And you tried to believe in a future so easy and bright.

You see Josh's mother, Irene, winding toward you through the scattered circles of guests. You smile, nudge the chair next to you into a more welcoming position. You've always felt like you lucked out in this area. Josh's dad died before the two of you met, but his mom is warm and kind, noninterfering, relatively drama-free.

She sits down next to you, sets her glass of wine on the table. "You finally get a moment to yourself," she says, "and here I come to ruin it."

"No," you say. "I'm glad to have some adult conversation."

She squeezes your shoulder. "It's so nice of you guys to come. I know it's a long trip."

Seven and a half hours, factoring in traffic, meals, and bathroom stops. But you shrug. "We're happy to be here," you say.

"Tilly seems good," she says. It's not a question, exactly, but she's providing a blank space, drawing a box in the air where your answer should go.

"Yeah," you say, your tone upbeat. "I mean, it's a work in progress." It's hard to explain to anyone who isn't right there in the middle of it. You could say that there are good days and there are bad days, and that makes it sound like her struggles aren't any different from anyone else's. But you know the difference, even if you don't know how to convey it to anyone else: on the good days, she's still telling her father she wants to fuck him. On the good days, she's still hitting her little sister if you can't manage to put yourself between them in time.

Tonight, though. Tonight, everyone is nicely dressed, and no one's yelled even once. Tonight, you are filled with good wishes, and you're going to dance with your husband, whether he likes it or not. You glance around until you spot your girls: Iris is across the room with Josh, saying something that's making all the grown-ups around her laugh, and Tilly's coming through the doorway, on her way back from the bathroom. All of your life here, in front of you. *I spy, with my hopeful eye . . .*

After dinner, there are toasts, and then the newlyweds cut the wedding cake, which turns out to be a wedding pie, causing nearly uniform disappointment at your table. Pie seems more sophisticated than cake, you think, perhaps more of an adult choice. But that doesn't mean you have to prefer it.

This is one area, though, where you and your husband disagree. "Mmm," he says. "That looks amazing. Why didn't we think of doing that at our wedding?"

You stare at him. "It's like I don't even know you anymore." Your girls laugh, the sound bright, like little birds.

"Aw, come on," he says. "Pie is great."

"I don't know," you say. "Maybe pie is more of a guy thing."

You've lost them. "Mom, that's sexist," says Tilly.

"Yeah," says Iris. "It's offensive."

You shake your head at them, these monsters you've created, and you walk away to join the line for dessert.

And when the DJ interrupts the pouring of coffee to ask that all of the married couples report to the dance floor, you stand up and take Josh's hand to pull him along with you. As you walk away from the table, you hear Tilly say to her grandmother, "Grammy, did you know I can get pregnant now?" but when you turn back to see if you're going to be needed, your mother-in-law smiles and shoos you away. The song is "The Way You Look Tonight," bland and lovely. It's timeless and generic in all the best ways; it smooths away the specifics and turns this wedding into everywedding. The DJ keeps his microphone in his hand, ready to winnow the dancing couples down until only the oldest remains.

You put your arms around Josh's neck and rest your head on his shoulder. You're forty-two, and you've known him since you were nineteen. Impossibly lucky, you think sometimes, to love someone so thoroughly and so long.

"Okay," says the DJ, midway through the first verse. "Anyone who's been married for five years or less, please leave the floor."

Four or five couples, the newlyweds among them, step away and join the crowd of onlookers. Look at them, the bride and groom, the way they stand close and continue to hold each other's hands, happy to be young and flushed, happy to be the first ones to leave. You don't mind, you realize, being left behind in this middle place, alongside the old folks. At least you get to dance for a while longer.

Your own wedding was lovely, but looking back now you're mostly amazed at how young you were. You said the words, and you meant them, but really you had no idea how it would feel to stick together through the bad times. You tighten your arms around Josh, as he drops a kiss onto the top of your head. This is it now: your sickness, your poorer. "Someday," one of Tilly's doctors once said to you, "you'll look back on this and wonder how you ever got through it."

"Okay," says the DJ. "Only couples who have been married ten years or more."

You're still safe; it's fifteen years since you stood where that girl in the white dress is standing. Here's what you have in common with the couples still moving around you: you know, all of you, what these newlyweds are in for, these starry-eyed fledglings who think this is the moment where everything good begins. You're dancing alongside veterans of wars and miscarriages and a thousand day-to-day disappointments. You cling to your husband, happy in his arms, until it's time to move to the side, to make way for couples who have lived through even more.

chapter 18

Iris

June 10, 2012: New Hampshire

My dad's the one who drove Scott to the ER after he got hurt last night, so I already know most of the details before we get to breakfast on Sunday: he has a second-degree burn on the palm of his right hand, and he'll have to wear a bandage for a while and do some rehab (which I thought only meant that thing about getting over a drug addiction, but I guess not), but other than that, he'll be okay. And Tilly asked a bunch of gross questions, like how much skin was hanging off and what color it was, so I also know the answers to those things, even though I'd rather not.

When we get to the dining hall, Scott's there, and he seems pretty normal. His hand's all wrapped up in a giant ball of white gauze, and he looks like he hasn't slept or taken a shower or anything. But in a strange way, he seems happier than usual. He's grinning all over the place and practically bouncing off the walls with excitement.

"Big day," he keeps saying to people when he runs into them at the buffet table or on their way to the kitchen. "Big day."

And with all the stuff about Scott getting hurt, I'd forgotten that today's the day the first GCs are getting here. I have a weird feeling about it, like when your parents are having people over for dinner that you don't know, or when your friend is trying to convince you that a movie's good, but you still don't want to watch it. Not dread, exactly, but . . . the idea of a bunch of strangers coming and staying at our camp just doesn't sound fun.

Scott comes and sits down at our table, carrying his plate of pancakes with his left hand.

"Good morning," my mom says. "Were you able to get any sleep?"

He grins. "Sleep is for the weak."

"So I heard you didn't have to get anything amputated," says Tilly. I see my mom close her eyes for a second and shake her head, the way she does when she can't quite believe something Tilly's just said.

"Nope," says Scott. "Everything's still attached."

"That's good," says Tilly. "I read this thing online once about this guy who had to . . ."

And then she just stops talking. Which is weird for Tilly, weird enough that we all turn to look and see if she's like having a stroke or choking on her breakfast or something. But she's just sitting there, looking surprised.

"You okay there, Till?" asks my dad.

It takes her a minute to answer. "Yeah," she says slowly. "I was going to say something inappropriate, but I stopped myself. Because I didn't want to get AD Block." She's smiling and she looks really proud of herself.

Then all the adults are falling all over themselves to congratulate her and tell her what a great decision that was, and my mom reaches across the table to give her arm a little squeeze.

"Yeah," says Tilly. "That was kind of weird. I was totally going to start talking about this guy I read about who had to have his penis amputated because he had cancer . . ."

And of course, being Tilly, she doesn't even understand what she just did. While my mom and dad are pointing out the flaw in her reasoning, I notice that Scott is having a hard time trying to cut up his pancakes with his fork, using only one hand, so I say, "I can do that for you."

Scott looks up at me and smiles. He has really nice eyes. I don't mean that like I have a crush on him or anything, it's just hard not to notice when he's looking right at you so closely.

"Thank you, Iris," he says, passing his plate to me. "You can be my right-hand girl."

After breakfast, Scott talks for a little while about the Guest Campers, and tells us all the things he was planning to say last night at the Saturday Campfire, before he got hurt: that he's proud of us, and we've learned so much in the past few days, and now we have the chance to help other families. And we should just be friendly and be ourselves and whatever.

Tilly raises her hand to talk. "Here's what I don't understand about the GCs," she says. "Why are they coming here?"

Scott laughs, and so do some of the other grown-ups. "Good question, Tilly," Scott says. "Let's see if one of the other kids can answer that for you. Candy? Iris? Ryan?"

Ryan's not even paying attention, as usual, and I'm trying to decide if I want to answer, but Candy gets her hand up first.

"So, okay," she says. "The reason that *any* of us are here is because our parents think that living a little bit separate from some of the parts of the modern world will be good for us. Right? Like getting away from computers and texting, and growing our own food so that it doesn't have any mutant additives or whatever."

"'Mutant additives,'" says Tilly. "LOL."

"Go on," says Scott.

"So that's the same reason that the GCs want to come. Except they're only coming for a week, instead of moving here forever. It's like at a Renaissance fair where there are some people who are just there because it sounds like fun, and there are some people who are super into pretending it's the Renaissance, and they have all the right clothes and call people wenches and squires and won't sell you a smoothie unless you call it 'grog.'"

"Wait a minute, wait a minute," says Scott. "So you're saying that we're the . . . what, the freakish true believers, while everyone else is just dabbling in our lifestyle?"

"Maybe we're the Amish," Tilly says. "That would kind of make sense."

"Yeah, that works," says Candy. "We're the Amish and the GCs are the tourists who want to take a ride in our horse and buggy."

"That sounds dirty for some reason," Tilly says. "Like if 'horse and buggy' were a euphemism for . . . never mind. I'm not going to say it."

"Good plan," says my dad.

Scott holds up a hand to get our attention. "If we're all done with questions and . . . metaphors, I think I'm going to see if I can get a nap in before our guests arrive."

As everyone starts to get up and clear their plates, Tilly leans in close to me. "Penis," she says, not whispering, but at least in a lower voice than usual. "I was going to say it was a euphemism for 'penis.'"

"Duh," I say, because even I knew that. Everything's *always* a euphemism for "penis."

Cars start pulling into the camp driveway around lunchtime. Not that there are that many of them—there are only going to be three GC families each week—but it's surprising to see anyone new after a week of being by ourselves.

Scott stands on the lawn with a clipboard and greets each family as they arrive, giving them welcome packets and taking away their phones and other electronics. He's got his hurt arm in a sling now, for some reason, and when people ask him about it, he just says, "A little mishap in the line of duty."

We all have jobs, and mine is to be the Welcome Guide for the Russell family: I'm supposed to show them where their cabin is, help them bring in their stuff, answer any questions they have, and then take the kids out to show them around while the parents have a few minutes to themselves.

The Russells are the last family to arrive. There's a mom and two boys, ages six and eight. They've come all the way from South Carolina and have real Southern accents. The mom asks me a million things about our family and how long we've been here and stuff like that, and then she asks me to go get them some towels; we have a bunch of extra linens that we keep in the laundry room. As I walk across Town Square, I make up a game where this is a hotel, and I have a job here as a chambermaid. My mom and dad run room service, and Tilly works at the front desk, even though she makes lots of mistakes with people's reservations. And Scott is our boss, except he broke his arm, so I have to help him run the place. I'm not sure what his job is, I guess he's the manager or something high-up like that. Maybe he even owns the whole hotel.

chapter 19

Tilly

Date and Location Unknown

On cold nights, when the elders gathered by the fire to tell stories and their talk turned to the Great Autism Panic of the early twenty-first century, we children were never quite sure how much to believe. The details were so odd that we were tempted to dismiss it as Hammondite folklore, no more or less true than the story of the strange summer camp where families went to learn how to be families.

Either way, though, it was an intriguing period of history: the quaint euphemisms ("special needs," for example, and "on the spectrum"), the fearmongering and misinformation, the chaos caused by the lack of an agreed-upon medical and therapeutic protocol. The elders lingered on the era's rudimentary understanding of neuroscience, the dissent within the medical community itself as to nomenclature, classification, and diagnostic criteria. Celebrities giving advice based on superstition, rather than medical fact. The worry that a child's natural inclinations and tendencies might become more destructive if left untreated. Parents seemed to be afraid of their own children's brains.

Most fascinating to us was always the idea that afflicted children were often segregated, confined to separate schools away from their "neurotypical" peers. It was a dark time, the elders conceded when we marveled at the cruelty, but you had to take it in context. Given the challenges that twenty-first-century parents faced, they said, perhaps we could cut them a little slack. We have to believe that they were doing the best they could.

Years later, in classrooms and libraries, when we learned from our own studies that the tales had been true after all, we weren't really all that surprised. Stranger things have happened. We simply shook our heads, like every generation does, and felt glad to be living in an age more enlightened than the one that came before.

chapter 20

Iris

June 10, 2012: New Hampshire

By dinnertime on Sunday, I've met all three GC families. There's the Southern mom with the two boys that I helped earlier, there's a family with a mom and dad and twins (one boy and one girl), and a family with a mom, a dad, and one boy. Tons of names to remember, and I'm trying to get them all down, even though they'll be leaving again in six days, and we'll have another new batch to learn.

After dinner on Sunday, Scott stands up in the dining hall and gives a welcome speech to the Guest Campers. After talking about what time breakfast is and what kinds of activities we'll be doing and all that kind of stuff, he says, "Now, several of you have asked about my injury."

He gestures to his arm, which is still in a sling. "The truth is, we had a little campfire mishap last night. Luckily, no one else was hurt, but we're all aware that it could have had a much more unfortunate outcome. I just want to take this opportunity to assure you that we take fire safety very seriously, and we're redoubling our efforts to make sure that nothing like this happens again."

He pauses for a minute and looks down, then shifts to a more cheerful tone. "And I think that's pretty much it, so . . ."

"Wait a minute, Scott," someone calls out. It's Janelle. She pushes her chair back from the table and stands up. "I'd like to say something, if that's okay."

"Of course," says Scott. He sounds concerned.

"Thanks," says Janelle. "So okay." She looks around the room. "I think I've met all of our Guest Campers, but if I haven't, my name is Janelle Ruffin. This is my husband, Tom, and that little guy sucking on his fingers over there is our son, Hayden. And the part of the story that Scott left out is that he only got hurt because he was trying to protect my child from harm."

"Oh, hey . . ." Scott interrupts. He's shaking his head.

"No," says Janelle. "This is important. Because I know that these people who just got here today are probably feeling a little bit unsure about a lot of things. And I just want them to know that they're in good hands, because this man standing up there in front of you . . ." Her voice is starting to shake a little bit, like she's trying not to cry. "I am so grateful that he's come into our lives. Before I met Scott Bean . . . I swear, I was starting to lose hope. Hayden is the most precious thing in my life, but I was starting to think there was nothing I could do to help him. Tom and I . . . we just felt so alone, you know?" She's crying now, full-on sobbing, and for a minute that's the only sound in the dining hall. Tom gets up and puts his arm around her. I look down at my plate, roll my leftover corncob from one side to the other. I hate it when adults get all embarrassing and sappy.

"Okay," says Janelle. "I'm finished. I didn't mean to get all emotional on you. I just wanted to say that Scott Bean is a hero. He's *my* hero."

"Oh, Janelle," says Scott. He sounds like maybe he's going to start crying, too, which makes me so embarrassed I kind of want to put my head down on the table. He walks over to Janelle and hugs her. My mom starts clapping softly, and other people join in.

Tilly says, "I was going to say 'Get a room,' but I stopped myself." Luckily, there's enough noise that I don't think anybody else hears her.

It turns out that things are different when we have Guest Campers here. At first, it seems fun, like a party: we're meeting new people and showing them all the cool things we've made, and even the food is better than usual.

But there's a lot more work, which I guess makes sense because there are almost twice as many people. After a day or two, I'm starting to feel like the GCs are all on vacation, and we're not. We have to get up super-early to make breakfast for everybody, then it's chores all morning until lunch. In the afternoons, there are fun activities, but it's still like the focus is on the visiting kids, and the rest of us are there to help set up or whatever. Plus, there's this feeling that we're on display; the visiting parents are watching us all the time, to see if we're normal or well behaved or whatever it is they want their kids to be after coming here.

On Monday afternoon, I'm helping Scott set up an obstacle course, and he asks me to get a pitcher of water and some cups to bring down to the lake, so I end up in the dining hall during one of the Parent Conversation Sessions. Before I go in, I can see through the screen that my mom is sitting right by the door, and I hear her say to one of the visiting moms, "No, Iris doesn't have a diagnosis. She's NT."

Then I open the door, and she sees me, and I go stand behind her and put my arms around her neck. "What's NT?" I ask.

"I'll tell you later," she says softly, and pulls me into a quick hug before she sends me on my way.

That afternoon, I spend a long time imagining what those letters might stand for, both good and bad possibilities. First, I decide it means "natural talent," and that makes me happy, but then I think about the kids like Tilly; they might be a little off-balance, but some of them are totally amazing at art or math or spelling or whatever. (Does memorizing whole TV episodes count as a talent?) And then I think, maybe the N stands for "negative," and there aren't any good combinations that can come out of that.

Later, before bed, I ask my mom again, and she tells me it stands for "neurotypical," which apparently isn't good or bad, it's just . . . normal. Tilly's not NT; there are a million different ways she's not normal. But I'm totally average, and it's kind of disappointing to know that *that's* the way my mom describes me to people when she doesn't know I'm listening.

On Friday, while we're getting breakfast ready, Scott asks Ryan and Tilly to help him hang up a big banner that says "Happy Mother's Day!" Which doesn't make any sense, because it's June 15, and Mother's Day was more than a month ago. But when I ask Scott, he says he won't answer any questions until everyone's arrived.

Finally, once all the Guest Campers are here, and we've all gone through the line and gotten our food, he bangs a spoon on a glass.

"Good morning, folks," he says. "Are any of you wondering about this sign here?" And a bunch of people yell "yes," just like you do in school when the teacher asks a question and wants you all to answer at once.

"Well, allow me to explain," says Scott. "I've always felt that once a year is not nearly often enough to celebrate mothers and all the wonderful things that they do for their children and for their families. So here at Camp Harmony, every Friday is Mother's Day!"

Some of the adults laugh, probably because they're surprised, rather than because they actually think it's funny. Right next to me, Tilly speaks up and calls out, "If we're doing extra holidays," but my mom puts a finger over her lips, and my dad starts whispering in her ear, and she quiets down before she can start demanding extra Halloween and Christmas and whatever else she was going to ask for. But she's already given some of the other kids ideas, and they start yelling out "Valentine's Day!" and "Thanksgiving!"

"Okay, okay," says Scott. "I hear you. There are lots of great holidays, and we've all got our favorites. And before any of the dads can ask, I think that Father's Day is important, too. But here's the thing: I've only got you here for a week—I'm talking to our Guest Campers now—and we've got a lot to do in that time, without trying to re-create Arbor Day and St. Patrick's Day and what have you."

"No one said Arbor Day," yells Ryan. Scott ignores him.

"But unlike St. Patrick's Day and all the others, Mother's Day carries a message that fits in quite nicely with the other things we've been talking about all week. It's about celebrating a family member who doesn't get celebrated all that often. It's about love and respect for the person who, more often than not, holds all the pieces of the family together from day to day. It's about stepping out of our usual roles for a little while, and taking care of her, instead of letting her take care of us. And I think that's a worthwhile pursuit, no matter what day of the year it happens to be.

"So here's how this is going to work. Moms, you get to relax. Get in your bathing suits, sit by the lake, read a book, take a nap. Whatever: your time is your own, which I know isn't something you get to hear very often."

"I wish I was a mom," says Tilly, but quietly enough that nobody yells at her. It's a weird thought, Tilly as a mom, and I'm not sure if it sounds like a bad idea because she's thirteen or because she's Tilly.

"As for you kids," says Scott, "Guest Campers and Core Family both: you're coming with me. I've got a few special activities planned."

Scott leads us out into the woods, to the spot where we had Saturday Campfire last week, when Scott got hurt. There's still a circle of wood and ashes where the fire was.

"All right," says Scott. "We're going to play a game called Werewolf."

chapter 21

Alexandra

February 2011: Washington, DC

A week after winter break ends, Tilly has a half day at school: teacher in-service or one of those kinds of things. On the way home, you stop at McDonald's for lunch, and you notice that suddenly—since this morning, even—Tilly has developed a compulsion to lick every surface she comes into contact with. She licks the counter, while you're waiting for your food. She licks the display case where the Happy Meal prizes are kept. She licks the table you sit at and the window that looks out on the gray air of the parking lot, the asphalt covered with rough salt and dirty snow. She stops to lick the doorjamb as you pass through it, and you try not to look at the three or four customers who watch it happen.

There's another change, too, though it's harder to quantify: an increase in defiance, in inappropriate language, in not following directions. In doing things she knows she's not supposed to. An increase in pushing your buttons, basically. She tries to open the car door while you're driving; you flick on the child locks. She throws a paper cup out the window; you pull over and walk her back a few hundred yards, so she can pick it up. And all the while, you don't freak out, not when she licks gum on the pavement, not when she calls you a bitch in front of an old lady. You hold her hand tight, you keep your tone mild, and you wonder what the hell is going on.

Is this a medical issue? She has a cold, and—in addition to thinking of the germs she's spreading and the germs she's taking in—you wonder if there's some connection. These kinds of sudden changes (including the one that got her kicked out of pre-K) have all taken place in winter. But it seems like a tenuous link.

You phone her pediatrician's office, with all the usual misgivings; it's a big practice, connected to a teaching hospital, and your kids never seem to see the same doctor twice. You take her in, do your best to keep her contained in the waiting room, as she giggles and runs for a door that says "Employees Only," as she tries to knock over an infant in a baby seat, as she sings a song that contains no lyrics except the word "vulva."

But the doctors—she sees a resident first, and then, briefly, an attending—don't find anything wrong with her, not anything they know how to treat, at any rate. As usual, the medical personnel seem faintly baffled by the mysteries your daughter presents. The attending mentions conversationally that Tilly has "cryptic tonsils" (which apparently means that they have folds in them where bacteria can gather) and you almost laugh. When has anything about Tilly *not* been cryptic?

You get her to sit on your lap for a throat culture; you squeeze her tight and nuzzle her hair like you did when she was little. But she ends up being too frightened, and you have to join a team of two nurses in holding her down and getting her mouth open while a resident jabs at her throat. You're almost crying, too, by the end of it, and the rapid strep test is negative, in any case.

Afterward, you think about taking her for ice cream. It's easy to be fierce and brave in the car: the hell with it, you think. Your little girl has had a hard day, and she deserves a treat. The important thing is to tamp down your own anxiety. That's one of the tips you took away from Scott Bean's seminar, and it's a good one. Any embarrassment her behavior causes you, any worry about what other people are thinking: it's a waste of your time and energy. Your number one job is being your kid's advocate, and you can't do that if you're nervous about what the people at the next table are thinking.

Easier said than done, of course, and your nerves already feel ragged. In the end, you get her a cone to go, and you count it as a victory.

If you're hoping that this will end as suddenly as it began, you're out of luck. It goes on for weeks and weeks. You speak to Tilly's teacher and to the therapist she sees at school; no one can really explain it. *Just ride it out* seems to be the best advice anyone can give you.

At school, she's not able to behave any better than she is at home, and even in a school designed specifically for kids with special needs, there are limits to what they can handle. When Tilly is too disruptive for the teacher to allow her to stay in the classroom, she gets sent out to "take a break," sometimes in a counselor's office and sometimes just in whatever empty room they can find. Eventually, the school asks you to keep her home for a little while. Among other things, the current situation is hurting her social interactions with her classmates; they're grossed out by the licking.

Throughout January and February, you and Tilly spend long, difficult days at home. Josh takes time off from work, when he can, to give you a break. When you leave the house, you wonder how you're able to walk around in public without people seeing that you're a complete mess.

It doesn't get better, and it doesn't, and it doesn't.

Sometimes you imagine getting sick—nothing serious, but perhaps something that would require a few days' hospitalization. Sometimes you wish you were invisible. You wish you'd never made yourself important to anyone at all.

Here are some of the things you're not posting on Facebook during February of 2011:

Alexandra Moss Hammond has kept her daughter home from school again, because she's licking the walls and cursing like a sailor.

Alexandra Moss Hammond's daughter has changed the name of Shel Silverstein's poetry collection to "Where the Pussy Ends."

Alexandra Moss Hammond's daughter just said in the post office, "Your tits are huge. Did I really used to suck on those?"

In the evenings, or what's left of them after the kids are finally, finally asleep, you and Josh sit in the living room and look at your separate laptops. He's researching fringe theories about autism; you're reading pornography about the characters of a TV show you've never seen a single episode of. The porn thing—and perhaps "erotica" is a better word because you like prose better than pictures— is a successor to the "build your own city" game. You cycle through diversions fairly rapidly; there's a lot that you're trying not to think about, and you find that novelty is the best strategy. Find something new and sink yourself in deep. So last month it was video games and this month it's amateur writing on LiveJournal. Next month, maybe it'll be crossword puzzles or biographies of serial killers. Celebrity gossip or a religious devotion to *So You Think You Can Dance*.

"Here's how it's going to happen," says Josh, after a long period of mutual silence. "Here's how it's going to turn out that vaccines *are* responsible, but not for the reasons we think."

You look up. "Okay," you say, waiting.

"So we know that the immune system detects and kills pathogens. But what if that's not all it does? What if it's responsible for figuring out what the individual needs to do to adapt to the particular environment he's born into?"

You're nodding, but you let your gaze fall back to the screen. Your characters are making out in an alley, despite the fact that they're both on-duty cops and someone is currently shooting at them.

"So we take this baby, this newborn, and we give him doses of like four major diseases in one day. What's the immune system supposed to make of that? It thinks we're living in plague days."

You look up for real. "Huh. That's interesting."

"Yeah. So the cortisol level shoots up, because the fight-or-flight mechanism has to be on super-alert. In plague days, it's every man for himself."

You pick up your glass of wine from the coffee table; it's the last of the second bottle, and there's a good chance you've had more than half. You pick it up and consider. Just because you poured it doesn't mean you have to drink it. But it's the color of a garnet, an inch and a half of promise. You take a sip.

"So how come it doesn't happen to every kid?" you ask. "They're all on the same vaccine schedule, more or less."

"Some kids are just predisposed to be extra-sensitive to it."

You nod. "Maybe." You go back to your reading: orgasms had, perp caught, Miranda rights read.

Josh looks over at your screen. "How's your porn? Are they fucking yet?"

"It's not really about that," you say. "But yes."

You close your laptop and put it on the coffee table. "Will you help me make the lunches?" Using the plural is optimistic; there's a good chance you'll only be needing one lunch in the morning.

"Sure," he says. He's back to his reading. "In a minute."

Hard to say what kind of effect all of this (and depending on your current outlook, "all of this" can encompass anything from the current month up to the last ten years) will have on your marriage. Sometimes you fight, but more often you go days without finding the time or energy to say anything private to each other at all.

In the kitchen, you cut up fruit and seal it into small Tupperware containers. Josh comes up behind you. He brushes your hair aside and presses his lips to your neck.

You consider it. "I haven't showered all that recently," you say.

He barks out a laugh. "That's hot."

You close your eyes and lean back against him. You are lucky here, if nowhere else. This is what you can't afford to forget. You believe, fervently, that falling in love is the one holy mystery in an otherwise secular life.

"Okay," you say. "Let me just put this in the fridge."

Alexandra Moss Hammond can't seem to keep her house clean or her daughters' hair free of tangles.

Alexandra Moss Hammond really should stop crying while she drives.

Alexandra Moss Hammond wonders if it's possible to drown on dry land.

In the morning, you're hungover, and Tilly has to stay home again. She freaks out when you burn her toast; you snap at her; she punches you in the arm. You're all edges today, both of you. You take away an hour of computer; she throws a glass of water in your face.

When you've both calmed down (and her hour has passed), she settles in front of the family computer to read about her current obsession, which is Greek mythology, and you open your laptop to see if you can find anything that might give you some hope. Social skills groups. Lymphatic therapy. Probiotics. Grapefruit seed extract and young coconut kefir.

Look at your Google history, and there it is, your mind, all its secret curves rolled out flat, like a map. Preoccupations and idle curiosities, mottled hopes and scribbled-out fantasies beating wildly on the screen. Everything you were, are, could be.

You read about home remedies and dietary supplements: Sodium citrate reduces inflammation. Vitamin B3 can have a calming effect. Bitter orange helps with sleep, but the NIH says it isn't safe. Red and green natural clays have antibacterial properties and can cleanse the body of yeast—but are you really going to feed your child clay?

At this moment, autism treatment is still an empty frontier. There are special prayers and crystals for sale. There's a man in Brazil who will perform long-distance "psychic surgery" if you send him your child's picture. But even among respectable doctors and researchers, crazy things are being tested: fecal transplant and chelation, elective tonsillectomies and transcranial magnetic stimulation. Electroshock therapy is being given another chance, and why not? No harm in paging through the history books, as long as you keep a jaundiced eye. Stop before you get to "lobotomy." Stop before you start tying children to their beds.

The day feels interminable, but together the two of you ride it out. The solace of life is that each day has an end. This one will, too.

chapter 22

Iris

The thing about Werewolf is, it's the most fun game ever, but it's really hard to explain. It starts out with one person being the Werewolf—today it was Scott—and everyone else has to build a shelter because the Werewolf is coming. You can build it out of leaves and sticks or rocks or whatever you can find. But there's a secret rule that only the Werewolf knows, like today it was that any shelter built up against a tree trunk doesn't count. Everyone can ask one yes-or-no question about the rule, to try to figure it out, and you can also listen to everybody else's questions. Then you hide in your shelter, and the Werewolf comes to town. Anyone whose shelter doesn't fit the rules becomes one of the Werewolf's spies, and everything begins again.

And it gets even more complicated, because each spy gets to make up a new rule, and they don't even have to be about the shelter. Like Candy was a spy today, and she added this whole truth-or-dare thing that was really fun. And also, spies can betray the Werewolf, and there's probably other stuff I'm forgetting.

So anyway, when we get back to camp around dinnertime, we're all talking about Werewolf and everyone's trying to explain it to their parents, but the adults are all acting like it's too convoluted and they can't understand it. My mom says, "That sounds like a very intricate game," and my dad says, "So when do I get to be the Werewolf?" and Tilly and I just look at each other and shake our heads. I have a feeling that Werewolf isn't going to be a parent thing, just a thing between Scott and the kids. If the other grown-ups don't get it, fine. We don't have to tell them about it again at all.

On Saturday, we say goodbye to the GCs and get ready for a batch of new ones. Tilly and I get put on laundry duty: we have to wash and fold all of the sheets and towels, so they'll be ready for the new people tomorrow. So we're in the little laundry building, sitting in these uncomfortable plastic chairs, the kind with a little desk surface attached, waiting for the dryers to finish.

"I wonder if there'll be any good boys this week," Tilly says.

"'Good boys'?" I ask. "What does that mean, exactly?"

"I don't know," says Tilly. "Cute, or maybe hot."

"Yeah, that'd be nice," I say. "They're only here for a week, though. That's not a lot of time to get a romance going."

"Maybe I don't want a romance," she says. "Maybe I just want to have sex."

"Tilly!" I'm shocked, like actually shocked. I've heard her say tons of inappropriate things about sex before, but not like this. Not all casual, like it's something that might actually happen.

"What?" she says.

"I just can't believe you said that." I mean, I know about sex and everything. I just don't get why anyone would want to do it, if it's not for having a baby.

She shrugs. "I can't wait to have sex. It's going to be amazing. Like going on a roller coaster, kind of."

I start laughing. "A roller coaster? How . . . like you're going up and down giant hills? And it's really fast and sometimes you scream and think you're going to die?"

She starts laughing, too. "No, I don't know, just . . . it's exciting, but in a physical way, you know?"

"What . . ." I stop to catch my breath. I'm picturing the world's weirdest amusement park. "What would you call that ride?" I ask. "The . . . Thunder Penis?"

"Oh, my God." Tilly's whole body is shaking, she's laughing so hard. "The Fuck Blaster!"

"Eww," I say. "The . . ." I can't talk for a second, and I put my hands on the desk in front of me, trying to steady myself. "The . . . Vagina Cannon!"

Tilly almost falls off her chair, and right at that second, the laundry room door creaks open. Scott comes in, but stops when he sees the two of us laughing our heads off.

"Just coming to check on you guys," he says. "Looks like the laundry's going well."

"It is," I say, willing myself to stop. "We're just waiting for the dryer to finish."

"I see." He sounds sort of sarcastic, like he's just going along with the joke, but the sun's shining through the door behind him, and I can't see his face. "And may I ask what's so funny?"

Tilly and I look at each other, and I almost crack up all over again. "We were just wondering," I say, "if there are going to be any cute boys coming tomorrow."

"Ah, boys," Scott says. He sounds more normal now. "Well, there will be boys. Whether they're cute or not, I really couldn't say."

"Why not?" Tilly asks.

"Because I haven't seen them yet," he says. "And even if I had, I'm not a good judge of what makes a teenage boy 'cute.'"

"You could be a good judge," Tilly says. "Like if you're gay." She starts giggling again. "Or a pedophile."

I suck in my breath. I only sort of know what that second thing is, but I know she shouldn't be going around accusing people of being one.

Scott's face is still dark and shadowy, but I can see his whole body go stiff for a second. Then really quick, he moves toward Tilly and grabs the edge of her desk with his one good hand. He leans close to her face, and when he talks, his voice is quiet but angry.

"Listen to me, Tilly," he says, enunciating each word. "For the love of God."

Tilly's leaning backward, trying to move her face away from his, but he just goes with her. "You," he says. He's talking like each word is its own sentence. "Are. Going. To get. In enormous trouble. If you don't learn. To watch. Your fucking. Mouth."

Tilly lets out a breath that's like a laugh at the swearword, but she looks terrified.

"Do I have AD Block?" she asks.

Scott shakes his head. "This is not about AD Block. This is not about Camp Harmony. This is about functioning. In the goddamn world."

"Okay," Tilly says. She squirms away from him, and he finally takes a step backward. "I get it. Jeez." Her voice is shaky, like she might be about to cry.

Scott shakes his head again and walks toward the door. "Get the laundry done," he yells over his shoulder. "And think before you speak." Then he's gone.

For a minute, Tilly and I just sit there. The dryer timer buzzes, and it makes me jump, but I don't get up right away.

Finally, Tilly says, "I have a good one." Her voice sounds totally normal. "The Flying Cock. Wouldn't that be funny?"

"I'm going to get the laundry," I say, and I leave her there by herself.

When the new GCs arrive on Sunday, it turns out that there really aren't any cute boys. And there's one family that right away I don't like. They're named the Bakers, and their kids are Jason and Kylie. Partly, I'm annoyed because their mom keeps calling me Lily (which happens more often than you'd think; people get introduced to our family and the thing they remember is that I have a flower name, so they think it's Lily, probably because it rhymes with Tilly). But also, Kylie's kind of snotty—she always has this look on her face like she doesn't believe you, even before you've said anything—and Jason's just really nervous and worried all the time. Right away when he got here, he started asking us about what we do all day, really specifically, like do we brush our teeth before or after breakfast, and what we do if we have to go to the bathroom while we're doing an outdoor activity.

After dinner on Sunday, I'm doing dishes with Candy, Tilly, and Ryan. So far, no one's gotten AD Block, so we're all still in the running for candy. But since we've all been behaving so well, it means those extra chores go right back into the roster.

I'm at the sink, doing the actual washing, while Candy dries. Tilly and Ryan are sort of sharing the job of putting things away, because it takes them both twice as long to do anything. Which is maybe mean to say, but it's also just realistic.

Candy's talking about how Kylie keeps acting like we all work here, like we're servants or something, and Tilly (who's been quiet for a while in that way that makes you think she's probably not even listening) suddenly says, "We should totally mess with the new kids."

Ryan's head pops up from over by the cabinets. "Your ideas are intriguing to me," he says, "and I wish to subscribe to your newsletter." (*Simpsons*, as usual.)

"What do you mean?" I ask Tilly, ignoring Ryan.

"We could do some pranks, or maybe make up something that would scare them. They don't know anything about this place; we can tell them anything. We can say that there's like a monster who lives in the woods, and we've heard all these weird noises . . ." She's getting excited, the way she always does when she's making up a story.

"A werewolf," I say. It just suddenly all comes together in my head.

"*The Werewolf says you have to hide . . .*" says Ryan. That's something from the game.

"*Are you on the Werewolf's side?*" Tilly answers.

"So what do you mean?" says Candy. "Like the game?"

"Well, they don't know about the game yet. We're not playing it till Friday. So we could just start making comments about a were-wolf, and make it seem like we're talking about a real thing, instead of a game."

"That's awesome," Candy says.

Ryan is totally into this idea, and he and Tilly start talking over each other. "We can have someone hide . . ."

". . . fur and fake blood and stuff . . ."

". . . scare the shit out of them . . ."

"Don't make it too crazy," I say. "It has to be believable."

"Yeah," says Candy. "And it all depends on whether you bozos can keep a secret."

"Shut up," says Ryan. "Of course we can." I'm not convinced that's true; even though he's my age, he's not particularly good at keeping his mouth shut. And Tilly's not much better.

"Because no grown-ups can know," Candy warns. "Especially not Scott."

"Duh," says Ryan.

"Okay," says Tilly. "Let's get our stories straight."

After we get back to the cottage and go to bed, Tilly keeps me awake late, talking about the monster. We decided earlier with the other kids that it's going to be *like* a werewolf, but a little bit different. It only comes out at night, but it doesn't matter whether it's a full moon. And we don't know if it's a person who turns into an animal, or if it's just an animal all the time. Candy said that we should keep the details vague, that it's scarier if we don't know what it is exactly, just that there's *something* out there in the woods.

But Tilly can never leave anything at "vague." I'm only half-listening, because it's not really a conversation; she's making up all kinds of background stories and coming up with a plan to have a different monster every week, something new for each new group of Guest Campers. This kind of thing is always a problem for her with other kids, because she has such specific ideas about how things should go that she gets upset if anyone else wants to do things differently.

I was tired when we went to bed, but now I'm wide awake. Tilly's voice is getting sleepier and sleepier, and there are longer and longer pauses between sentences, but she never really stops talking. The last thing she says before she falls asleep is, "And you don't need a silver bullet to kill it. That's an urban legend." And then she's finally quiet.

I can hear my parents in the living room; I can't hear everything they're saying, but the walls are thin enough that I get most of it. First, they're talking about some of the other parents—my dad really doesn't like Ryan's dad, and he's making my mom laugh by telling a story about a conversation they had. Then my dad asks, "Hey, do we have any cranberry juice left?"

"No," my mom says. "Just OJ."

"Can I interest you in a nightcap?"

"What kind of nightcap? The Evian bottles are empty."

"I've got a couple of tricks up my sleeve," my dad says. "Airplane bottles. At the bottom of my shaving kit."

"Ooh, tricky."

I sit up in bed. They're talking about alcohol, I think, which is definitely not allowed here. It's sort of exciting to find out that they're not following all of the rules exactly. Because they're grown-ups, and why should Scott get to be in charge of them? I don't really understand what Scott is to them here. I don't think he's their *boss*, even though he tells them what to do. I don't think anyone gets paid, but then again, we never have to buy anything, so I guess it works out.

I get out of bed really quietly and sneak out to the hallway. My dad's gone to the kitchen, and after a minute, he comes back with tall glasses of orange juice (and, I guess, alcohol) for them both. They clink glasses and take a sip, and then without looking at me or anything, my mom says, "Are you just going to sit there in the dark, Iris?"

I start laughing. "How did you know?" I ask.

She turns and smiles at me. "Moms have secret powers. Do you want to come sit with us for a few minutes?"

"Yeah." I get up and walk to the couch. They were sitting close together, but now they move apart to make room for me in the middle. I get in between them and put my head on my mom's shoulder. She strokes my hair.

"Couldn't sleep?" asks my dad.

"Nope." I point at the glass he's holding; there's ice clinking in it, and it's already got beads of water rolling down the sides because the room is warm. "Can I have some juice, too?" I ask.

"Sure," says my dad.

The couch bounces as he gets up. As he's walking to the kitchen, I call after him, "No alcohol in mine."

They both look surprised for a minute, and maybe a little bit guilty. And then my mom hugs me closer, and we're laughing together, all three of us.

chapter 23

Alexandra

March 2011: Washington, DC

One Saturday in March, you take the girls to the toy store, so they can pick out a birthday present for their cousin. On the way there, everyone seems to be in a good mood, talking about possible purchases, both realistic and fanciful.

"Maybe we could get her a machine that sings songs to you when you're sad," says Tilly. "It knows when you're sad, because it has eye-recognition technology, and it can see when there's a tear." In the front seat, you shake your head. It's amazing, the way this child's creativity has come to be an ordinary part of your life. You should write this down, though you know that by the time you have a chance to, you'll probably have forgotten the peculiar Tilly-phrasing that makes it so good.

"Maybe," says Iris, doubtfully. "Or we could get her a toy pony. She really likes ponies."

Once inside the store, you let the kids wander a little bit, and you give yourself the luxury of browsing. You love this place; it's a neighborhood business, and it's been here a million years. Higher prices than, say, Target, but more interesting toys. You like to support them when you can.

Things have been going better lately, at least a little. The licking hasn't disappeared, but it's calmed down, and the new tics she's developed aren't quite as disruptive. She's back at school again most days, which is good for both of you.

You've been listening to Scott Bean's CDs and reading his newsletters, and you believe firmly that it's made a difference. The advice he gives, the techniques he suggests, are sensible and easy to implement, and they make you feel less helpless. You've got a set of tools, even if you're not always sure which ones to try.

He emails you, too, periodically. His notes are brief, but personal; not a form letter, but a real note from the real guy, using your kids' names and asking how they're doing. "Just checking in," he always says. You see it for what it is—a clever piece of marketing, keeping his name on your radar—but even so, the notes touch you. You appreciate the effort, however small it might be.

You've stayed in touch with Janelle, the mom from Philadelphia who you met at Scott Bean's workshop, and that's been helpful, too. You email each other during the day with updates and grim jokes; a couple of times a week, you talk on the phone after the kids are asleep. It's not that you don't have other friends. But you don't have many other friends you can talk to about this.

You don't want to jinx anything, but you feel like maybe, maybe, this most recent crisis has passed. And if it hasn't, you've got a secret weapon in reserve, in case you need it: at the bottom of Scott's messages, right below his name, there's always an automated signature line, listing some of the services that Harmonious Parenting offers. And the first entry, three words, is like a candy that you've hidden away where no one else will find it: *Private consultation available.*

You walk through the toy store, making mental notes to save for future birthdays and Christmases. You're thinking that you'll give the girls a little time to browse and pick out their gift recommendations. But it's only a minute or two before you hear Tilly begin to scream.

Anatomy of a meltdown: it can happen anytime; it can take you completely by surprise. You know to watch for certain triggers—hunger, fatigue, impending illness. But there are also times when it seems to arise out of nothing. Times when you never do figure out a cause, not even afterward, when you and Josh and Tilly's therapist sit down and do the Miss Marple thing, breaking down every external factor and personal interaction, every food eaten and cartoon watched in the hours leading up to it.

You know this much: it happens when she doesn't get what she wants. But not in a selfish way, not like a toddler who doesn't understand why she can't have every toy. It's more that if she doesn't get what she wants, she gets scared. She feels trapped. In an instant, she's lost. She can't see her way out. Everything seems bigger than it is. If she's been told that she can't use the computer, it means that maybe she'll never be allowed to again. For all she knows, you or Josh might unplug the computer, pick it up, and carry it out to the trash. If she's not the one in control, then who knows what might happen? The world is an unpredictable place.

You're always trying to stay on alert, three steps ahead of her, but it's not really possible, because her brain is such a fine and complicated machine. Say she wants to play a game with her sister. Great, right? This is what you want. Reaching out, moving out of the sphere of her own mind a little bit. But before they even begin, she's got it all planned out. They're not going to be just any aliens; they're aliens from the planet Hammondia. She's already expecting it to go a certain way, and there's not a lot of room for compromise. If she thinks that the aliens have names like Zogox and Glaptu, then it's a disaster for her sister to want to be called Lauren.

The way it manifests today is that one minute you're browsing wrapping paper, and the next you can hear Tilly, half a store away, yelling at the top of her lungs. No words, just a high-pitched shriek, piercing the hushed air.

You drop the gift bag you're holding and run toward the scream. You find them in the doll section, and you round the corner just in time to see Tilly raise her hand and take a swipe at Iris.

"Stop," you maybe-say and maybe-yell. "Tilly. Stop. Now."

You get to her before she can hit again, and you grab her hands in yours. She's found her words now, and she chokes them out between sobs. "I hate her! She's a bitch! Fuck her!" In the corner of your vision, you see Iris slip out of the place where she's been standing, pressed against a shelf of doll beds, and run toward the end of the aisle.

The problem with Scott Bean's bag of tricks is that they only work if you're able to stay calm. And right now, you're not calm at all.

You squeeze Tilly's wrists, hard. "What's going on?" you whisper, furious.

"Stop it," she says, her voice twisting. "You're hurting me. Do you hate me?"

And maybe in the washed-out heat of this moment, you do. Your children have told you many times that there's no difference between being angry with somebody and hating them for just a little while. And right now, you're angrier than you've been in a long, long time.

When the four of you are together, it's usually Josh who gets this job, talking Tilly down while you do damage control with Iris. But Josh isn't here, and you need to be the fucking adult.

You bite your lip and loosen your grip on Tilly. Breathe and breathe and breathe. You cross your arms over your chest, grab hold of your forearms, hidden beneath your coat sleeves. Dig your fingernails into your flesh, someplace where your clothes will hide it. It's a kind of currency exchange: the physical pain creates a tangible jolt that disrupts the circuit, turning fury into sadness. It focuses you, giving you a place to pin your attention. By the time your throat swells and your eyes begin to ache, you're finally ready to speak.

"No," you say, your voice breaking. You can feel the tears on your cheeks now. "I don't hate you. I love you so much."

You put your hands on her arms. Her body is practically vibrating; she's still fuming, though about what you may never know. What you'd like is to get her out of here, take her outside to scream in the open air, where there aren't a dozen happy people trying to buy toys. But you know you won't be able to get her out, because to her, that will sound like a threat, and it will make things worse. You'd have to bodily drag her through the store, and that's not a good idea. Once you get started on any kind of physical struggle, it's going to trigger a whole other set of bad events.

So you hold her in place and keep your talking to a minimum, get her to count and breathe and all those other things that are written in her "angry notebook" from school. When you're sure that she's a little calmer, you leave her where she is and go looking for Iris.

You find her in the art section, hiding. You crouch down next to her and hug her tight. "It's one thing when she does this at home," she whispers.

God. God. "I know," you say. "I know." Sometimes you don't know how you're going to stand this.

After a moment, Tilly wanders over. "I'm sorry, Mommy," she says. "Sorry, Iris." She's on a fairly even keel now, and she wants to put it behind her. But you . . . you just can't. When you don't immediately say, "It's okay," her face rumples, just a little. "Are you mad?" she asks, her voice quavering.

You keep your words steady. Firm, but not angry—this is key. "I'm a little bit mad," you say. You've still got your arms around Iris, keeping her at a safe distance. You look up at Tilly, who's standing above you both. "This was hard for me, Tilly. You need to learn to control yourself. This was very embarrassing and upsetting for both me and Iris."

You've devastated her. You watch it happening. It turns out that it doesn't matter how not-angry you sounded; you've still done damage. When you tell her, "I was embarrassed," she hears, "You're a fucking idiot." You say, "You need to learn to control yourself," and she hears, "This family would be better off without you." You watch her face absorb the blow. She's going to be crying in a minute, but right now she's still in the process of letting your words hit her all over, leaving little welts. You close your eyes for a long moment.

You need to help her with this. She needs to understand the way her behavior affects other people. But it's not worth it to crush her this way. She's sobbing now. You did this to her. She starts to wail, and she's hitting herself in the stomach, over and over again.

"I should die," she says. "I should commit suicide."

You take a breath. It's too much, too dramatic for such a little thing, and it allows you to get a little perspective. Where have you seen this sort of thing before—this instant globalization, jumping to the worst possible conclusion? She's her mother's daughter all over.

You're very, very good at beating yourself up. And you so wish that you hadn't passed it on to your little girl. Because the traits you've given Tilly, the good ones and the bad, aren't just reflected back at you; they're magnified all out of proportion. Where you're smart, she's brilliant; where you scold yourself during car trips, she sobs in the aisle of a toy store, believing that she deserves to die.

You take her by the hand and pull her down onto the floor next to you. You put your arms around her. "Okay, sweetie, okay." All you can do is comfort her. Iris stands and watches the two of you on the floor; she's a different kind of creature entirely.

"Okay, my baby," you whisper to Tilly. "It's going to be okay." And maybe, if you can create a soothing enough rhythm, maybe there's a chance that you'll start to believe it, too.

When your kids were little, there was a brief period when reality shows about comically strict nannies were popular: *Supernanny*,

Nanny 911. Programs about families in chaos, needing a firm hand to guide them. They became a guilty pleasure of yours. It was partly schadenfreude—*well, at least we're not as bad off as they are*—but you also hoped that you might learn something you could use. The thing that always came through, crystal clear, is that it was never the kids who were causing the problems. It was like an autopsy, a cause-and-effect diagram: these are the mistakes the parents made, and this is how they led us here. That child deliberately pouring juice on the floor? It's more than likely that you created this situation yourself; all she did was adapt to it.

When you get home from the toy store, without a present, you sit down and open your laptop, scanning for the information about private consultations. You email Scott and ask for a quote.

chapter 24

Iris

June 20, 2012: New Hampshire

We begin Project Werewolf at lunch on Wednesday. I'm actually really excited about it; it's like being in a play. I know it's kind of mean, but the thing is, I don't really care that much. These kids are just passing through. They're not part of the CF, and after they leave on Saturday, we'll probably never see them again. They just show up for a week and make our lives harder.

So Ryan and Candy and Tilly and I all fill up our plates at the buffet and then go sit down at the same table with Kylie and Jason. And then I just start eating my sandwich and wait for the right moment to come.

In movies and TV shows, when kids come up with a plan that the adults don't know about, it always goes so perfectly. Like they've thought of every detail, and broken it down into parts, and every person knows practically how many *seconds* until it's their turn. But in real life, especially when you've got kids like Tilly and Ryan, who you can't really trust to behave the way a normal person would, it's a lot less smooth. That's why I've set it up with them that I'm the one who's supposed to start, and even though they're both giving me these looks like *come on*, I wait until we're almost halfway through lunch.

Jason's nervous, because he's heard we're having a campfire tonight, and he's afraid that he's going to get burned like Scott did. So he's asking all these questions, and instead of eating, he keeps putting little pieces of his napkin into his mouth to *chew* on them, before he takes them back out and leaves them on the table in a gross, soggy lump.

Candy's telling him about the fire-starters and about how we'll probably sing the Camp Harmony song and whatever, and then she mentions that it'll be dark by the time it's over, and she gives me this little look, too quick for anyone else to notice. And finally I pipe up and say, "Make sure you stay with everybody else, though, because the light of the campfire keeps away the wild . . . well, anything that's wild in the woods."

Tilly and Ryan make a big show of glaring at me and saying "shh," and I think they mostly pull it off.

Kylie's bored and not paying much attention, but Jason looks up at us so quick it's like a cartoon. "What do you mean?" he asks. "Like mosquitoes?"

We all can't help laughing at that, because (a) that's so dumb and (b) we've all been covered in mosquito bites for weeks now, and these kids are probably used to their moms spraying them down with toxic bug repellent.

"No," says Tilly. "Actually, the light attracts the bugs. But it keeps away . . ."

And then I hit her hard in the arm, like we planned. "Tilly," I say, whispering, but loud enough that the other kids can hear. "We're not supposed to mention that."

Candy says, "She just means like rabbits and chipmunks and stuff."

"The esquilax!" says Ryan, which was definitely not one of our planned lines and is probably a *Simpsons* thing that he can't resist saying. "It's a horse with the head of a rabbit"—and he pauses, but not really long enough for anyone to cut in—"and the body of . . . a RABBIT!"

Afterward, he bursts out laughing really loud, and Tilly looks annoyed, but I think it's actually probably good. It'll make the adults think that everything is business as usual over here. If they glance over to see what we're doing, it's just Ryan quoting *The Simpsons* and Tilly with her hair in her mouth. Just lunch the way it always is.

"Yeah, right," I say. "It protects us from the big bad esquilax."

"Or anything bigger," says Tilly. It might be better if she just lets it go and waits for the new kids to ask us questions, but I think she's too excited to do that.

"Like what?" asks Kylie. She's still acting all cool, but her forehead's sort of wrinkled, like maybe we're getting to her a little.

Tilly and Candy and I all look at each other, like we're trying to decide whether to say anything. Ryan puts his hand over his mouth, so he doesn't start laughing, but luckily no one else is paying attention to him.

"We don't really know," I say, "but we think there might be something bigger out there in the woods."

"Like what? A bear?" asks Jason. His eyes are really wide.

"No," I say. "Something bigger. Something . . . worse."

"We think . . ." Tilly begins, but I cut her off before she can say anything stupid. I don't want her to say the word "werewolf," or it'll ruin the whole thing. It'll make it sound silly, like a cheesy ghost story. The thing that's scary should be that there's *something* out there, but we have no idea what it is. What's scary is that it's something none of us have ever heard of before. Something so weird and freaky that it doesn't even have a name.

"We don't know," I say, talking over Tilly, which isn't easy to do, I can tell you. "It's just noises and shadows. It's probably nothing." I look straight at Jason then, careful to keep my eyes away from his spit-pile. "You don't have to worry at all," I say, and even I can hear that my voice sounds mean.

Then Scott gets up to make afternoon announcements, and we don't have time to say anything else, which is just exactly perfect. I feel light and bouncy, like I've got helium inside me. I made this work. I made it go exactly the way we wanted it to.

I keep feeling that way until about a half an hour after lunchtime, when Scott comes to get me out of the Red Rover game and pulls me hard by the arm into the office.

I can't believe how short a time it took. Scott tells me that Jason (of course) got scared (of course) and told his mom what we'd been saying. And somehow, because of whatever he said, I'm the only one who's in trouble. Right away, the helium's gone, and I'm starting to feel worried. Because I can tell that Scott is really mad at me, like *a lot*. More than it seems like he should be for the situation, actually, and I have no idea what he's going to do. I wish for a minute that my mom were here, or my dad, but then I realize that it probably wouldn't help. They'd probably back him up. "Every adult is your mom here"— that's something Scott likes to say. "Every adult is your dad."

Scott paces through the little office, around the chair that I'm sitting in. He's squeezing and unsqueezing his hands into fists, and then all of a sudden, he picks up a stapler from the desk and throws it at the wall behind my head. It doesn't hit me, but it makes a loud noise, and when I turn around, I can see that it's cracked the paint. The paint that I put up there on our very first day. I scrunch down in my chair and pull my legs up, like my knees are going to protect me somehow.

"I am trying to figure this out," says Scott. His voice is practically burning, like it's *red* with anger, almost. "But I cannot for the life of me figure out why you would do something like this. Do you know who you are?"

He stops and looks at me, waiting. It seems like one of those questions you shouldn't have to answer, but I don't want to make him madder. "Iris Hammond?" I say, in a tiny voice.

"Yeah," he says. "Iris Hammond, fine. But beyond that, you know who you are? You're our *good* kid. You're the one we trust."

I make a little sound that I didn't even mean to make. What he said, it *hurts* me, like an actual pain in my chest, and it keeps hurting more, the more it sinks in. For a minute I feel like I can't even breathe. Then I really am crying, the worst sort of crying, where you sound like you're moaning, and you can't stop, no matter what you do.

"I . . ." When I try to talk, it sounds all wrong, my voice going up and down like waves. "I *am* a good kid," I say, finally, but in my head, I'm going through the whole conversation with Jason, thinking about how I *wanted* to scare him, wanted him to . . . I don't know, wet his pants or something, or be so scared that he wouldn't be able to sleep. And I know it's not true, what I'm saying. I'm *not* a good kid.

I put my head down on my knees and cry for a long, long time. The thing is, I should be mad about what he said, but it should be for *Tilly's* sake, not just my own. Because if I'm the good kid, then it means Tilly's one of the bad ones, and no matter how mad I get at her, I know that's not true. So I'm crying for everything in the whole world, it seems like. It's partly because I was mean to Jason, and because Scott just told me I was bad, and as soon as he said it, I knew he was right. But more than that, I'm crying because I'm realizing that this is what I've wanted, maybe my whole entire life: for someone to take me and Tilly, look us both up and down, and tell me that I'm the one who's good and smart and special and nice. And feeling that way just might be the worst thing I've ever done to my sister, whether she knows about it or not.

By the time I finally look back up at the rest of the room, I'm gasping, almost like I'm going to throw up from crying so much. Scott's looking at me, not mad anymore, but not particularly concerned, either. Just kind of blank. I reach out and take a tissue from a box on the desk.

"Let me tell you a story," he says. "When I was growing up, I had a little brother named Jesse. He's dead now, but that's neither here nor there."

I look up, surprised. I wonder if I should say something, like "I'm sorry," but there's no chance. He just keeps on talking.

"Now Jesse was a little bit like Tilly, and a little bit like Jason. And that didn't always sit right with me, as I'm sure you can understand."

I don't know if I'm supposed to nod or agree with him or whatever, because that means I'm saying that I don't always like Tilly. Or you know, that I don't always like the way she *is*. But Scott isn't even looking at me, anyway.

"So when I was about eleven, and Jesse was about ten, he used to collect these stickers called Wacky Packs. They were like parodies of brands, like things you might find at the supermarket. Like there would be a picture of a Snickers bar, but it would be called Sneakers, and it would say that it tasted like old gym shoes, or something like that. They were stupid, but kids thought they were funny, and Jesse was wild about them."

Scott wipes his good hand across his forehead; we're both sweating. I wish he'd just turn on the air conditioner, but I don't think I should ask when I'm still in trouble and he's in the middle of telling a story.

"He didn't just have a normal collection, either. He studied up on which ones were rare and hard to get, and he wrote letters to people who collected them in other countries. And this was before the Internet, so it was a lot harder than it is now to hunt down whatever you were looking for. I'm a little amazed when I think about how he managed it. He had hundreds of those things."

He stops talking, obviously thinking about these stickers, or his dead brother or whatever. I scratch a mosquito bite on my arm, kind of just to remind him I'm still in the room.

"So anyway," he says, finally. "One day, I got mad at Jesse because he knocked a bunch of stuff off my dresser—we shared a bedroom— and so I took all his Wacky Packs, and I brought them to the woods behind our house, and I burned them all up."

I gasp, like actually make a little gasping noise. I don't know what I thought he was going to say, but this is worse.

"Jesse was devastated, of course. And I got a beating, because that's what childhood was like back then. But the worst part was that when I tried to fix it, by saving up my spending money and buying him whatever new ones I could afford, Jesse wouldn't even look at them. It was like I hadn't just ruined those individual cards; I'd ruined the whole thing for him forever."

I'm going to start crying again; I can feel my throat getting tight and sore. But I don't really understand why he's telling me this. Is he saying that the stupid werewolf story I told Jason was really as bad as this horrible thing he did to his brother when they were little? Or that it ruined something for Jason forever? For a while, neither of us says anything. We both just sit there, sweating in the little room while I try to even out my breath.

"All right," he says, after a while. "Try to calm down. I'm afraid that there has to be a consequence, no matter how sorry you are. So AD Block tonight, and no swimming this afternoon." He sighs. "You've lost a little bit of my trust today, Iris. Start trying to earn it back."

"How did he die?" I ask. My voice is still all wavery.

Scott shakes his head. "That's a story for another day."

He leaves the office, and I put my head down on my knees again. I'm waiting to see if I'm going to cry again, and almost *want* to, like otherwise there's no place else for this hurt in my chest to go. But I feel . . . empty. My head hurts, and my mouth is dry, like I've cried out all the water in my body.

I get up and throw away my soggy tissue in the little trash can. In with the other garbage, there's one little scrap of paper that catches my eye. It's all covered with Magic Marker swirls, and I recognize it right away: it's one of Candy's envelopes, from the letters she writes to her dad. Which is confusing, because why would it be here in the trash? But my head feels empty, like I don't have the energy even to wonder about anything, so I just focus on the pretty pattern of flowers and swirls. I keep the picture in my mind, as I walk back to our cabin and lie down on my bed, and when I fall asleep I don't dream about anything besides white paper being filled up with color.

When I wake up, it's almost dinnertime, and my mom is sitting on the edge of my bed.

"Hey, sweet girl," she says when I open my eyes. I reach my arms around her waist and give her an awkward hug, pressing my face to the skin just above her knee.

"Are you feeling all right?" she asks.

I shrug. She puts her hand on my hair. "I heard about AD Block," she says. "I'm sure you're disappointed about the candy."

I hadn't even thought about the candy. "Are you mad at me?" I ask, my voice muffled by the fabric of her shorts.

She pulls me up into a sitting position. "No," she says. "I don't think that was a nice thing to do, but I know you've already been scolded by Scott. Honestly, I think he's being a little rough on you."

"So I don't have to go to AD Block?" I ask.

She breathes out a laugh. "No, you still have to go. But I can tell you that you won't be alone. I don't know the details, but I heard that Candy got in trouble for something, too. I'm not sure what. And on my way here, I heard Ryan yelling at Scott, so he may very well be on the AD Block roster by now."

"Huh. So now only Tilly and Charlotte are eligible for the candy award? And I guess maybe Hayden?"

My mom shakes her head. "I guess, I don't know. That's really Scott's department. Listen, your hair's tangled from napping on it. Let's get it brushed before dinner, okay?"

AD Block takes place in the kitchen, so I just hang around the dining hall until everyone else leaves. And my mom's right: I'm not the only one who got in trouble today, even though I guess I'm the only one who got in trouble for the werewolf story. Ryan and Candy are both here, plus Hayden's dad, Tom, who's here to supervise. And it actually ends up being fun, at least for a while.

"Okay," says Tom, once we're all there. "I'm supposed to start by reading you this task list that Scott left for us. One, clean up from dinner . . . and then there are like fifteen subsections. Wash dishes, dry dishes, wipe tables . . . you guys think you can figure out what 'clean up from dinner' means, or do I have to read you every single step?"

"READ US EVERY SINGLE STEP," yells Ryan, just to be annoying. He's bouncing around like he can't stay still for even a second.

Candy hits him in the arm. "We get it," she says.

"Yeah, I think we can handle it," I add.

"Okay, good," says Tom. "Basically, there are three major tasks: clean up from dinner, set up for breakfast, and talk about what you all did to get here. If we multitask and do our talking and our cleaning at the same time, we may be able to get out of here fairly quickly."

So we divide up the chores, and we get started. I'm washing the dishes, Candy's sweeping, and Ryan is cleaning the tables, pretending that his spray bottle of vinegar and water is a laser gun.

"All right," says Tom. "Looking good. Now tell us, Iris: why exactly did Scott suggest that you grace us with your presence this evening?"

So I tell him about what happened with Jason, and I say all the right things about how I shouldn't have done it, and it was mean and I'll never do anything like it again. Tom watches me carefully, and it looks like he's going to ask me some more questions, but then he just shakes his head.

"Okay," he says. "Ryan, what brought you here this evening?"

Ryan stops wiping. He's spraying way too much cleaning stuff; his towel is sopping wet already. But I guess the tables won't be dirty, at least.

"Sir, yes, sir!" he shouts. I don't get his brain sometimes—like, is he acting like a military guy because it fits in somehow with the laser-gun thing he was playing a minute ago? Or is it just as random as it sounds, because he has too many ideas in his head, fighting to get out? "I called Scott an asshole, sir!"

Tom's face twists, and he turns away so we won't see him smile. "Yeah, that'll do it," he says. He bends down to hold a dustpan for Candy to sweep stuff into. "And how about now? Are you thinking that was a good decision?"

"Sir, yes, sir!" says Ryan and laughs like crazy.

Tom turns to stare at him. "Really," he says, not even a question.

Ryan shrugs and sprays some more vinegar-water on the table. "No, not really," he says. "I guess. But it was a joke. It was funny."

"Which one was a joke? Calling Scott an asshole, or saying it was a good thing to do?"

Ryan's eyes get wide when he hears Tom say the word "asshole." I can tell he wants to laugh or say something about it. *Just answer the question*, I say in my head, trying to send him a telepathic message. I do that all the time with Tilly, when I can see that she's about to do something stupid or inappropriate. It never works.

But somehow, Ryan pulls himself together and just says, "Both. They were both jokes."

"Okay, well, that's where your problem is," says Tom. "It sounded like a joke to you, but I didn't think it was funny, and I sure as heck don't think Scott thought it was funny."

I see Ryan's lips move. "Sure as hell," he whispers. He thinks he's quiet enough that we won't hear him, but he's totally wrong.

Tom sighs. He carries the dustpan over to the big, gross garbage can where everyone scrapes their dinner plates, and empties in all the scraps and junk he's collected. He pulls up the edges of the garbage bag, getting ready to tie them together.

"You're an interesting kid, Ryan," he says. Candy kind of snorts, hiding her mouth behind her hand.

"No, I'm serious," Tom says. "I don't mean it in a negative way. You know what you are? You're like a scientist, doing tests in a lab. You don't just take it for granted that you're going to get in trouble if you cuss at Scott; you have to like perform an experiment to find out exactly how far you can push him, and exactly what sort of trouble you're going to get in."

Ryan sort of jolts upward, excited, and he says, "My dad told me this story about a scientist guy who spilled some kind of acid on his hand, and his hand got all burned and shriveled up, and it had to be amputated."

Tom shakes his head and gives up a little. "Yeah, okay. Hey, you want to know a secret, Ryan? When you're a grown man you can swear as much as you want. Until then, try not to say every single thing that comes into your head, okay?"

"Okay," says Ryan, though I'm not even sure he's listening. He's spraying some of the vinegar-water on his hand and looking to see if it does anything.

"No, but I know what you mean," I say to Tom. Sometimes around adults, like teachers and other kids' parents, I get this feeling, like it's up to me to show them that some kids can act smart and mature, even if nobody else is behaving that way. But also, what Tom was saying reminded me a little of Tilly. "It's like there are these invisible signs everywhere, you know what I mean? Most of us just have them in our heads. Like if you come to a busy street—I mean, if you're old enough to walk around without holding a grown-up's hand—then you know there's an invisible sign there that says, 'Don't Cross Until the Cars Stop Moving.'"

"Or you could just look at the 'Don't Walk' sign, which *isn't* invisible," says Candy. It's kind of funny, because I hadn't thought of that. But I want to get my point across.

"No, okay," I say. "But like if you see some kind of machine, and it has a big red button on it that says, 'Danger, Do Not Press,' there's also a little invisible sign in your head, telling you that you should follow those directions. But some people want to press it anyway, just to see what happens."

"Yeah, exactly," says Tom. "That's a good way of putting it."

I finish up the dishes and start drying bowls and spoons for cereal in the morning. And then Tom asks Candy for her "misbehavior narrative," as Scott calls it.

Candy shrugs. "Scott caught me trying to call my dad."

Tom looks confused. "Your dad? You mean Rick?"

"No, my *real* dad." She sounds a little annoyed, like everyone should already know. "He lives in Boston."

"Okay," says Tom. "So what happened?"

"I was trying to use the phone in the office, but . . . I don't know, it wouldn't work. I got a message about long-distance service or something. And so I was going to try to find out how to have my dad pay for it? I think there's a way to do that, but before I could figure it out, Scott came in and he went ballistic."

"Hmm," says Tom. "That's rough." He doesn't say anything else for a while, just takes a clean rag and starts drying all of the tables that Ryan has left wet. I'm looking down at a spoon I'm drying, and suddenly something clicks in my head. The scrap of paper in the trash in the office: it means that letter never got mailed.

"So why *can't* she call her dad?" I ask. "Is it just because we're not supposed to use the phone or something? Because it's technology, or because it would cost money?"

Tom's quiet for a minute longer. "I'm not really sure," he says. "I think that Scott wants to keep our group separate from the outside world for now. Just for a little while, until we're completely settled in."

"But we *are* settled in," says Candy. "And we're not separate from the outside world, because we just had this whole new group of people show up. I saw one of the kids with an iPhone, for goodness' sake."

Just as a side note, I smile a little when she says "for goodness' sake." When we first got here, she was saying "for God's sake" all the time, and Scott kept bugging her about it. Now it seems like her brain's all trained, and she just uses the appropriate version without even thinking about it.

"Yes, and you probably saw Scott take it away about two minutes later," says Tom. "Look, I don't have an answer for you, Candy. I really don't. But Scott's kind of our visionary here, and he's got his own ideas about things. And even if I don't always agree with him, I respect him and trust him completely. So for now, I think you're going to have to do the same."

Candy still looks mad, and I don't blame her. It would suck not to be able to see or talk to my dad. I have this sudden memory of what it was like every night at home, when my dad got home from work. We were always so happy to see him, and it was like a turning point for the day. Everything felt more cozy or something, once all four of us were there together.

It makes me feel sort of lonely and nostalgic, which is weird, because now I can see my dad any time of the day. But it's not the same, because we're both always busy with chores or listening to Scott or something. It doesn't feel cozy here very much at all.

We finish up in the kitchen, and Tom turns off the lights and leads us outside. We all head toward the lake, where I can see there's still a campfire going on, even if the singing's over. Candy and Ryan run ahead, so I'm left walking next to Tom. It's kind of good, because maybe it's better to talk about this to a grown-up who's *not* my parents.

"Tom?" I say. My voice sounds high, like I'm nervous. "You know what Scott said to me this afternoon, after he found out about the story I told the other kids? He said that I was supposed to be the good kid."

He doesn't get it. "Well, you are a good kid, Iris. Absolutely."

"No, that's not it. He said it like I'm supposed to be the best kid here. Or maybe the *only* good kid." I hope it doesn't sound like bragging for me to repeat that.

I can't see Tom's face very well in the dark, but he actually stops and turns to look at me.

"Really?" he says. "Scott said that?"

"Uh-huh." Now I'm a little bit nervous, like maybe I shouldn't have said anything.

Tom nods slowly and then starts walking again. "Well," he says, finally. "In spite of what I just said about how we all have to trust and respect Scott's decisions, I'm going to come right out and say that I don't think he should have said that to you. And it's not because I don't think you're a good kid."

"Okay," I say. "Um, thanks."

He's quiet for a minute. "Here's the thing: One, I don't think you should make anyone feel like they have to be good *all* the time, because that's just not possible, especially for a kid. And two, I think you must've caught Scott at a bad moment, because I am certain that deep down he believes that all our kids are good. Look at it this way: if you're the 'best' kid here, then by that scale, Hayden's gotta be the worst, don't you think?"

I nod and shake my head all at the same time, because I see what he's saying, but I don't want to look like I agree with that.

"Yeah, and you know that's not true, right?" he asks.

"Right." I wonder suddenly if it's hard for him and Janelle, seeing all these other kids all the time who can do things that Hayden can't. I mean, I don't know what everyone thinks is going to happen from being here, all the grown-ups, that is. But I think they must be hoping that this whole experience is going to help their kids be more . . . I don't know, normal, I guess. But no matter how hard Hayden's parents work at it, there are just some things that he's never going to be able to do.

"I really like Hayden," I say. "He's so sweet, almost like a baby." Then I wonder if that's the wrong thing to say, like I'm putting him down for not being mature enough or something.

But Tom smiles and looks down where we're walking. "Yeah," he says. "He is. And you know what? There are worse ways to be."

"Yeah," I say. "There are."

chapter 25

Tilly

Date and Location Unknown

Imagine a world in which people disappear from photos when they die. Like in *Back to the Future* when Marty McFly is almost missing his chance to get his parents together, except that there's no blurring, no gradual fading. They're there, and then they're not. A million widows crying over pictures of themselves. A million mothers, smiling at a crook in their elbow. A million babies, floating in midair.

School photos empty themselves, one by one. First the teachers, probably, leaving behind a crowd of unsupervised kids wearing old-fashioned clothes. Then the group winnows slowly, until nothing remains but the faded rug, the outdated maps on the walls. (Check out the names: Czechoslovakia. Rhodesia. Zaire.)

At senior mixers, potential lovers show each other photos of their young selves in wedding finery. Look at that lace. My mother sewed it by hand. A bittersweet game, layering the photos together, so that those young strangers appear to be standing side by side. Here's how we would have looked. What a handsome couple!

On Facebook, deaths are announced through blank bathroom mirrors, cameras holding themselves. Old *Playboy*s show empty staircases, classic cars with no one posed on the hood. Lists of turn-ons next to rumpled, unmade beds.

Posters of people gone missing hold new measures of hope, right up until the moment when they don't. The FBI knows exactly when to remove a fugitive from their list.

Families gather together to pose and smile, knowing that sooner or later, the only thing anybody will see will be an empty room.

chapter 26

Iris

June 22, 2012: New Hampshire

When Friday comes, and Scott announces Mother's Day again, I wonder if we're going to play Werewolf at all, after the whole problem with Kylie and Jason. But Scott takes us out into the woods, back to the campfire site, just like last week. This time, there's a table set up that Scott must have had some of the other grown-ups bring out, because he's still got his arm in a sling. I don't know what's on the table because it's covered with a sheet, but it's all lumpy, so I know there's something under there.

"Before we begin," Scott says. "We all know there's no such thing as monsters, right?"

We do.

"And we all know that there's nothing scary or dangerous out here in the woods, right?"

We do again. "Good. So remember that. Whatever happens out here, it's all made up, and it's all a game."

And then he starts it up, the same way he did last week: "We're going to play a game called Werewolf. And the best thing about Werewolf is that it's a different game each time you play, but it always starts the very same way." Last week, I wasn't sure if he was rhyming intentionally or just by accident. But now I know it's on purpose.

"Okay, those of you who were here last week, help me out." His voice gets quiet. *"The Werewolf says you have to hide . . ."*

And me and Candy, Ryan, and Tilly all chant, *"Are you on the Werewolf's side?"*

I check out the GC kids. Some of them seem like they're into it, but Kylie clearly thinks it's stupid, and Jason looks scared, even though not a single scary thing has happened.

"Now the thing about the Werewolf," Scott says, "is that he doesn't like kids who know how to survive in the wilderness. Because those are the kids he can't catch. So each of you has to be as smart and wilderness-savvy as you can be, and build yourself a house where the Werewolf can't find you."

I think that's supposed to be the educational/good-for-you aspect of the game, that we're learning things about staying safe in the woods. Whatever. That's not really the main part.

"Here are some building materials to help you out," Scott says. He goes over to the table and starts to pull off the sheet with his good hand. He's having trouble with it, though, because the fabric keeps snagging on the things underneath.

"I can help," I say. I go over and pull the sheet off with him. Underneath, there's all kinds of things: ropes and pointy metal posts, some random pieces of fabric, old couch cushions and pillows, even one of those dog-crate travel carriers, which is like a whole shelter in itself. This is awesome, and I can tell the other CF kids get it right away; Ryan says, "Whoa," and Tilly yells out, "Yeah, that's the stuff." We are definitely going to be able to build better forts this week than we did last week, when we could only use what we found on the ground.

"Welcome to the Building Store," says Scott. "The trick is that the store is owned by the Werewolf. And if you want to buy any of these materials for use in your structure, you have to gain the Were-wolf's trust."

"Can I be the Werewolf?" asks Ryan.

"The Werewolf doesn't like people talking out of turn, Ryan," says Scott. He's smiling, so it doesn't sound mean or anything. "Just FYI. And no, I'm afraid not. I'm the Werewolf today."

"Are you always going to be the Werewolf?" asks Tilly. "Oops, sorry, Mr. Werewolf. I didn't mean to talk out of turn."

"Nice save," says Scott. "And the answer is: that's for me to know and you to find out."

A bunch of kids say, "Aww" and "That's not fair" and whatever. I'm not really disappointed, though. Being the Werewolf looks fun, but it's also complicated and kind of a lot of responsibility.

"Speaking out of turn puts you at the back of the line for the Building Store," Scott says. Everyone quiets down.

"Now you have your goal, which is to build an awesome hide-away and stay safe. But the Werewolf has plans of his own: he wants to gain power. He wants to take over the town and turn it into a vast werewolf empire. So when he sells materials from his Building Store, he doesn't deal in money. He deals in secrets."

"What do you . . ." says Tilly, then shuts up really quickly. She raises her hand and waits for Scott to call on her. Then she asks, "What do you mean by secrets?"

"Let's just start playing," Scott says. "It'll all become clear. Okay . . ." He claps his hands twice and raises his voice. "Werewolf shop unlocks its doors—who's got a secret for the Building Store?"

Everyone runs over to the table to get in line. I end up fourth, right behind Tilly. Now that I'm closer to the table, I can see that all the items have numbers taped to them, like prices at a yard sale. All the numbers are between one and three.

Tilly turns around to talk to me. "What secrets are you going to use?"

I don't have anything in mind, but I decide it's a good strategy to pretend that I do. "I'm not telling you!" I say.

"Fine," she says. "I'm not telling you mine, either."

Candy's first in line, and Scott leads her over to a tree stump about ten feet away, where we can't hear them talking. I watch as she gets up on the stump and he leans closer so she can whisper in his ear. He nods and says something to her, then she whispers to him again. "Yes!" he yells. He gives her a high-five, and she runs over to the table and grabs the dog carrier.

"Aww," Tilly says. "I wanted that."

Next is a GC boy named Joey. He and Scott have their little tree stump conference, and he goes and picks out a sheet and a roll of duct tape.

"How come he got two?" Tilly asks.

"I think it has to do with the numbers on them," I say. "I think they're prices."

"Tilly and Iris," Scott calls out. "Family discount. Come on over together."

I'm not expecting that, and I'm not sure I like it—I just want to do my own thing, I don't want to be put on a team with Tilly or anyone else—but I walk over with her to where Scott is standing.

"You guys are lucky," he tells us when we get there. "Werewolf special, today only. Most customers are exchanging three secrets for three merchandise points. But in the unlikely event that there are two sisters, standing next to each other in line, and one of them is wearing . . ." He pauses to look us over. "A green flowered top, they each get a chance to earn an extra point."

"That's pretty specific," Tilly says.

Scott shrugs. "The Werewolf wants what the Werewolf wants. So here's how this is going to work. You two are going to take turns whispering secrets in the Werewolf's ear. Neither of you gets to know what the other one is saying. But think hard about your secrets, because whoever tells the best one gets four points instead of three, and that can make a big difference at the Building Store."

"But I don't really get it," I say. "What kind . . ."

"Uh uh uh," says Scott, holding up a finger. "Gotta be fast; go with your gut. We're going to have three rounds. Round One: a secret about yourself. Make it true and make it good. Tilly first." He points to the tree stump and she climbs up to whisper in his ear.

I don't know what she tells him, but he laughs out loud. "Good one," he says. "Iris! You're up."

Tilly and I switch places. Even on the tree stump, I'm not tall enough, so I stand on tiptoes. I lean right up to his ear and whisper, "Sometimes in the shower, I sing songs from *High School Musical* and pretend I'm one of the characters."

Scott laughs, just like he did after Tilly's secret. "Awesome," he says. "The Werewolf loves it. Round Two: a secret about each other. Tilly?"

This makes me nervous, but actually I don't think Tilly knows any of my secrets. Not that I have any major secrets, but you know. The ones I have I've never told her.

Still, she doesn't even take a minute to think about it. Just climbs up and whispers something right away.

"Really?" says Scott, looking at me. "I never would have guessed." He and Tilly laugh.

"What did you say?" I ask.

"Can't tell you," says Tilly.

Fine. My turn. The first one I think of seems too mean—it's about how Tilly told a boy in her class she had a crush on him, and he laughed at her—but then I think of a good one. "Okay," I whisper. "One time, Tilly went to get her ears pierced, but after the first one, she was too afraid to go through with the second. So she just had one pierced ear until it finally closed up by itself."

"You're kidding!" says Scott. "Wow!" He looks over at Tilly and then back at me. "Okay, so far it's neck and neck, so make this last one good. Round Three: a secret about somebody else in your family."

Tilly has to think about this one, but after she finally tells Scott, he says, "Wow. I think we may have a winner." So I know I'd better come up with something big.

I climb up on the tree stump, then hesitate. "Nobody's going to get in trouble, are they?" I ask Scott, talking in a regular voice. "Because of the secrets?"

He smiles and shakes his head. "Nope. It's just a game. All in good fun."

"Okay," I say, and rise up on my toes. When I'm finished, Scott lifts my arm up above my head like I'm a boxer or wrestler or something. "Sorry, Tilly," he says. "Our extra point goes to Iris."

I walk away smiling. And the shelter I make, using a rope, a blanket, and a two-point laundry basket, turns out to be the best of anybody's.

The GCs leave on Saturday, and I don't think anyone's sad to see Kylie and Jason's family go. I'm hoping the next group will be better. We spend the afternoon cleaning up the guest cabins, and we have dinner, and then it's time for Saturday Campfire. We go out to the Harmony Circle with our flashlights, and the adults get the fire going. Scott gets up to talk; he looks tired, and his hair's all messy, which is really weird for him.

"So it's been a tough week," he says. "We knew we'd have them, right? Nothing huge, just a few little things here and there, but it did make me stop and wonder why the heck we're doing all this."

I know he's probably talking about the "monster in the woods" incident with Jason and Kylie, though I don't know about anything else bad that happened this week.

"And I've been thinking . . . well, I'm not sure where to start here. But I've been thinking about the difference between truth and honesty."

He pauses and takes a sip from the water bottle he's holding.

"To do a job like this one, you have to know how to tell a story. Here's the story of how your life could be different if you let me help you. Here's the story of what I can do to make your struggles a little less difficult."

He pauses again, and for a minute he looks like he's lost his train of thought.

"I don't offer guarantees; I don't do magic. I tell the story that you need to hear in the current moment, and I'm always one hundred percent honest, even if I'm not telling the one hundred percent truth. You know what I mean?"

"Scott," says Janelle. Her voice is gentle, like when she talks to Hayden. "Have you been drinking?"

For a second I don't know what she means, like I don't realize she means *drinking* drinking. But then Scott laughs in a goofy way and sways a little without moving his feet, and I think she's probably right.

"Maybe a little," Scott says. "Water bottle full of vodka. I heard somewhere that that's a good way to do it . . . It may be true that you're here because you want to be, but if you're not one hundred percent committed, and if you're not being honest with each other . . . wait a second, I had a point here."

And then I get a little bit scared because I think this might be my fault. Because that was my winning secret, the one that got me the extra point for the Building Store: that my parents have alcohol hidden in our cabin, and that sometimes they drink it, even though they're not supposed to. And I mentioned Evian bottles specifically.

"I have reason to believe," he says, and he's not looking anywhere near me, which is a relief, "that some of us have been playing a little fast and loose with the rules, when it comes to contraband and so forth." He shrugs. "I don't know. I'm not too hung up on the actual details. Do you get that? I don't care if you have a drink once in a while. It's just . . . it's about trust."

"Maybe we should head back to camp," my mom says.

Scott nods. "Yeah, in a minute. Just let me get this out, okay? I've never really had any kind of a family, not since I was young, anyway. And . . . just what are we doing here, you know? What are we to each other? Are we all on the same team? Are we . . . can we at least pretend to be some kind of a family?"

And then his face wrinkles up, and he goes to put his hand over his eyes, except he's got one arm in a sling and the other one is holding the bottle of alcohol. And I'm so afraid all of a sudden. I'm so afraid that he's going to cry and it's all because he's covering up for me. He's making sure I don't get in trouble.

"Okay, Scott," says Tom. He's been holding Hayden, but he sets him down and walks over to Scott. Janelle follows, almost running, and pulls Scott into a hug.

"It's going to be okay," I hear her say.

"I should go," Scott says. His voice is all wobbly with tears. "I should leave camp. I don't deserve to be here, after acting like this."

"Now that's not true," Janelle says. She pats Scott on the back and then lets go of the hug, turning back to face the group. I notice the way that the group is divided now, with the three of them on one side of the campfire and the rest of us on the other, flames crackling and rising in between us.

"I think we can all agree that we're not seeing Scott at his best right now, but I, for one, am not about to judge him for it," Janelle continues. And I'll confess that I'm one of the rule-breakers he's talking about. Last week, I took my car keys from the office, and after curfew I snuck out of my cabin like a teenager, drove down the driveway with my lights off, and went out to a convenience store, where I bought a bottle of wine and a pack of Reese's Peanut Butter Cups."

"That's not fair!" says Tilly. My parents both lean forward at the same time to shush her.

"Anyone else want to speak up?" Janelle asks. "Let's not forget that we're here by choice. We all made the decision to tie our fate to this man, and that's not something to take lightly. Two weeks ago, this man was seriously injured *saving my son's life*, and I'm not about to throw that all away because he made a mistake today."

"Yeah," says my mom. She squeezes my shoulder and then pulls away from our little family group and walks over to join Tom, Scott, and Janelle. "I'll go next," she says. And pretty soon, we're all lining up to talk about all the things we've done wrong.

chapter 27

Alexandra

April 2011: Washington, DC

The doorbell rings, and you look around. Neat enough. You open the door, step back, and there he is: Scott Bean, in your house.

He's taller than you remember, and skinnier. You feel shy as he gives you a hug. For a moment, you wonder what the hell you're doing. This first meeting is just between you and him—there's no one else home. Maybe this was a stupid thing to do. What do you know about this guy, really? Not a lot, even with all the time Josh has spent Googling him, looking for cracks in the armor.

Josh is skeptical about this plan, but then Josh is skeptical about a lot of things. He's done enough research to be sure that Scott isn't an ex-con or a sex offender, and that there aren't any former clients suing him for fraudulent parenting advice, or whatever. And once you got Josh to agree to listen to the CDs on his way to and from work for a week, he grudgingly agreed that Scott had some good points, and that a consultation with him might not be completely worthless.

So you won the argument, and now Scott Bean is here. You've been planning this for weeks, so you'd better let him in and ask for his jacket. Sit him down and offer the healthful, carefully thought-out snacks you've prepared.

Luckily, he's got that easy warmth you'd almost forgotten existed, that ability to put people at ease. "So," he says, settling into an armchair. "Tell me about Tilly." And you do.

He'd asked you in advance to put together a "narrative history" of Tilly's issues, nothing formal, just a few notes about key events in the journey from birth to diagnosis and beyond. *The story of how you got here*, he'd said, *to put it another way*. So you've got your anecdotes lined up.

You begin: when Tilly was eighteen months old, you enrolled in a parent-child music class. You were pregnant with Iris and wanted to have a little special time with Tilly before the new baby came. The classes were very sweet, overpriced, and clearly more for the adults than for the toddlers. The teacher would play a CD (available for twelve dollars and now burned indelibly into your brain), and the "caregivers"—moms, babysitters, and occasional stay-at-home dads—would lead their little ones in dancing, shaking maracas, and waving colorful scarves in the air. Everyone took it very seriously; everyone seemed to be terribly in love with their children and not the least bit panicky about the empty hours that stretched ahead after class was over.

What's notable to you now is that it was one of the first chances you had to watch Tilly with other kids her own age. She was . . . the same, and not the same. Here, in a room full of one-year-olds, you began your secret note-taking. She was on target with all her milestones, a little bit advanced verbally, certainly as curious and adorable as any one of the others. But she balked at the structure of the class, refusing to take part in activities if something else caught her eye. She couldn't seem to be taught not to put the instruments in her mouth. Bubbles and parachutes didn't fill her with glee; instead, she preferred playing with the shoes that all the moms and kids took off before class started. Later, when you'd go through autism checklists you found online, you'd do this same sort of tallying: she fits this criterion, but not that one; her motor skills aren't great, but she gives hugs and kisses; she melts down when she's frustrated, but she doesn't mind looking you in the eye. And the thing that was always so heartbreaking was how close she came to fitting into the category of "normal."

At the end of each session, the teacher would turn the lights off and play a slow song, a uniquely haunting version of "Shenandoah." Caregivers would scoop their charges into their laps and settle them in to sway and cuddle. It reminded you of high school dances, of that last desperate slow song before the lights went up. And here you were, without a partner. Because you had given birth to an adventurer. And there was no way she was going to submit to five minutes of quiet hugging when there were dusty rec-center corners to explore.

She's always been a little bit confounding, in all the best and worst ways. If she hadn't been your first, you might have let yourself wonder sooner. Another story: once at a friend's wedding, you were talking to a very nice woman—you can't remember who she was now; bride's aunt?—and as you were trying to explain something about the enigma that was Tilly, you mentioned that she had taught herself to read before the age of three.

"Reading before she was three?" The woman burst into laughter and put her hand on your arm. "Oh, honey, that's not good."

Scott interrupts here. "Wait—explain that to me. Why isn't it good?"

"It's not that it's bad, in and of itself," you say. It's important to you that he get this. You and Josh have returned to this discussion, over and over again. It was a transformative moment, like a superhero origin story, or maybe the opposite of one. It signals a change in your understanding of who your daughter was and what type of parent she needed you to be. It's when you first understood that "extraordinary" can have more than one meaning. "But it suggests that *something's* not proceeding typically, in terms of development, you know?"

He's nodding, and you're relieved. "Right," he says. "It means things may be uneven. If she's off the charts in one direction . . ."

Good. He's got it. It was easy for you and Josh to focus on all the ways she was ahead of the game, racing past the achievements of other toddlers. But you weren't doing any of you any favors until you started paying attention to the ways she wasn't.

Scott listens, occasionally nodding or interrupting to ask for clarification. You tell him the long saga of Tilly's school life, the ongoing problems of tics and tantrums. You explain that if Tilly wants your attention, it is nearly impossible not to give it to her. That normal forms of discipline have little effect. That you don't intend to turn everything into a power struggle; it just seems to happen. You tell him that when someone doesn't quite get Tilly, or approaches her with the wrong set of intentions, things can go terribly, terribly wrong. You've had more than one babysitter call you in tears.

"And what about Iris?" Scott asks. "How is she affected by all this?"

You have stories about this, too. When Iris was three years old, she had a favorite element. She chose carbon (for reasons that remain impenetrable to you), so that when her big sister told people that her favorite element was mercury, Iris would be able to chime in, too.

Iris adores Tilly, but she's also beginning to be embarrassed by her. "That's where my sister sits," you overheard her telling a friend a few weeks ago, explaining a cluster of crumbs on the dining room rug, "and sometimes she eats with her fingers."

You've tried hard not to define Iris by the ways she's different from Tilly, but you haven't always succeeded. Once, when Iris was about four, she said something clever and you called her "my smart girl." "No," she corrected you, her little voice stretching out the vowels. "I'm not your smart girl. Tilly is."

Iris is complicated and fascinating. But she has the luxury of being an ordinary mystery, in the curious, endearing way that all children are.

Potential waiting to be unlocked, consciousness unspooling from nothing to something. A bud gathered up taut, working hard at growing itself. You may know that this particular bud is going to open to reveal a rose or a daisy, and that it will develop in a way that's consistent with every other rose or daisy since the beginning of time. But there are endless variables: warmth or coolness of color, number of petals, placement of thorns. You don't know which rose, out of all the possible roses in the past and future of the world, this one will turn out to be.

Tilly is a flower, too, of course—but you already feel like you're using the wrong metaphor. What terms could you possibly use to describe her to someone, if you had to use images instead of terminology? Imagine, maybe, what it would be like to take care of a child who'd been born with wings. Is it a blessing or a curse, or somehow a little of each?

"And how about you?" Scott Bean asks. "How are you doing?" Kind. He is very kind. And you don't think he's pretending.

You find that you're a little less willing to talk about yourself. You've been listening to Scott's CD series in your car again; you're midway through your second go-around. The disc that's currently running is about "self-talk" and mantras, and while you've found it helpful, you're not quite ready to spill out your actual feelings for this man to examine.

"I want to die" is not an unusual bit of self-talk for you, but you wish you could get rid of it, because you suspect you're just being dramatic. You and despair are on . . . friendly terms, but there are a number of reasons why you think you'll probably never kill yourself, and one is that you're too dedicated to keeping track of minutiae. Every life has as many lasts as firsts, and if you knew the date of your death, you'd feel compelled to make note of them: The last time you yell at one of your children. The last time you sing a song out loud. The last time you hold a baby. The last time you go on vacation. The last time you cry as if your heart might break.

In any case, this isn't (quite) a therapy session, and you're not going to spell out your every neurosis. Instead, you tell him that there are times when you feel like you can hold everything together, but just barely. You tell him that you need help, but you're not sure how to ask for it, and that you don't even know what sort of help you need.

Revealing even this much is a risk. Your words in the air, their pitch of desperation. *Label me*, you might as well say. *Give me a checklist. Show me how to fix it.*

But Scott won't let you be embarrassed. "The first thing you need to know," he says, "is that you're not alone." He leans forward, takes hold of your hand for a moment. "Do you believe me?" he asks.

You know what the right answer is, but you pause for a minute, waiting to see if it's true. "Yes," you say, surprising yourself. "I do."

"Good," he says. "That's the beginning. That's the most important part."

He sets up a time and date to come back and meet the rest of the family. He gives you homework, and you promise to do it, like the eager schoolgirl you are: yes, you'll look at these handouts on environmental toxins and behavior; yes, you'll try eliminating dairy from Tilly's diet; yes, you'll arrange for a night out with Josh.

"Before we meet next time," he says, just before he goes, "I want you to think about these two things: happiness and purpose. What do those things mean to you? And do you believe I can help you fulfill them?"

"I . . ." you say, and you're not even sure where the sentence is heading, but he stops you anyway.

"Not now," he says. "Next time." He opens your front door, and he's gone.

You feel exultant, almost light-headed. What is it, exactly, this vital warmth, this bird in your chest taking flight? How can you give it a name? You might call it joy and relief; you might call it fellowship

and communion. Faith, with its edge of magic, its unspeakable certainty, has always eluded you. The beauty of prayer: sending messages out into the universe and believing they'll be heard. How must
it be to have that kind of singular, compelling purpose? A life labeled
with both a direction and a goal? You've never realized that maybe
it's not something that just happens. You've never realized that it may
be something you can actually choose.

chapter 28

Iris

June 24, 2012: New Hampshire

On Sunday morning, before the new GCs arrive, Tilly, Ryan, Candy, and I have a talk about Project Werewolf. You might think we'd give it up after last week, after we got in trouble and everything. But if there's something special about being in the CF, like Scott keeps saying, then there must be something special about being in the CK. (That means Core Kids. Tilly made it up.) When new kids show up, thinking that we're like the housekeeping staff or something, we need to show them we're powerful, and that's what the Werewolf story does.

Like Scott said at Saturday Campfire, sometimes you need to tell a story, even if it's not one hundred percent true.

We're changing our strategy, though, this time around. We're not going to *tell* the new kids anything. We're just going to set out the evidence and let them figure it out for themselves.

The nicest part about Sundays is that there's usually a little time after lunch, while the new campers are getting unpacked and whatever, when we all get to go back to our cabins and just hang out together as a family. Today, my mom goes to take a shower, and my dad sits down on the couch with a book. I remember suddenly how much he used to like to read the newspaper; that's something none of us have seen in a while.

I sit down next to him and lean my head back on the couch cushion, staring up at the water-stained ceiling. "Hey," I say. "I think we completely missed Father's Day."

He looks over at me and squinches his eyes, like he's trying to remember. "You know, I think you're right," he says. "No big deal. We have enough Mother's Days to balance it all out."

"You know what I'd get you, if I could get you a Father's Day gift?"

He puts down his book and smiles at me in one of those weird parental ways, like he's proud of me just for asking the question, when I haven't even told him the answer yet.

"What?" he says.

"A newspaper."

He laughs, surprised, and puts his hand on the top of my head, stroking my hair. "I would love that," he says. "I really would."

Then Tilly walks in from the bedroom and starts talking to us, the way she always does, like we've been with her in her head for the past ten minutes.

"So how come we know so much about like George Washington, but nothing about the guy who was his blacksmith or whatever? Or the blacksmith's wife and kids? Even if someone never gets to be president or a famous general or something, that person still lived a whole life. They were still important to their family and the people they loved."

"Well, that's a good . . ." my dad starts to say, but Tilly isn't done, so she just talks right over him.

"I mean, why can't there be a big giant statue of George Washington's blacksmith or like Napoleon's cook? And if there could be a giant statue of Napoleon's cook, then there could be a giant statue of you or me. Our whole family."

"Well, there can't be big giant statues for everybody, obviously," I say. "We'd run out of space." It's a cool idea, though. I'm picturing a humongous Iris statue standing on top of a mountain somewhere. High up, where people could see it for miles around.

"I see what you're getting at, though, Tilly," my dad says. "All of these billions of people have lived on the earth, and most of them have been just ordinary people. But if you don't do something that makes you famous, your story gets kind of lost."

"I wish we were famous," I say. "Maybe we could start a band or something."

"Yeah," says Tilly. "But why can't we just be famous because we're awesome people? Or just because we're people, period." She starts pacing, the way she does when she's thinking about something. "The Hammond Family," she says, like she's seeing the name all lit up on a billboard or something. "There could be books about us and movies. There could be a whole museum—the Museum of Hammond Family Artifacts."

My dad smiles. "What do you think it would have in it?"

"There could be baby pictures of us, and those envelopes with a little bit of hair from our first haircuts," Tilly says. "Things we did in school, and souvenirs from our vacations, like that snow globe I got in North Carolina with the lighthouse in it . . ."

"What about the Galaxie?" asks Dad. "Would there be room for it?"

"Of course!" says Tilly. "It would be in its own special display area, and people could get inside it, like we always did."

The 1971 Ford Galaxie was this old car that we used to have in our house in DC. When I say "in our house," I mean it literally, because we had this garage that was actually part of our basement. I don't really know why we had the car—I think my dad bought it before I was born, because he likes old cars, but as far as I know, it never worked enough for anyone to turn it on. I didn't even know about the Galaxie until I was three or four. And then one day, Tilly showed it to me, and it was like one of those dreams where you're in your house, and you discover a room you've never seen before: *Really? This was here all the time?*

Tilly and I used to go inside the car and play in it. It was really big, wider and roomier than most cars I've been in. And it had this really big steering wheel, and jump seats in the back that folded up when you weren't sitting on them, and funny cranks to put the windows up and down. We used to pretend we were old enough to drive, or else we'd pretend that it was our own house, where we lived without any grown-ups. There were all these random toys in the backseat, ones that we'd brought in to use as props and never took out. We didn't go in the Galaxie as much as we got older, but suddenly I wish that we could go inside it now. I wish it more than anything.

I'm starting to feel sad, and no one's noticing. I feel like I might even start to cry. "So what you're saying"—I pause, waiting until I have their attention—"is that the museum would have all the stuff we left in Washington. All the stuff Mom and Dad got rid of or put in storage."

Dad makes a sympathetic little sound. He sits up straighter on the couch and puts his arms around me. "Poor sweetie," he says, his voice muffled against my head. "I know you miss a lot of the things we left behind."

Tilly comes over and wraps herself around us, making a three-person hug.

"Don't be sad, Iris," she says. "Just pretend it's all in the museum. And we can go there and see it anytime we want."

We stay like that for a minute, and then Tilly gets another idea, and she's off, walking in circles around the room.

"Hey, what do you think they would sell in the Hammond Museum gift shop?" she asks. Her voice is all happy and excited with ideas.

"They could have postcards with pictures of us, and jewelry with our birthstones . . ."

"Snow globes with us inside," I say, because I like the idea, and I know it will make Tilly happy.

We all have secret assignments to lay out werewolf clues, in addition to all our chores, and the plan is to get them all ready by Wednesday. My thing is, I've got an old T-shirt of Tilly's that we ripped up and spattered with fake blood. We had some trouble figuring out how to make the blood, because of course there's no artificial food coloring here. So we tried mixing together some honey and cocoa powder, because Candy said she had heard that in the movie *Psycho*, the blood they used was actually chocolate syrup. And then we smushed in some cherries, and blended it all together. It actually looks pretty good; it's a little bit thick and chunky, but that's okay because that makes it more gory, like there might be . . . I don't know, bodily *tissue* or something in there.

So I've got a big piece of T-shirt crumpled up and hidden in my pocket. A little while after breakfast, when I'm supposed to be feeding the chickens, I walk into the woods and leave the shirt on the ground at this one place we picked out yesterday. I can see that Tilly's already been here, because her job was to stick little bits of hair and fur around in different tree branches. (The fur is from this stuffed gorilla that belongs to Ryan's little sister, and the hair we just pulled out of everybody's brushes and combs, so it's all tangled and gross.)

I spend a minute or two deciding where to drop the shirt. It's really quiet here, and I like being on my own for a few minutes. When we first got to Camp Harmony, I thought there was going to be a lot more time like this, just hanging out in all the pretty nature and chilling. I mean, half of what my parents said about moving was that we'd all benefit from being able to roam around freely, and hear our own thoughts without a million computerized distractions or whatever. But really, most of the time we're with all these other people, doing exactly what Scott tells us to.

There's rustling behind me and I turn quickly, worried that I'm about to get caught. But it's just Ryan, coming with some chicken bones and the rest of our fake blood to dribble on leaves and rocks and stuff. As we pass, we both smile and give the secret signal Tilly came up with: cross your fingers on both hands and then tap your index fingers together twice. I walk out of the woods and go back to my chores, feeling that happy-sneaky feeling of knowing that I have a secret.

My favorite chore is taking care of the chickens. We have six little chicks—there were supposed to be eight, but one died and one egg didn't hatch—plus a full-grown hen named Henny Penny. Kind of a stupid name, but Scott had everyone vote on it, and all the littlest kids got two votes instead of one. Most of the time, we just call her Penny.

Penny's my favorite. I never thought I would like a chicken. Like before we came here, I don't think I'd ever even seen a real live chicken, and I figured they wouldn't have much personality. They're not particularly cute, and you can't play fetch with them or anything. But Penny knows who I am, and maybe I'm just making this up, but I swear she clucks in a special way when she sees me coming.

So on Thursday, I'm hanging out with the chickens, and some kids' voices start drifting in from the woods, close to the area where we left all the werewolf stuff. I look around to make sure there are no adults nearby, and then I put down my bag of chicken feed and duck into the trees.

When I get to the place with all the fur and fake blood, I see there are two boys there: Ryan and a guy named Lincoln, who's one of this week's visiting kids. He's older than me; about thirteen, I think. Tilly's age.

They see me before I get to them, and Lincoln leans over and whispers something into Ryan's ear, and then the two of them start laughing crazily. I hate when kids do stuff like that. It suddenly changes everything, you know? Like a minute ago, things were all normal. I was on my way to talk to these other two kids, and everyone was . . . equal, pretty much. I mean, there were various ways you could group us together, like those activities teachers used to give us in kindergarten: you have three beads, and none of them is exactly the same. If you group them by color, then the two red ones go together, and the blue one is the odd guy out. Or you can group them by shape, and then the two square ones go together, and now one of the red ones is the odd guy out, because it's the only one that's round.

So right then, it seemed like it didn't matter that they're both boys and I'm a girl, because Ryan and I are both permanent camp kids, plus we're the same age. Lincoln should definitely be the odd guy out. But now I feel all worried, because I don't know what they're saying about me. And if anyone's the odd guy out, it's definitely me.

"Hey, guys," I say when I'm close enough to talk in a normal voice. "What's up?"

"Not much," says Ryan. "Lincoln wanted to show me this weird stuff he found." He's pointing at the fake blood, and trying not to give me a knowing look, so that evens things out a little again.

"Huh," I say.

"Oh, fuck that," says Lincoln. "It's obviously fake as hell. We were just shooting the shit."

Tilly and I used to have a secret swearword bingo game when we were watching grown-up TV shows and movies. Lincoln would only need a "bitch" and a "damn" to win the whole board.

"Anyway," he's saying, "things are a lot more interesting, now that you're here."

I can feel my mouth drop open a little, and I concentrate on closing it again. I don't know where to look. It's a compliment, but it's not. Because the way he says it kind of creeps me out.

"I'm going to go back and finish feeding the chickens," I say.

"No, wait," says Lincoln. "You should see this." He puts his hand into the pocket of his shorts. "I found a little baby mouse."

"You have a mouse in your pocket?" I'm confused and, honestly, worried for the mouse. I don't think it would have a lot of room in there.

He turns away from me a little, still moving his hand around in his pocket. I'm feeling a little bit anxious, but only because I'm wondering if he's going to show me a dead mouse. I'm not expecting at all that when he turns back he's going to have his pants unzipped and be holding his penis in his hand.

"See, look," he says, making a move toward me. I step back. "Isn't it cute? Do you want to pet it?" And he laughs uproariously.

I feel nervous inside and a little like I might throw up. But I also don't want to run away like a scared little girl. I try to think of what Tilly would do in this situation.

"Asshole," I say. It sounds stupid and wishy-washy. When Tilly says it, you can tell there's real feeling behind it.

"Ooh, hot," says Lincoln. "I like a girl with a potty mouth."

He's rubbing his penis a little, and I can see it getting hard, which is kind of fascinating, even if it's also the most repulsive thing I've ever seen.

"Show me your tits," says Lincoln. "If you've got any."

I say, "I don't, really," which is really not the right thing to say, because it's like I'm joining in this conversation with him. Like maybe I'm acting like I like him or something. I should just turn around and go. But there's part of me that doesn't want to be rude, if you can believe I'm actually thinking that. And there's part of me that feels a little flattered, or at least like I'm *supposed* to feel flattered.

"I've seen 'em," Ryan says. It's the first thing he's said since all of this started.

"You have not!" I yell. I'm furious at Ryan, suddenly, way madder than I am at Lincoln. I mean, it's easy; I *know* how to be mad at Ryan.

"Last week, when you were changing for free swim in the bathroom at the dining hall," he said. I can see he's totally torn here. He almost sounds apologetic for a minute, but then he remembers he wants to be all tough to impress Lincoln. "You know how there's that lock that's a hook, and it doesn't always close all the way?"

"So how were they?" asks Lincoln.

Ryan looks back and forth between me and Lincoln, before saying "small" in a low voice that he doesn't think I can hear.

Lincoln practically collapses in fake laughter, bending over with his penis still in his hand. "Did you hear that?" he asks me. "He said they were small."

"Yeah, I know. Just like I already said."

"You know, Ryan's got a little mousie, too." Lincoln says. "Go ahead, Ryan. Get it out. I bet Iris wants to see it."

"I do not," I say. My voice is quiet but vicious. I stare at Ryan, waiting to see what he's going to do. It's suddenly really important for me to know.

Ryan looks scared. Actually scared. He looks at me with his face almost crumbling, like he might cry. But what he says is, "Okay," and he reaches for the snap on his shorts.

And no. No freaking way, no FUCKING way. I am not going to stand here and let Ryan show me his penis. "Fuck you," I say to him. I lunge forward and shove him back into a tree. His head makes a big thunk against the wood. I hope it hurts.

I turn around, and then I'm running out of the woods, back to camp. I don't want to see anybody; I don't want to talk to anybody. I don't stop until I get to the door of our cabin, which I open and close with a smash. My mom's in the kitchen, but I don't answer her when she asks me why I'm crying. I don't have a single thing to say.

I slam the door of our bedroom and lie down on the bed. It's quiet, except for the noises I'm making, which keep going for a while, no matter how hard I try to stop.

After a few minutes, Tilly comes into the room. She walks over to my bed and tries to give me a hug, but since I'm lying down, it turns into her practically lying on top of my back. It doesn't feel bad, though, that heavy weight pressing me into the soft mattress. It feels like she's getting between me and everything else in the whole giant, stupid world. It feels like she's my big sister, and she's protecting me.

chapter 29

Alexandra

May 2011: Washington, DC

This spring, it's clear that puberty has arrived, full force. Lately, you've had to remind Tilly (over and over again) not to rub herself idly through her pants. The concepts of "public" and "private" have always been difficult for her, especially as they relate to her body. But the stakes are higher here than picking her nose or lifting up her shirt to scratch her belly; somehow, you have to get it across to her that she *cannot* touch herself in front of other people.

"I don't like it," she says to you one day. It takes you a minute to understand that she's talking about sexual arousal. "It's annoying; it kind of hurts, almost. It feels like I need to pee or something, but there's no way to make it go away. At least if I rub it, it doesn't feel as bad."

You speak to her frankly about masturbation, you give her a few books to look through, and you tell her to spend some time alone in her room. A half hour later, she emerges, red-faced and pissed off. "I can't do it," she says. She's almost in tears. "I don't know how to have an orgasm. It doesn't work. Can't you help me? Can't you show me or something?"

You close your eyes, take a breath. She's asking a genuine question.

She doesn't understand why you won't. You've just told her it's natural and normal; you told her everyone does it, and when she pressed further, you admitted that you do, too. From her perspective, here's what just happened: you told her she needs to learn a new skill, but she can't ask anyone to show her how it's done. From her perspective, you're being kind of a bitch. Add it to the long list of anecdotes you're never going to post on Facebook.

Josh, at least, is appropriately horrified.

"I mean, what are we supposed to do," you ask him, "buy her a vibrator?"

He lets out a strangled groan, half fake, half real. "Stop it," he says, covering his ears and making a face. "Good God."

You sigh. It seemed natural that all the period stuff should fall to you, but there it was a lot clearer what the "right way" was.

"Well, okay, so what if she were a boy? What would we do then?"

"If she were a boy, I don't think she'd be having this problem." He shrugs. "Or if she did . . . it's a lot easier to explain using metaphors and crude hand gestures."

In the end, you say fuck it and you order her a damn vibrator. You find a few educational websites and YouTube videos, and you walk her through it without actually . . . walking her through it. Eventually, she gets it and you all move on to the next step. Which is apparently learning not to tell your family about your orgasms at the dinner table.

Introducing Scott to Josh is weird; you can't shake the feeling that you're introducing your husband to the man you're having an affair with. Which is not an image you want to dwell on; there's nothing even vaguely sexual in the vibe you get from Scott, or the interactions you've had with him. But there's something illicit about the way you've slid him into your lives, sideways: dressing up a little bit to go to his evening seminars, while Josh takes over homework and bedtime duties; engaging in a private email correspondence with him; inviting him over to the house when the children are at school.

Probably, Josh would be less threatened by the guy if you *were* sleeping with him. He's suspicious of Scott's motives, dismissive of his credentials, and resentful about the four hundred dollars per session you're paying him for his time. He's also twenty minutes late getting home from work on the night of the meeting, which is fine, because you suspected that something like this might happen, and you told him the wrong time deliberately. You've picked up a few tricks over the years.

Truthfully, though, this isn't much of a battle. He knows as well as you that you both need help. He knows that the older Tilly gets, the less time you have before she's expected to manage on her own.

The two of you disagreed about how to present Scott to the kids, and you've settled on introducing him as "a teacher who likes talking to kids." Which you think actually sounds creepier than just calling him "a friend of Mommy and Daddy's," but whatever.

The kids don't really care what you call him, though. Tilly, in particular, is excited to meet him, excited that you're bringing someone new into her life. This is one of Tilly's many wonderful traits: the enthusiasm with which she greets every new endeavor. Wonderful, but sometimes heartbreaking, because you can never be sure how she'll be received in return.

"Hi, Scott," says Tilly, before he's even got his coat off. "Do you know what the tallest statue in the world is?"

This is her thing, lately, her "special interest": that seems to be the polite term that everyone's agreed on. "All-consuming obsession" would be closer to the truth. She's pretty much always had one. Before big statues, it was Greek mythology, and before that, dolphins.

In fact, you're pretty sure that Scott *does* know what the tallest statue is, since he's been briefed on Tilly's interests, but he doesn't give it away. "Huh," he says. "Good question. I'm afraid I don't know."

He's barely finished speaking before Tilly's filling him in. "It's the Spring Temple Buddha, in the Zhaocun township of Lushan County, Henan, China. They started building it in 1997, and it wasn't finished until 2008. It's 420 feet tall, but if you count the base, which I don't, it's 502 feet. The next tallest one is the Motherland Calls, in Volgograd, Russia, which is 279 feet, but that includes the sword she's holding over her head. The statue itself, from head to toe, is 171 feet."

"Wow," says Scott. You put a hand on Tilly's arm to remind her to give him a chance to talk. "That's really interesting. I think the tallest statue I've ever seen in person is the Statue of Liberty. How tall is that one?"

"Well, actually, most people consider the Statue of Liberty the second tallest statue in the world, but that's only if you count from the bottom of the pedestal to the top of her torch, which is 305 feet. But if you just count how tall the statue would be if she climbed down from the base and went walking down the street or something, she'd only be 151 feet tall."

You watch her chatter away, pacing around the living room as she talks. You think, *She is my life*, and it is of course both true and not. The day after she was born, it occurred to you that all of the categories had changed now. When you filled out medical paperwork related to the baby, everyone had slid forward a peg: "parents" meant you, "grandparents" meant your own parents and Josh's. For a brief, dark time—approximately the first week of her life—you couldn't escape the feeling that you were one step nearer to death. And all because of this tiny, eight-pound creature.

The plan tonight is that Scott will spend about an hour observing the kids, and then he'll spend some time talking to Josh alone. Later in the week, he'll write up a report and then meet with the two of you to discuss it.

Tilly has brought out her "statue notes" now, for Scott to look at: a spiral-bound notebook where she's recorded all of the research she's done on this new topic. As if the passion she feels, the giddy infatuation these structures inspire in her, can be summed up by a list of relative heights and dates of completion. Such depth of feeling. When she talks about it to you (or to anyone else), you can see how much she wants to convince you that this information is worth your time. To make you see the beauty that she sees.

And what you want, the *only* thing you really want—from Scott, from this consultation, from all of the therapists and special-ed teachers and therapeutic service providers who are doing their best to help you—is to preserve this child's enthusiasm and charm, even as you teach her that she can't always have everyone's attention, that grabbing strangers' arms and insisting they talk about statues isn't exactly the right way to live among the people of the world.

Scott never did ask you to give him an answer about happiness and purpose, but you wonder if maybe the question itself was its own exercise. How is it that we ever manage to forget how brief and fragile our lives are? The time will come when your body will stop working. Your mind—now in constant movement, containing vast galaxies—will no longer think. Of course, you know this; you, as much as anyone else, are subject to those brief, terrifying moments of clarity. Bright bursts of anxiety, blooming and swelling.

But is that all you're supposed to do with that knowledge—fear it? Or are you supposed to hold on to it, use it to figure out how you want to move through the world?

Happiness, as it exists in the wild—as opposed to those artificially constructed moments like weddings and birthday parties, where it's gathered into careful piles—is not smooth. Happiness in the real world is mostly just resilience and a willingness to arch oneself toward optimism. To believe that people are more good than bad. To believe that the waves carrying you are neither friendly nor malicious, and to know that you're less likely to drown if you stop struggling against them.

While Scott hangs out with the kids, you and Josh sit in the next room and look over brightly colored handouts. The one you're holding is about the effect of pesticides and other environmental toxins.

So many things to worry about. Which ones do you decide to fight? Last summer, small yellow signs began appearing on lawns all over your neighborhood: "This yard treated by the Mosquito Experts! Keep children and pets off grass for 24 hours." You looked it up on their website, to see exactly what they were using and how safe it was; the phrase they used was "low mammalian toxicity." It didn't reassure you much, but you liked the wording. Think of your children as the mammals they are: slippery seals, wide-eyed monkeys. Curious and mischievous, embodying your dearest hopes.

In the end, you hired the Mosquito Experts, too. Because you're a good neighbor, and because a yard infested with mosquitoes carries its own hazards. And anyway, "natural" doesn't necessarily mean harmless—what makes us imagine that it does? Arsenic and deadly nightshade, hurricanes and tsunamis and poisonous scorpions—all one hundred percent natural. Water alone can probably kill you ten different ways.

Tilly's still talking on and on to Scott; you can almost move your lips along with her. You've learned more about giant statues than you ever imagined you would. You know that the Colossus of Rhodes was toppled by an earthquake. It broke first at the knees. It stood in place, whole and intact, for a mere fifty-six years, but the ruins lay where they fell for nearly a millennium. "Even lying on the ground, it is a marvel," wrote Pliny the Elder. "Few people can make their arms meet round the thumb of the figure."

But "the truth" is not something that exists in a vacuum, static and unchanging. For hundreds of years, people believed that before the earthquake, the Colossus of Rhodes stood astride the entrance of a harbor, with one foot on each side of the water. The statue is depicted in this pose in artwork and illustrations; Shakespeare wrote about it this way, and so did Emma Lazarus, in the poem that would be affixed to the Statue of Liberty on a bronze plaque. But modern scholars agree that this is nonsense. It's a mechanical and logistical impossibility. As nice a picture as it makes, no ship ever sailed between those bronze legs.

There is currently no cure for autism; there is no universally agreed-upon treatment plan. Whether we should aim to "cure" it at all is a matter of some debate. But no one can say what will be true about autism in a thousand years, or a hundred, or twenty. Anything that is built can topple. Anything written can be revised.

Josh has set the timer on his phone for an hour, and when the table you're sitting at begins to vibrate, you get up and follow him into the other room.

Scott and the girls are sitting on the floor in front of the coffee table. They've all got paper and crayons; they're drawing (they are excited to explain to you) their own giant statues. Iris has created a monument to bunnies; Scott has drawn a monument to roller coasters. And Tilly, in true Tilly fashion, has designed a monument to monuments. On a hillside, a thousand feet high, a dozen statues stacked one on top of the other. And she's glowing like she's never been happier.

This is, you believe, the instant when Josh decides that he approves of Scott. It's not that Scott has done anything particularly amazing; this is an activity that any teacher might come up with, or any good babysitter. But he's paying attention to your girls, meeting them at their level. Listening to what they have to say.

People who have parenting philosophies, Josh used to say, *have too much time on their hands.* He used to say, *I know what works and what doesn't. I know my kids better than anyone.*

Now he sits down on the floor, between Tilly and Iris. He slides over a piece of paper and picks up a red crayon.

"My turn," he says. "Make some space for me, too."

chapter 30

Iris

June 29, 2012: New Hampshire

The day after the stupid Lincoln penis thing is Friday. That's good because it means only one more day until Lincoln and his family leave and I never have to see them again, but bad because it means it's Mother's Day, and so I'll have to see a lot more of his ugly face all afternoon in the woods.

I mean, I'm okay. It's not like they raped me or sexually abused me or any of those things that older kids have special assemblies about at school. But ever since it happened, there have been times when I've been around some of the men at camp—really embarrassing people, like Scott or Tom or even my dad—and I think, out of nowhere, "He has a penis." It just floats into my head by itself; I don't even mean to be thinking about it. It's like when I was little, and it occurred to me that everyone goes to the bathroom, even people like teachers and actors on TV. But that was kind of funny, whereas this freaks me out.

The whole Werewolf thing is messed up, too, because Candy and Tilly don't know what happened, and they want to keep making plans for the next group of kids. But now I don't want anything to do with it. Because whenever I think about werewolves, I get this slide show in my head of Lincoln's ugly penis and Ryan's stupid scared face and all the fake blood and fur scattered on the dirt. And then I just feel like puking my guts out.

I just have to get through Werewolf today; that's the last time I'll ever have to be in the same place as Lincoln. On the way into the woods, I stick close to Tilly and Candy. We're walking slowly, so everyone else is passing us. When Lincoln walks by with Ryan, he calls out, "Hey, pussycats." He emphasizes the "pussy" part.

"Shut up," says Candy. And then, once they're a little farther from us, she says, "Lincoln's a dick."

"Lincoln *has* a dick," I say, and then feel embarrassed because Candy gives me a strange look, and I realize it's kind of a weird thing to say.

But Tilly doesn't look like she thinks it's weird. She just throws her arm around my shoulders to pull me into a clumsy half hug and laughs like it's the funniest thing she's heard all day.

By the time we get out to the Harmony Circle, I'm starting to think that maybe it will be okay. Maybe I'll just be able to avoid him completely.

But then Scott gets up in front of us and says, "Today, the Werewolf wants to do things a little bit differently."

Doing something a little bit differently turns out to mean that we're going to build shelters in groups of two instead of by ourselves. There are eight of us, and I'm sitting way across the circle from Lincoln, so I don't think we'll end up together, but then Scott makes us count off and has one go with five and two go with six, etc. And there's Lincoln walking toward me with an ugly grin.

I don't even talk to him. I just stand up and walk over to the Building Store and wait in line to buy supplies. I see some of the kids in front of me getting some of the good stuff—like Candy has the big double sleeping bag, and Ryan has the dog crate—but I don't even care because I've got other stuff on my mind. I wait my turn, and when I get up to Scott, I say, "I have to talk to you for a minute."

He puts on his "concerned grown-up" face, and leads me a little bit away from the table and the other kids. And I'm thinking that saying the word "penis" to Scott might be the most embarrassing thing that's ever happened to me, but if it gets Lincoln in trouble and means I don't have to be his partner for this game, then maybe it'll be worth it.

So I tell him what happened, and my face is hot and probably bright red, but I get it out and I wait to see what Scott's going to do about it.

At first, he doesn't do anything but look at me. And he doesn't seem shocked or mad or even a little bit upset. He just stares at me, and after a minute he says, "Iris, if that's a lie, it's a very bad lie to tell."

I suck in my breath, and it sounds like a gasp. I start to say something, to tell him that it's *not* a lie, but he holds up a finger to stop me.

"And if it isn't a lie," he says, "it's going to get all of us into a whole lot of trouble."

My mouth is still open from before, but now I don't have any idea what to say. I don't . . . does he mean that I'm in trouble, too?

Just then, Ryan comes running up, yelling something about Charlotte acting like a baby, and for just a second, Scott looks absolutely furious. He reaches out and puts his hand across my mouth, warning me to stop talking. Then with his hand still pushing against my face, he says, "Ryan, you will work this out, or no *Simpsons* talk for two days. And I swear to God, if you don't stop whining, I'm going to put you in that dog crate myself."

Ryan's eyes get all big, and I can tell he's really scared. I almost feel bad for him, because that doesn't seem fair, threatening that he can't talk about *The Simpsons*. I'm not sure he could even stop doing it if he tried. But then I think about the way he looked yesterday when he was talking about peeking at me naked, and I feel like I wouldn't even care if Scott taped his mouth shut and locked him in the dog crate forever.

"Go," says Scott, and Ryan turns around and runs back to his sister. Scott waits until he's gone before he takes his hand away from my mouth.

"So what I'm going to do," he says to me, just like we were never interrupted, "is I'm going to pretend you didn't tell me what you just told me. I don't want to hear another word about it. And you're going to play the game along with everybody else."

Then he smiles at me really wide and shrugs his shoulders with an expression like, "There's nothing I can do." He says, "The Werewolf wants what the Werewolf wants."

I can feel my face curling into something ugly. I'm mad. I'm so mad, but I'm not going to cry. I just turn around and walk over to the table at the Building Store, and I grab up a whole bunch of stuff: an old blanket and a plastic laundry basket and some duct tape. As much as I can carry in my two arms.

"Hey," Scott calls after me. "That's not how the Werewolf does business."

"Too bad for the Werewolf," I yell over my shoulder. And then, still loud enough for everybody to hear: "I already gave my information. It's not my fault if the Werewolf doesn't want it."

I walk over to Lincoln, who's looking at me like maybe I'm more interesting than he thought. I don't care, though. I don't care what he fucking thinks.

I drop all the junk I'm carrying at his feet, and then I just look at him, wondering what comes next. I can tell it's sneaking in, that feeling like I should be nice to him because I'm a nice girl. And if I'm *not* a nice girl, then who else can I be?

It's not really a literal question, *who else can I be*, but for just a second I imagine that it is. I try out Tilly in my head, but she probably wouldn't even notice there was an awkward situation going on. And then I hear Candy, talking to someone across the field, and it's like an answer traveling through the air.

I look at Lincoln, who's staring at me with his ugly mouth hanging open. "What's your problem?" I ask. It sounds really rude. Good.

"Did you tell him?" he asks me.

"Did I tell who what?"

"Scott. When you were talking to him just now. Did you tell him what happened?"

I pretend I have no idea what he's talking about. "What happened?" I say. "Oh, you mean yesterday? When you showed me your"—I take a breath and put a mean smile on my face—"tiny little dick?"

He goes all red and splotchy. "You fucking bitch." He pushes me, hard, and I fall back onto the grass. But there's something about his stupid blushing face and the way his voice cracks in the middle of the word "bitch," and I just start laughing.

"Shut up," he yells, and I think maybe he's going to kick me or try to stomp on me or something, but I also think maybe he's going to just freak out and start crying in front of everyone. And that makes me laugh harder, because I suddenly get it that, oh my God, he's just like Tilly. Except, of course, that Tilly doesn't have a penis—and that's such a bizarre thing to think that I just keep laughing and it feels like there's no way I'm ever going to stop. I'm laughing when Candy sees me lying on the ground and comes to ask if I'm okay, and I'm laughing when Scott comes over to grab Lincoln, who's started to hit me with these sad weak punches that barely even hurt.

I laugh until there are tears running down my face and my nose is all gross and slick with snot. And if there's any chance that maybe I'm crying about some other thing entirely, it doesn't even matter, because who would ever be able to know for sure? Nobody, not even me.

• • •

The week of the Fourth of July is a little less busy than usual, because we only have two Guest Camper families instead of three. I overheard my dad talking to Tom about it; I guess they didn't get many people signing up, because it was a holiday week, so Scott decided to charge more money for it and call it a "special intensive workshop retreat" or something like that. But other than the fact that there are fewer people than usual, we don't seem to be doing anything differently.

The Fourth is on a Wednesday this year. On Tuesday, after dinner, I'm on my way down to the lake, because Scott said we could have a Moonlight Swim, when I run into Ryan's mom, Diane, who's looking for Henny Penny. She gets out of the henhouse fairly regularly. I think maybe she's smarter than all of us, or maybe we're just not as good at building things as we think we are.

"I'll look for her," I say. "I know all her hiding places."

I drop my towel on the ground and head toward the woods. Sometimes Penny wanders in there. It's dusky out, and the sun is starting to go down, but it's still light enough that I don't need a flashlight.

I walk past the point where the path ends, past the place where the stupid thing with Lincoln and Ryan happened, and I continue through the trees, making soft little clucking noises as I go. Right when I'm starting to think that I should turn around, because she's obviously not here, I search the trees to my left, and my eye catches on something that's a royal blue kind of color. It's not like I'm paying much attention, but my brain notices that that's not a color you usually see in the forest. I stop walking, and look for a minute, trying to figure out what it is.

And suddenly, my heart is beating fast, and I want to get back to camp as fast as I possibly can. Because I think maybe there's something hiding out there in the woods, after all.

• • •

By the morning, I've pretty much calmed myself down. It's a tent; I'm pretty sure that the thing I saw in the woods was a tent. I don't know why it got me so scared—people go camping, it's not like a supernatural occurrence. And maybe it even belongs to somebody here at camp. No reason to get freaked out.

It is kind of a mystery, though, and because it's the Fourth of July and a holiday and everything, it seems like it might be fun to investigate it. After breakfast, we have some free time, and Tilly and Candy and I head into the woods.

At first, I get us all a little bit lost, because I can't remember exactly which way I went when I was looking for Penny (who we found behind the dining hall, by the way). But eventually I recognize some of the trees that I walked past.

It's a hot day, even in the forest, where there's more shade. It doesn't really feel like a holiday. I don't even know if we're going to get to see any fireworks.

We keep walking, but I'm starting to figure out that the tent's not there. I retrace my steps a little, until I'm sure I'm in the right place, but no. Nothing.

"I swear it was here," I say, but I don't sound too convincing.

"Maybe it was just someone camping, and they left," says Tilly.

"Weird place to camp," says Candy. "The closest water is the lake, and to get there, you'd have to walk through all our cabins and everything."

"Maybe you imagined it," says Tilly. She's not really joking, exactly. It's just that whenever something happens that doesn't have an easy explanation, she starts looking for ways to make it work.

"No," I say. "I didn't imagine it."

"Or maybe it was a dream," said Tilly.

"Well, anyway," I say, "it's not here anymore."

"Maybe somebody was filming a movie, and they had to film a camping scene . . ."

"Tilly," I say. It gets annoying sometimes. "I really doubt there was a film crew out here. Whoever it was . . ."

Candy stops me from talking by putting a finger in the air. She looks like she's listening for something. And then I hear it, too: leaves rustling, just a little. And then a branch snaps.

We all turn around, the three of us. There's a man—someone I've never seen before—walking toward us. I let out a little scream, not because he seems particularly scary, but because I'm so surprised. Tilly grabs my arm, and we're both ready to run if we have to.

The man raises his hand in a wave. Candy's leaning forward like she's trying to see better, and then she takes a few steps toward the man.

"Daddy?" she says.

The man smiles the kind of great big smile that almost turns into laughing. "Candy," he calls out.

He opens his arms, and she runs into them.

Tilly and I stand there awkwardly while Candy and her dad have their reunion. Before they're even done hugging Tilly asks, "No offense, but why are you here? I thought you and Diane were divorced."

Candy's dad pulls away from Candy and turns to us and smiles. It's a weird smile, not mean, but just the way people look sometimes when they've just met Tilly and don't really get her yet.

"Uh, yeah," he says. "Candy, do you want to introduce us?"

"Yeah, sure," says Candy. She's beaming and holding on to her father's arm. "Dad, these are my friends Tilly and Iris. Guys, this is my dad, Michael McNeil." Her voice has that formal kind of tone that you get when you have to use your parents' real names.

"His last name isn't Gough?" asks Tilly.

"No," says Candy, sounding annoyed. "Neither is mine."

"What about Ryan and Charlotte?"

I nudge my elbow against Tilly's arm a couple of times, because I don't think Candy and her dad want to explain their whole family history right now.

Candy's dad is looking around, like he's making sure no one else is coming. I think maybe he's nervous. "Hey," he says. "Do you guys like fried dough?"

"Oh my God," says Candy. "That would be amazing. You would not believe the healthy crap we've been eating here."

"I've heard of that," Tilly says, "but I've never had it. It's like a funnel cake, but flat, right?"

Candy's dad makes an exaggerated face like his eyes are bugging out. He seems nice. "You guys've never had fried dough?"

We shake our heads. "Oh my gosh," he says, shaking his head. "We have got to remedy that ASAP. I am taking you guys to Weirs Beach."

Candy lets out a little shriek, and Tilly says, "Yes! Score!"

We've been hearing about Weirs Beach ever since we got here. Seems like most of the Guest Campers either go there before they get to Camp Harmony or else right after they leave. There's a boardwalk and bumper cars, pizza and arcade games and mini-golf. It sounds so fun.

"Okay," I say. "Let me just run and tell my mom." I didn't even think I was hungry, but now I'm thinking about cotton candy and whatever that funnel cake thing is, and I can't wait. My mouth is actually watering.

"Well, wait just a sec," says Candy's dad. "I don't want you to do anything you're not comfortable with, but I have a feeling that if you tell your parents, they're not going to let you go."

"You want us to just go, without telling anybody?" asks Tilly. I can see her thinking about it.

"He's right, though," says Candy. "They'll never say yes."

"Yeah," says Tilly. "I guess they wouldn't."

"How long will we be gone?" I ask.

Candy's dad shrugs. "It doesn't have to be long. I'll drive you back and drop you off whenever you want."

"They probably won't even notice we're gone," says Tilly.

I sigh. "I don't know." I sound so whiny, like a little kid. But I'm afraid we'll get in trouble.

Candy's dad reaches out a hand toward my arm, but doesn't quite touch it. "Hey, Iris," he says. His voice is serious. It's nice that he paid attention to my name and remembered it. He says, "It's totally okay if you don't want to go. It's completely up to you."

"Yeah," I say. "I know . . ." I hear Candy sigh. Ugh, I hate this. Now it's like I'm the baby who's messing things up for the older kids. God, it's hot. I wipe some sweat away from my forehead.

Candy's dad is still leaning toward me, and now he smiles, just a little. "No pressure, but you know what else they've got there?"

He waits until I look up at him. I shake my head.

His lowers his voice to a stage whisper. "Snow cones."

It's strange to be in a car again. Candy's sitting up front with her dad, and Tilly and I are in the back. It took us a while to walk to the road from the woods without going through camp, but Candy's dad seemed to know his way.

"So were you actually camping out there?" Candy asks, as we're putting on our seat belts.

"Yeah," he says. "I've been here since Monday."

"Were you spying on us?" asks Tilly. She sounds sort of excited at the thought.

He throws us a quick look, kind of apologetic. "Well, a little bit." He pauses. "Not my finest moment, probably, but I've just been so worried." He keeps his eyes on the road, but reaches across to Candy and squeezes her shoulder.

"Why were you worried?" she asks.

"Oh, you know," he says. "I couldn't get in touch with you or your mom, I hadn't heard a thing from you in a month."

"I sent you a letter," Candy says. I don't know why I never told Candy about the envelope I found in the trash. It just seemed . . . like something Scott would want to be a secret, I guess.

"Well, I didn't get it. And you're out here in the middle of nowhere with that nutcase . . ."

"What nutcase?" asks Tilly.

"Do you mean Rick?" asks Candy. Her voice is tight, like she's ready to fight about this. It's funny because I didn't think she liked Rick much, but I guess it's one of those things where you can make fun of people in your family, but other people can't. Not even your real dad.

"No, sweetie," says her dad. "Rick's fine. I know we've had our differences, but . . . no, I'm talking about the head guy. Bean."

"Scott?" I say.

"Scott's a nutcase?" asks Tilly. Like it's a factual question, like whether he has Italian heritage or something. Like if this guy says yes, she's just going to take his word for it.

"Dad," says Candy, with that irritated-teenager voice. It occurs to me that she must not get to do that very much: be annoyed with her dad. In addition to all the ordinary stuff, like not eating dinner with him every night, she also doesn't get a chance to get mad at him because he's telling lame jokes or he won't let her go out after dark or whatever.

"Okay," says Candy's dad. "Maybe not 'nutcase.' I just mean that your mom and Rick are the ones who signed up to join this thing and go live in the woods with a bunch of strangers. It's not something I picked, and I don't have to trust the guy just because they do."

"Why don't you trust him?" asks Candy.

Her dad shrugs. "I've done some research. He's not a doctor, he's not a psychiatrist. Not that he claims to be, I guess. He just says he's an educator, but still, where does he get the expertise? I set up a Facebook page a couple of weeks ago, when I couldn't get in touch with you. It's called Families Against Scott Bean, and it's taken off like crazy. People have just been coming out of the woodwork. Turns out that this guy's past isn't as squeaky-clean as he wants people to think. Like he got fired from a teaching job for hitting a kid, and . . ."

"Hey, can I use your phone?" Tilly asks. She's pointing at an iPhone sitting in the cup holder next to the driver's seat; she's already reaching out to take it.

Candy's dad scoops up the phone before she can grab it. "Well, wait just a minute there," he says. "What do you want it for?"

I can tell he's thinking the same thing I am, which is: Is she thinking about calling Scott? Or maybe looking up that website?

But she says, "I just want to see if you have any good games," and he passes it back to her, after taking a minute to put it in airplane mode. Like that would stop Tilly if she really wanted access to the Internet.

The rest of the ride is just Tilly playing *Angry Birds* and Candy and her dad talking quietly in the front seat about people I don't know. I watch the scenery out the window, which mostly doesn't look familiar, even though I know I saw it all a month ago when we first got here. It's kind of funny to realize that we haven't left camp once in all that time; I hadn't thought about it much. But I don't think I've ever stayed in the same place like that for so long. I feel almost like claustrophobic in retrospect; now that we're away from Camp Harmony, I don't really want to go back anytime soon.

Finally the Weirs Beach sign comes into view, and I'm the first one to see it: blue with big white letters and a curvy red arrow made of lightbulbs. I bet it looks awesome at night when it's all lit up.

Candy's dad parks the car, and we get out. The parking lot is right next to the beach, which looks not all that different from the beach at camp, but nicer somehow. Wider and more festive, with lots of people swimming and stretched out on towels. Everything seems a little more colorful. There are people sitting at picnic tables, and kids playing with beach toys, even though lake sand sucks for building sand castles. For a minute, I wish that we had our bathing suits, but then I remember that we couldn't go back to get them, because we didn't tell anyone we were leaving. It makes me feel kind of scared. I look across the lake, at the ring of green trees all along every edge, and wonder where exactly my parents are, and whether they've noticed we're gone yet.

"This way, girls," says Candy's dad. We walk past a random wooden gazebo sitting on some grass right in the middle of the parking lot, and go up a flight of stairs to the boardwalk. Tilly and Candy and I all stop and look around for a minute. It's pretty crowded here, and we feel funny after not being anywhere public for so long. Tilly moves a little closer to me and nudges me with her arm. I take her hand and hold on to it as we start walking again.

"Okay," says Candy's dad. "I see pizza, video arcade, old-time photos. Looks like the food stands are down this way."

He takes us to the fried dough counter and buys us all some. It's really good, maybe even better than a funnel cake. Less crispy, more . . . well, doughy, I guess.

Then Tilly wants to go to the arcade, and Candy's dad says, "Hey, you know what I'd like to do, Candy? Let's get one of those old-fashioned pictures taken, like we did that time on the Cape, remember?"

So he gives me and Tilly twenty dollars to play games, and they go off to the photo place.

We finish eating, and then we're thirsty, so we buy some lemonade. By the time we walk away from the fried dough stand and head to the arcade, Tilly's shirt is covered with powdered sugar. We stop for a minute, so I can help her brush it off, and when I'm done I see that we're standing right in front of the vintage photo store. I look through the window, trying to see if I can see Candy and her dad, all dressed up. I love those old-fashioned dresses. But the store is totally empty, except for the guy behind the counter. Candy and her father are nowhere in sight.

chapter 31

Iris

July 4, 2012: New Hampshire

They're not in the antique photo place, and when we walk back to the parking lot, the car is gone. I feel scared, all of a sudden, and kind of dizzy. I sit down on the hot grass, setting my paper plate and cup down next to me.

"Hey," says Tilly, patting her pocket and leaving a smear of powdered sugar on her shorts. "I still have his phone. We can call him. Oh, wait . . ." She laughs.

"Tilly," I say. I don't think she's getting it. "How are we going to get back to camp?"

"Well, Candy will probably tell them that we need to get picked up when she gets there."

I shake my head. "I don't know if her dad is taking her back to camp," I say. "He didn't seem to think she should even be there."

I can see Tilly start to panic. "Oh no, oh no!" she says, her voice getting louder until she's almost yelling. Now she's *more* freaked out than she needs to be. I get what my mom means about Tilly seeing everything in black and white, with no gray. "What are we going to do? What if we never get back to camp? What if we never see Mommy and Daddy again?"

"That's just stupid," I say. I'm feeling mean, but then Tilly's face crumples up like a little kid's, and instantly I regret it.

She starts crying (wailing, really), so loud that people are beginning to stare at us. "You don't have to yell at me," she gasps when she has enough breath for it. I didn't really yell, but I guess that's not the point.

"Okay," I say, patting her arm. "I'm sorry. I'm really sorry. We'll figure this out, okay?" I give her one of the napkins I'm holding, and she wipes her nose. Tears are still leaking out of her eyes, but she sniffles and calms down enough to take another bite of her fried dough. She looks so worried and so sad that I have to give her a hug.

"So, okay," I say. "We have a phone. We could call the camp, except I don't know the number."

"We could look it up on the Camp Harmony website," Tilly says, which is really smart and actually not something I would've thought of.

"Good idea," I say.

"We're going to be in a lot of trouble."

"Yeah, probably." Something occurs to me. "What time is it?" I ask.

Tilly pulls out the phone. "11:14."

"So not even lunchtime. They might not even know we're gone yet. They probably think we're still out in the woods."

I'm thinking while I'm talking. Here we are in this really fun place, more exciting than anything we've done in weeks; do we really have to turn around and leave right away? I know we're going to get into trouble either way. Might as well enjoy ourselves first.

"Know what I mean, Til?" I ask. "They probably don't even know we're gone."

She's not getting it.

"You think we could get back without them noticing?" she asks.

I shake my head. "No. What I was going to say is, we've still got like fifteen dollars left. Why don't we have some fun?"

In the end, we never do get to call the camp. About an hour later, we're in the arcade playing Skee-ball, when a voice behind me says, "Matilda and Iris Hammond?" I turn around and it's a cop.

Tilly says, "Are you going to arrest us?" and the policeman speaks into his walkie-talkie and says, "They're here." He takes us with him to a little police shack on the boardwalk, and fifteen minutes later, our car drives up with Scott sitting behind the wheel.

We're in trouble, obviously, but it takes a while for us to get to that part. First, there's just a lot of confused talking, with the policeman asking us questions and us trying to explain the situation with Candy. There's a lot of stuff about her dad's phone; the police seem to think that he left it with Tilly on purpose, so they wouldn't be able to track where he went, but as far as I can tell, it was just a random mistake. Tilly ends up having to hand it over to them; I can tell she was hoping that maybe she'd be able to keep it.

Once they let us go and we're all in the car—my dad's up front in the passenger seat, while me, Tilly, and Mom are all squished into the back—everything's just silent for a couple of minutes. I feel really tense, like it'd be better if they all just started yelling at us already.

It's weird to have Scott driving, because it's *our* car. Except it's way cleaner than it ever was before, which makes me wonder who cleared out all of our junk, and whether Scott or somebody actually took it to a car wash.

Tilly must be thinking the same kinds of things, because after a minute, she leans forward and starts looking in the seat-back pocket.

"Hey," she says. Her voice is really loud, after all that quiet. I feel my mom flinch a little, where her leg is touching mine on the seat. "Where are my statue notes?"

I sigh, keeping the noise as quiet as possible. I'm younger than Tilly is, and *I* know that the best thing for us to do right now is just to keep our mouths shut and wait to hear whatever the grown-ups are going to say. But she doesn't get it, or maybe she gets it but she's distracted by this other thing, and now she's probably going to freak out, and it's going to make everything worse.

Sure enough, Scott says, "Do you really think that's the most important question right now, Tilly?" His voice isn't mean or angry, but it's so cold it scares me.

"Yes," says Tilly, her voice rising as she talks. "Yes, I do think it's the most important question. What happened to my statue notes?"

"We cleaned out the car," my mother says softly. "I'm not sure . . ."

"Where are my notes?" Tilly yells. "They're mine, I need them . . ."

"QUIET!" roars Scott. The tires screech as he pulls over to the side of the road. The car turns so fast that I slide sideways into Tilly, and my mom slides sideways into me.

Scott turns off the car and yanks the keys out. He twists around so he can look at the backseat. His face is all red, except for one little white patch on his forehead that gets whiter when he's angry. I guess it's a birthmark or something.

"What the hell were you two thinking?" Scott yells at us.

"Scott," my dad says, just as I say, "You don't have to yell."

"You," Scott says to me. He's taken his seat belt off, and he lunges toward me, putting his face right up to mine and poking me in the chest. "You need to be quiet, too."

"Enough," says my dad. He grabs Scott's arm roughly. "That's enough."

Scott sighs and pulls himself back into the front seat. We just sit there, by the side of the road.

"I hate you," says Tilly quietly, her voice cracking. "I fucking hate you."

"Listen," says Dad, turning to look at us. "I don't think you guys know how scary this was for us. We couldn't find you, we didn't know if you'd been kidnapped or if you'd gotten hurt in the woods somewhere. We were counting the canoes to make sure the three of you hadn't taken one out without asking . . ." His voice sounds tight, like he's trying not to cry.

"Oh," I say. It's a tiny little sound that just slips out of my mouth. He's right; I didn't think about what they would think had happened when they realized we were gone.

"You thought we were dead?" asks Tilly. She sounds weirdly amazed at the idea.

"Yeah, we did," says Mom. I put my head on her arm. "We thought it was a possibility, anyway. We were really worried."

"I'm sorry, Mommy and Daddy," I say. "I'm so sorry."

"Me, too," says Tilly. "I'm really sorry." I can see that she's got her head on Mom, too, over on the other side.

There's a problem, though, with Tilly and apologies, and I don't think she even knows about it. The problem is that she thinks that when you say you're sorry, it means everything's all over. She doesn't get that sometimes people are still mad at you afterward, or that sometimes there still has to be a punishment. So when she says it, she sounds kind of happy and relieved, like she's glad the problem has been taken care of.

"I know you're sorry," says Mom. "But that doesn't . . ."

And that's where I can tell we're about to get to the bad part, the part about consequences and what happens next. But Tilly cuts her off before she can finish her sentence and asks, "What if we were really dead? What would you have done?"

"Oh, for fuck's sake," says Scott. He turns the car back on and pulls back onto the road.

Tilly starts laughing. I reach over Mom and poke her. When she looks at me, I mouth the word "Stop."

But she doesn't shut up. "What?" she asks. "Scott? Why did you say for fuck's sake?" And then she's giggling harder. "If we were dead, you would've fucked us?"

"Tilly!" says Mom. "Cut it out now!" My dad says, "Oh, my God, Tilly . . ."

"Do you see?" says Scott. I can see over the back of his seat that he's shaking his head. "Do you see what I'm saying?"

Mom sighs. "Yeah," she says. "I guess I do."

"Josh?" asks Scott.

My dad nods. "Yeah. Okay."

"What?" I ask. "What's going on?"

"No," says Dad. "It's nothing big. Just that we've been talking about what type of consequence we're going to give you guys."

"Are you going to kick us out of camp?" asks Tilly? "Are we going to have to go back to Washington?"

Seriously? This is so obviously not what the punishment will be, and also so obviously what Tilly would *want* to happen, it's ridiculous. Maybe they'll also buy us new iPads! I roll my eyes but stay silent.

"No," says Scott. "We don't give up at Camp Harmony; we just work harder. Which is exactly what you two will be doing."

"So more AD Block?" I ask.

"No," says Scott. "I think we can all agree that this goes beyond the scope of AD Block. You'll be taking on extra chores—we'll go over specifics when we get back to camp—and you'll be doing it in a very visible way."

"What do you mean?" asks Tilly.

"We mean that you're going to be working where the GCs can see you," says Scott. "And we're going to make sure it's very clear that you're being punished and that you understand the severity of what you did today."

Tilly and I both talk at the same time. I say, "How?" and she says, "Why?"

"Why?" says Scott. "Because in addition to the events of this morning being very frightening, they were also very damaging to the reputation of Camp Harmony."

"So what?" says Tilly, which, honestly, is kind of what I'm thinking, too.

"How do you think it looks?" asks Dad, turning around in his seat again. "These people are paying money to come to our camp and learn our parenting tips, and three of our own kids disappear one morning without a trace."

Tilly starts laughing. "Probably not good," she says. I close my eyes.

"Do you get that this is a business?" asks Scott. "Do you understand that this is how we earn a living?"

"Yes," says Tilly, though I've never actually thought about it, and I bet she hasn't, either.

"Back to the question of how," says Mom. I've still got my head on her arm, and I can feel the vibration of her voice as she talks. "You'll be wearing something on your clothes—a tag or a sign of some kind. Saying what you did."

"This is just like the Nazis," says Tilly. "We're living with Nazis now."

"It is *nothing* like the Nazis," says Mom, "and that's not an argument we're going to have right now."

"We think it's important," says Dad, "both that you don't forget why you're being punished, and that the GCs can see that we're not just sitting back and letting our kids run wild."

"Mommy?" I ask in a small voice. I still have my eyes closed. "What about Candy?"

"What?" asks my dad.

"Candy," says Mom.

"That's a good question," says Scott, "and the answer is that we don't know. This has all happened very quickly, and we're still trying to piece it all together. I can tell you this, though: right now, Candy's mother, Diane, is at the Laconia police station, filing a report."

They all keep talking, about kidnapping and custody laws and I don't even know what, but I breathe in and I breathe out, and after a while, I manage to stop listening. Even though I know we're almost back at camp, even though I can feel it when the car turns from smooth road onto gravel driveway, I stay pressed against my mom and let my mind take me away to sleep, for however long the grownups will let it last.

When we get back, the adults let us get some lunch before we start our new chores. When we're finishing our sandwiches, Janelle walks into the dining hall.

"Hello, ladies," she says. "I'm sure you're not going to be happy about this, but Scott asked me to make these for you. They go around your neck."

She holds up two rectangles of white cardboard with strings attached to the top corners. They both say the same thing: "I GOT INTO A STRANGER'S CAR AND LEFT CAMP WITHOUT PERMISSION."

"I'm not wearing that," says Tilly.

"I'm afraid you are," says Janelle. "And I've already heard your Nazi argument, so don't think that's going to sway me." She sounds like she's almost smiling, though.

So we have to spend the afternoon of the Fourth of July wearing these signs while we weed the garden and clean out the chicken cages. And every time anyone walks by, either GC or CF (and even if it's somebody we've seen three times already), we have to stop what we're doing, stand up, and read our signs out loud. But for something that's supposed to be such a terrible punishment, it's not really that bad. Tilly and I practice saying the words in unison, and then if anybody laughs, we say (together), "Stop it! This is serious!" By the end of the day, we barely even mind it anymore. Candy's entire family is gone by dinnertime.

I can hardly believe that it was only this morning that I was at Weirs Beach with her. And I don't mean that just as an expression. I literally don't understand how it's possible that this is still the same day, and it's still the Fourth of July, and that this morning I woke up in our regular old family cabin with my parents in the next room, and I had no idea that any of this crazy stuff was about to happen.

After everyone's eaten, Scott sends the Guest Campers back to their cottages for some "quiet time" and tells the rest of us to stay where we are. Of course "the rest of us" is a smaller group than ever before: just our family, and Scott, and Tom, Janelle, and Hayden.

After all the visitors are gone, Scott stands up and clangs a glass to get everyone's attention. "So," he says. "Happy Independence Day." It's almost funny, because he looks so serious and grim. But nobody laughs.

"I think, by now, everybody's heard the news. You're all aware that Candy's biological father came to Camp Harmony today and kidnapped her."

That still doesn't really sound right to me. I don't understand how someone can be kidnapped by her own father, and anyway, it wasn't some violent hostage situation ransom scene, like in a movie.

"According to our witnesses," Scott says, sending a look in the direction of our table, "it's possible that she left willingly. But it's important for us all to remember that Candy is a child, that she was with an adult she thought she could trust, and that she almost certainly did not understand the repercussions that would follow from this act. I want to be the first to say this: Candy's loyalty is not in question here."

I've only sort of been half-listening, but this makes me sit up and look around. I don't get why he's talking about loyalty. It just seems like a weird thing to say.

"I'm afraid I can't say the same for the rest of the Gough family. Diane came to me this afternoon and told me that the police are investigating the case, but that they've made it clear that parental abduction cases are tricky. And Diane believes that it's in the family's best interests to leave the camp, if they're serious about getting Candy back."

"I don't understand," says Tom. "Why?"

Scott sighs. "For a number of reasons. One is that the New Hampshire police don't have jurisdiction, because the Goughs haven't lived here long enough to establish residency. And the other is that . . ." He pauses. His face is tight. "Apparently, Candy's father is saying that Camp Harmony isn't a healthy environment for her. And that Rick and Diane brought her here without his permission."

"How is it not a healthy environment?" asks Janelle. "That's . . . like our whole thing, to provide a healthy environment."

"I think I know," says Tilly, half-raising her hand as she speaks. "On the way to the beach, Candy's dad called Scott a nutcase."

"Yes, Tilly," says Scott. "Thank you for clarifying." He smiles, without it really looking like a smile. "Now since the Goughs' departure has left us especially shorthanded, I'd appreciate it if you could all pitch in and help with the after-dinner cleanup."

And because he heard us laughing about our signs earlier, Tilly and I are the ones who have to stay the longest and do the most work.

When we get back to the cabin, we both go to our bedroom. I flop down on my bed. It's still light out on the Fourth of July, and I have to spend the rest of the night in a tiny, hot room. What I'd like is just to have some quiet, so I can sit and not think, but that's not going to happen with Tilly in the room. She's pacing around and talking to me and to herself and sometimes singing. After a while, I notice that she's eating something.

"What's in your mouth?" I ask her.

She grins. "Check it out," she says, and pulls a bunch of stuff out of the pocket of her shorts: little Halloween-sized packs of Smarties and Laffy Taffy, a purple plastic ring, a mini green Slinky. Stuff from the arcade. Somewhere between the fried dough and the parental arrival, she must have turned in a bunch of Skee-ball tickets.

"Cool," I say. "Can I have one of those?" I point to the roll of Smarties. I don't say the name out loud, in case anyone can hear us.

"Of course!" she says. "You can have the whole thing."

"Thanks," I say. Sometimes I really love my sister.

We hang out on my bed and eat the rest of the candy, and play with the Slinky, which is too small to really do anything interesting.

When I go to the bathroom a little later, I blow my nose in a piece of toilet paper and then smush up the candy wrappers inside it. When I throw it in the trash can, it looks pretty normal. I don't really think any of the adults are going to be looking through every single snotty tissue.

Tilly's asleep by the time I get back to the room, but it takes me a while to get comfortable. And then, just as I'm about to fall asleep, I hear something that sounds soft and far away, a little string of pops, one after the other. Fireworks, maybe at Weirs Beach. I listen to the familiar rhythm of it, the waiting quiet in between each burst and crack, and I wonder about the colors, whether it might be possible to tell from the sounds which ones are blue and which ones are red or white.

As I fall asleep, I'm thinking that fireworks are shaped like Koosh balls, with all those stringy lines shooting out. I'm thinking about little sparks dripping down the sky like liquid, and smoke left behind when it's all over. What a weird thing, I think, that this is how we celebrate our nation's birthday: to go sit outside in the dark and watch things explode in the sky. And how weird that our parents thought our lives would be better if we moved to a place where we can't see it happen at all.

chapter 32

Tilly

Date and Location Unknown

In the land of Washington, DC, under the reign of Bo the Obama dog and Butterstick the baby panda, houses were made of bricks, and the best kind of family was the kind that contained a mother, a father, and two little girls. In one such house, in one such family, the daughters were named Tilly and Iris. And they were happy.

The world was full of mysteries. There were parks for dogs and classes for babies. The Washington Monument changed colors partway up and had red lights in the top that looked like eyes. Parents would yell out "*Exorcist* steps!" without explanation whenever they drove past a particular gas station in Georgetown. There was a TV show about a store that sold cupcakes, but no one ever went there because the lines were too long, because there was a TV show about it.

Parents were indecisive but powerful. Children were the most important people in the world. In those days, babies were rocked to sleep by mothers who murmured songs by Green Day and Oasis. The life of each child, the very fact of his or her existence, was celebrated yearly with baked goods and gifts. Sometimes a special sticker would be affixed to his or her clothing.

Goody bag technology was at an all-time high.

There were many things that didn't make sense. Children were supposed to tell the truth, unless the truth was that the man on the bus was fat or that fathers were loved a little bit more than mothers. Grown-ups contradicted themselves frequently.

There were secret meetings held by subversive societies that met underneath the dining room table. They planned missions called Operation Wide Awake and Operation Midnight Feast. There was a popular belief that sometimes mothers could see out of the backs of their heads. There was a rumor that fathers sometimes had psychic powers.

Christmas began the day after Thanksgiving with a mysterious and ominous event known as Black Friday and continued until early January, when fathers would drag dead fir trees outside to the curb, leaving behind a trail of needles that felt like shards of glass when they poked your feet through your socks.

It was a land of giants. There were presidents as tall as three grown men. There was a place you could go to have your picture taken, sitting in Albert Einstein's lap.

In all this land, in all this wonder, there was only one thing that anyone could possibly say was a problem. And that was that once you left, it was impossible to find your way back.

chapter 33

Iris

July 8, 2012: New Hampshire

Four days after the Fourth of July, when it's time for the new Guest
Campers to arrive, there's only one family that shows up. I hear my
mom talking about it with Janelle; apparently, there were two other
families scheduled to come, but they both canceled at the last minute. They each had different excuses—one family said their kid was
sick and the other said that the dad's aunt had died or something—
but Scott's wondering if maybe it's not really a coincidence, especially since it happened so soon after the thing with Candy.

The family that does come are called the Finchers. When they
arrive on Sunday, we're all there, waiting for them on the lawn, like
always. The car pulls up, and we all go over to say hi and offer to help
with their luggage, but they don't get out of the car right away. The
mom's looking at something on her cell phone, and when Scott goes
over to open her door, she puts up a "one minute" finger to him.

He smiles politely and waits, making faces at the kids in the
backseat—looks like a boy and a girl, maybe seven and nine—until
she's done. Then he helps her out of the car and holds out his hand
like he's waiting for her to give him something.

"Phone-free zone," he says pleasantly. "I'll take that."

She looks annoyed and starts to say something, but then her husband says, "Hon," in this warning voice, and she closes her mouth. She takes a minute to close whatever app she was using and turn the power off. Then she smiles tightly and hands the phone, which has this ugly green case with rhinestone shamrocks on it, over to Scott.

"Here you go," she says. "I guess we're not in Kansas anymore." She looks around at the other grown-ups nearby, but none of them seems to want to be part of her joke.

Tilly, though, is totally oblivious to the fact that a joke has even been made. "That's okay," she says to the mom. "You'll like it here better, anyway."

Right away, everything seems kind of strange and lopsided. We're used to having a more even mix of Core Family and Guest Campers, and a lot of the activities are for bigger groups. So now it's like we're all just hovering around this little group of people, focusing all our attention on them. And the mom really isn't very nice. Her name is Frances, but she wants all the kids to call her Ms. Frances. I guess it isn't that weird, but it's not the way we do things here. Which Scott tells her, but she won't budge, so finally he says that he wants her to be comfortable, and since we have a more "intimate" group this week, we can let some of the rules slide. It isn't until I'm thinking about it afterward that I realize: this is the first time I've ever seen anyone have an argument with Scott and win.

It's not a very good week. Tilly and I are still on extra-chore duty, and the signs we have to wear around our necks don't seem particularly funny anymore. Plus, until the Goughs left, it hadn't really occurred to me that any of us *could* just leave. Now that my brain knows it's a possibility, I seem to be thinking about it all the time.

On Wednesday, we're on our way to the dining hall for lunch, when the Fincher boy, Sam, comes running up and says, "There's something wrong with Henny Penny!"

He goes running back toward the chicken yard, with me and Scott and a bunch of other people following. When we get there, I can see that Henny Penny's just lying on the ground, not moving. And I don't want to start crying, in front of all these people, but if Henny Penny's dead, I just don't know if I can handle it. Tilly already looks like she's about to cry, and so does Sam Fincher, which is weird, because he's only known her for like three days, so what does he have to be upset about?

We all gather around in a circle while Scott moves toward her and gently picks her up. I don't know what we're waiting for, because it's not like he's a veterinarian. Or a magician. But he holds the chicken in his hands, warming and stroking her feathers. He's whispering something I can't quite hear; I think he might just be saying, "You're okay." We're all quiet; even Hayden stops whimpering when his dad picks him up. And then Scott closes his eyes, and his lips are moving, like he's praying or saying some kind of wizard spell. For a second, he pulls Henny Penny close to his chest and then, all of a sudden, he raises his arms and tosses her into the air. I gasp, and I hear a couple of other people making little noises, too, because what is he doing? Is he just throwing her on the ground? But he's not. I don't know if he knows this is what's going to happen, or if he's just hoping, but as soon as Henny Penny's body moves away from Scott's hands, her eyes open and she makes a surprised little clucking noise. For a minute, she's still falling, and I'm worried that she's going to get hurt again when she hits the dirt, but just before her feet touch down, she starts to flap her wings. And she's flying.

Scott's grinning like crazy, and it's such a relief to see him happy, and to know that Henny Penny's okay. A few people start laughing, and I hear someone ask, "How'd he do that?"

I feel a hand on my shoulder, and I turn around, and it's my mom.

She folds me up in a hug, and then Tilly comes over and throws her-self against us, and somehow, instead of falling over, we end up in a group hug. After a minute, my dad comes over and says, "Here are all my favorite girls," in that dorky dad way.

Eventually, people start to go back to whatever they were doing before the Henny Penny scare. My family is the last bunch of people to keep standing there in the chicken yard.

"Hey, you know what this reminds me of?" says Tilly. "*Danny, the Champion of the World*, by Roald Dahl. You know that part where Danny and his father want to poach some pheasants, so they grind up sleeping pills and put them into raisins? And then the pheas-ants eat them and fall out of the trees because they're so sleepy."

There's a pause, and then my mom asks, "You think Scott drugged a chicken?"

My dad starts laughing and shaking his head. "I wouldn't put it past him," he says.

My mom hits him lightly on the arm and says, "Shh. Don't say things like that."

"Why?" asks my dad in a stage whisper. "You think his spies are listening?"

"Maybe the chickens will tell him," says Tilly, in her usual way-louder-than-a-whisper voice.

On Thursday, I'm sitting next to Scott at lunch and I ask him, "So are we still playing Werewolf tomorrow? It'll be just me and Tilly and the Fincher kids."

Scott smiles. "I don't see why not," he says. "No minimum player requirements for Werewolf. It's a different game every time, right?"

"Right," I say. For some reason that makes me think about what happened the week that Lincoln was here, when I told Scott about the penis thing and he accused me of lying. I still feel kind of weird about that. But I guess there isn't really anything to say.

I notice that Scott isn't eating; he's just picking at something on the table next to his plate. I look at it and see that it's one of these stickers that the Fincher girl likes to plaster all over everything.

"Does that remind you of Jesse?" I ask, before I have time to wonder if it's a good idea.

But Scott just looks at me blankly, like he doesn't know what I'm talking about.

"Jesse?" he asks.

"Your brother," I say. "The one who died."

Scott wrinkles his forehead and smiles at me. He's looking at me like I'm some kind of puzzle. "I don't know who you're thinking of, kiddo," he says, "but it's not me." He shakes his head. "I don't have a brother. I never did."

chapter 34

Alexandra

January 2012: Washington, DC

It's been a long time since you've worried about getting a call from Tilly's school, so you're not particularly alarmed when you see the school's number pop up on your cell phone screen. You figure it's probably one of the administrators, wanting to set a date for her next IEP.

Instead, it's the head of the middle school, who wants to "give you a heads-up about an incident that happened this afternoon."

Tilly's class had been on a field trip, or rather, on their way to a field trip; more specifically, they were in a van on the Beltway. Tilly got into a disagreement with a classmate and was reprimanded (unfairly, she believed) by a teacher. She then unbuckled her seat belt and succeeded in opening the door of the moving vehicle.

No one was hurt; a teacher's aide with quick reflexes was able to grab her and wrestle her back into her seat, which gave the driver enough time to pull onto the shoulder. But it was scary for everyone in the car. Tilly will be facing three days' suspension, and the school would like you and Josh to come in to discuss a possible "safety plan" for Tilly, to prevent anything similar from happening in the future.

The thing is, you've been thinking lately that everything's going okay. Maybe not in a big-picture, larger sense, but in a day-to-day time-to-breathe kind of way. Lately, your weekly phone consults with Scott Bean—you've been doing these for several months, and Josh doesn't even complain about the money you're spending, because he can see they're helping—have been focused more on questions like "How can I get her to start her homework without a battle?" and less on things like "What do I do when she makes sexual jokes about her dad?"

This "incident" isn't something you process all at once. During the phone call, you're more puzzled than anything else, trying to understand the logistics of what happened. Later, when you pick her up, you're angry, and your mind is busy with setting consequences and asking her what she'd been thinking.

At home, after dinner, as you're going about the evening business of loading the dishwasher and supervising homework, you begin to have flashes of the different ways this day might have ended. But it's not until you hug her at bedtime that you begin to shake.

She's not little anymore. She's going to be thirteen on her next birthday; it's an age when plenty of kids are entrusted with the freedom to leave home without a parent, to walk to a friend's house, to take a city bus to school. But again (and again and again), you have to remember that Tilly is not the same as "plenty of kids."

You and Josh have a fight that night; of course you do. It starts when the two of you are still up in Tilly's room, getting her ready to go to sleep. You're both trying to get at the heart of what happened today, and to ensure that it won't happen again, but your strategies are taking you in different directions. Josh is gently prodding her about her feelings; you're using scare tactics, talking about exactly what happens to a body that goes flying out of a car at fifty-five miles per hour. You know this may not be the best approach, and you can admit that you're freaking out a little, but fuck it. This is important. You simply cannot let this day end without making sure your daughter understands the full impact of what she did today.

Josh is shooting looks at you—quizzical and then borderline aghast—and finally, as your voice gets tight and you're telling Tilly that you couldn't bear to lose her, he shushes you. The two of you have a brief, unsatisfying conversation through gestures and facial expressions, and then you kiss Tilly, pull up her blanket, and storm down the stairs.

He takes a few more minutes; you can't hear what he and Tilly are saying, but you can hear his soft, reassuring tone. By the time he comes back down, you're fuming. You don't really trust yourself; that's part of it. You don't trust your own instincts, especially when it comes to parenting and especially when it comes to Tilly. But he's not the only one who gets to talk. He's not the only one who gets to decide what's okay to say.

"You're an asshole," you say, with no preliminaries. You're whisper-shouting because you know that Tilly's still awake, and she has sharp ears.

"You know what?" he says. "Fuck you. Just . . . fuck you."

And that's as insightful as the discussion ever gets. Later, after you've stormed back up the stairs—Josh remains in the living room, where he'll probably fall asleep on the couch—and cried pitifully about a number of far-ranging things that may or may not have any relevance to the current situation, you wonder how it is that the two of you have never learned how to argue like adults, like thoughtful people who care about each other and know they'll come out stronger on the other side. You're the one who started it, this time around. Did you think you were going to get anything useful out of it? Because all you've done tonight is buy yourself an empty bed and an awkward morning still to come.

Unfortunately, it doesn't seem like either of you managed to get through to Tilly; it's less than a week before the next call. A conflict with her P.E. teacher this time, and a winding stairway with a steep drop down the middle; she made a move like she was going to climb over the railing.

Everyone—teachers, classroom assistants, counselors—is working hard to make sure she's supervised at all times. But she doesn't have a one-on-one aide, and there are eight other kids in her class, each with his or her own set of issues. You don't have any idea what you're going to do if the school decides that they can't manage her anymore.

There really aren't a lot of other options, once your child has been removed from a special-ed school. Well, there *are* other options, but they're grim. There are places that call themselves "centers" instead of "schools." There are "residence programs" for children you can't handle at home. There are psychiatric wards. There are real, honest-to-God padded rooms.

And there's homeschooling. The idea fills you with terror, but maybe it shouldn't. It's important work; it's not that different from deciding to stay home with your kids when they were tiny. You've known for a long time that sitting in a classroom might not be the way Tilly learns best, and you'd be able to tailor her studies to incorporate her interests. You could go on field trips: Washington is a city full of midsized "big people," and you still haven't found time to visit most of them. Jefferson and Lincoln, obviously: both nineteen feet tall, though one is standing and one is sitting, a distinction Tilly takes very seriously. If the marble Lincoln happened to rise up one day, stop slouching in that chair and walk down the steps of his odd neo-Grecian temple, exactly how tall would he be? Well, maybe you and Tilly could figure it out. A math project that meets both her interests and a seventh grade curriculum.

And there are tons of others. There's the new MLK memorial (thirty feet high, emerging in relief from his Stone of Hope) and FDR, oversized but not particularly tall, sitting in his ambiguous wheelchair-like seat. There's a twelve-foot Einstein, sprawling on a bench down by the mall. And a quick search turns up a few you've never even heard of, like a seventeen-foot-tall statue of Mary McLeod Bethune in Lincoln Park.

Tilly might say that it's not fair that it's the presidents and generals, the famous scholars and civic leaders, who get the monuments. But she's also too young to see the way that we're all acting out the same stories, over and over again. We are all, at any given moment, Adam or Eve, Bathsheba or Odysseus or Scarlett O'Hara. The Little Match Girl or someone you read about in the newspaper. Seen from a great distance, it might appear that none of us is ever doing anything new at all.

Imagine if ants made movies. We'd watch one or two of them, out of curiosity, but we'd tire of them quickly, and chances are, we'd miss a lot of the subtlety. We'd have trouble telling the players apart, for one thing, and the stories they told would start to seem like they were all the same. This one dies in the pupal stage, when the workers are forced to flee to avoid a predator. This one breaks off her wings as she prepares to care for her eggs. This one is digging; this one is guarding the nest. But the basic story? They work; they mate; they die. How many of these would we watch before deciding that all ant stories are basically the same?

It's only a matter of weeks before the head of the school calls you into her office and tells you that she's very sorry, that everyone adores Tilly and is going to miss her, but that the school simply can't meet her needs any longer.

You and Josh nod and thank her. It's not unexpected. There's already a list of homeschooling supplies in your Amazon shopping cart. The first thing you do when you get home is make the requisite clicks to place the order.

You don't know how this is going to work, if it's going to be a disaster or the best thing you've ever done. You're torn between seeing yourself as an ant and seeing yourself as a giant.

Imagine if our lives were treated as carefully as the rest of history. Imagine if we were documented as conscientiously, preserved as gently. Each birth at least as important as a naval victory. Each death a national tragedy. There are plenty of ways to remember someone: a park bench, a colossus, an epic poem. Your only job is creating a life that contains a story worth telling.

chapter 35

Iris

July 13, 2012: New Hampshire

On Friday morning, Tilly's acting strange, all giddy and secretive. She tries to hold out on telling me what's up, but I'm good at getting stuff out of her, so she gives in pretty quickly.

Finally, she closes the bedroom door and pulls something out of the pocket of her shorts. It's a phone, an iPhone with green shamrocks on it.

"How did you get that?" I whisper. Our dad's the only other one home, and he's in the bathroom, so I don't think there's much chance he'll hear us.

"It's Ms. Frances's," she says.

"I know, but why do you have it?"

"Last night, after AD Block, I was walking past the office, and I saw a light coming from the window. But not the normal light, just like a little square of light. So I got a little closer, and I saw that it was Ms. Frances, and she was using her phone."

"Really? How did she get it out of the drawer? It's supposed to be locked."

"I don't know," says Tilly. "But I had an idea that she might not remember to relock it when she left. So I waited until after everyone else was asleep, and I went back to the office to check. And . . . ta-da!"

The toilet flushes. "Shhh," I say. We stand there listening, until we hear our dad moving around in the kitchen.

"There's more," Tilly whispers. She's grinning. "I also thought it would be funny if I looked up a whole bunch of porn sites. So that when Ms. Frances gets it back, she'll see all that in the history, and she'll think Scott did it."

I'm smiling along with her now. I'm half horrified and half impressed.

She takes the phone out of her pocket and opens up Safari. The page that pops up is a Google search for "hot shaved teen pussies."

"Ew!" I say, jerking my head away. "How did you even think of that?"

She smiles. "I don't know," she says. "I just did."

"You've got to get the phone back to the office, though, before Scott or Ms. Frances sees that it's missing."

"I will." She stretches and yawns. "I'm really tired today, because I was up almost all night, using the phone. I also logged in to my old email account, to see if Mom and Dad had canceled it, but it still works. I remembered one time when Candy and I were talking about stuff, and she told me what her email address was. So I sent her a picture of Mom and Dad sleeping."

"Did you delete that?" I ask. This is exactly the kind of detail that always trips her up. "If Ms. Frances finds a picture of Mom and Dad sleeping, she'll know that someone else was using the phone. Because why would Scott take a picture of that?"

"Oh my God," says Tilly. "I didn't think of that." She taps away at the screen.

"Girls?" calls my dad. Tilly shoves the phone back into her pocket.

"Yeah?" I say.

"Ten minutes till lunchtime."

"Okay, thanks," I call.

I whisper to Tilly, "Are you going to put the phone back before lunch?"

"No," she says. "Dad will be walking with us. I'll make sure to do it this afternoon."

And so Ms. Frances's phone comes with us into the woods to play Werewolf.

Today, Scott's using Werewolf to teach us about tracking animals, which I guess could be a useful skill . . . if we ever get lost in the wilderness. He's made fake tracks that look like the paws of different woodland creatures, and he has each of us stomp in the dirt, so we can see what kinds of marks our own shoes make.

"What does this have to do with the game?" Tilly asks.

"Nothing," says Scott. "Yet." Then he makes his voice soft and mysterious and chants, "Little feet that run away, what kind of Werewolf is it today?"

The Fincher boy really seems to like that, and he repeats it a couple of times.

"Before we get to the tracking, let's take a look at the exciting items at the Building Store."

I get up and help him pull the sheet off the table, without being asked. I can still be his right-hand girl. There's all the same stuff as last time; I don't really see anything new.

"Now each of you is going to get a special item to help you build your shelter. But to find it, you each have to pick a trail of tracks and see where they lead you."

So we each pick a path and put our newfound tracking skills to work. My path leads me about ten feet into the trees, then right up to a big white box. I'm excited to see it's the dog crate. I haven't looked at it too closely before, but I do now. It's made of plastic, with little windows covered with crisscrossing metal bars. It's going to make an awesome shelter.

I see Tilly following her trail, a little ways off to my right; when she gets to the end, there's a plastic sled waiting. "Cool," she says. Then she sees what I have and yells, "No fair!"

"Too bad," I say in my sweetest/meanest sister voice. "The Werewolf wants what the Werewolf wants."

Tilly stares at me for a minute and then smiles. "I bet you'll look really nice in it," she says.

"Nice and safe from the Werewolf," I say. And then we go our separate ways to build our shelters.

Later, I keep watch for adults while Tilly returns the phone to the office. When she comes back, she says, "Guess what? I sent one more thing to Candy before I put it away. A picture of a sweet little puppy dog named Iris."

I shriek, then cover my mouth, in case anyone's listening. "You did not! I didn't know you even took a picture."

"I did." And then she puts on some kind of villain voice and says, "Never underestimate the Older Sister."

"I never do," I say. "As long as she doesn't underestimate me first."

"What does that even mean?" asks Tilly, and soon we're laughing so hard that it doesn't even matter that we have to put signs around our necks and do our chores.

Dinner is normal, and the campfire is normal, and singing the Camp Harmony song is normal. Tilly and I go back to our cabin, and go to sleep just like we always do. But in the morning, an hour or so after the Finchers leave, a police car pulls up and parks in front of the office. And after that, nothing's normal for a very long time.

chapter 36

Alexandra

March 2012: Washington, DC

Your first few weeks of homeschooling are shaky but successful. Getting set up was fairly easy: less administrative red tape than you'd expected, and tons of resources online. You have a couple of Facebook friends who have been able to make recommendations about schedules and curricula, and you've connected with a few people through local online groups. And you've been talking to Scott Bean on an almost daily basis. He's helpful with big issues and small ones, with advice both philosophical and practical. And he's giving you a discount, because you've been helping him out with things here and there, mostly related to publicity and marketing. He's about to launch a huge new project—a "family camp" somewhere in New Hampshire, with a core group of families living there year-round and weekly parenting sessions during the summer—and he needs help spreading the word. Josh has made snotty comments a couple of times, suggesting that he thinks you're becoming too dependent on Scott, but it's these phone calls that are keeping you sane.

The academic requirements take about five hours a day on average; you and Tilly generally work for three hours in the morning and two in the afternoon. You both go for a walk at lunchtime, weather permitting, and you've signed her up for weekend swimming lessons, to compensate for the lost P.E. component. Socialization is another piece of the puzzle, but you've decided to let that slide for the first month or two. You can't do everything all at once.

You schedule your first field trip for Theodore Roosevelt Island, a trip you owe her anyway, since she's finished filling in the sticker chart you made to help her remember to change her pads when she has her period. You structure the week's history lessons around Roosevelt's presidency (jumping forward temporarily from the Civil War), and you get her reading a kids' biography. For fun, you assemble a YouTube playlist: a clip of a *Simpsons* episode that centers around Bart's interest in TR, an educational cartoon from the '90s, a few sound recordings of Roosevelt's actual speeches. As a long-term plan, you're thinking that some time you should take her to a Nationals game, to see the fourth-inning Presidents Race, with giant mascot heads of Washington, Lincoln, Jefferson, Roosevelt, and (for some reason) Taft, Coolidge, and Herbert Hoover.

The two of you get in the car and head out to Virginia around 10 a.m. It's an easy drive; it's not far from National Airport (which you apparently still refuse to think of as Reagan National, even though it's been almost fifteen years since the name change). You have bottles of water and a picnic lunch. A worksheet full of questions for Tilly to find answers to, and extra sweaters in case it's chilly by the water. You're feeling good. Optimistic, even.

You park and walk over the footbridge that leads to the island.

"Okay," you say. "Easy question. What body of water is underneath us right now?"

"The Potomac," she says. You give her a high five.

Tilly wants to see the statue first, of course. You've printed out a map and studied the crisscrossing hiking trails, so you know that the monument plaza will be somewhere off to your left, after you reach the end of the bridge. Last night on the phone, Scott said, "You know, you and Josh and the girls are exactly the kind of family I'm looking for to help me set up the camp. If you ever decide you're tired of city life and all those daily battles, you let me know."

You laughed and thanked him, flattered but a little weirded out. It's an ambitious plan, this utopian country haven he's imagining for special-needs kids and their parents, but it's a little bit crazy. You're not really sure where he's going to find these families who are willing to give up their entire lives to go raise organic chickens or whatever.

You and Tilly find the right path and start walking. It's a beautiful winter day, chilly but sunny. You'll have to come back in the spring sometime, when there's more plant life and foliage to study. But it's pretty today, too: the starkness of the bare trees, the interlacing shadows on the ground.

It's a weekday so it's not very crowded, but you do pass a few people here and there, running or walking dogs. Tilly's chattering nonstop about the statue: who designed it, when it was built (and dedicated, a whole separate category in statue world), the fact that the architects wanted to showcase Roosevelt in "characteristic speaking pose," which is why he's depicted with one arm raised over his head. You get a few smiles, and an old lady walking a terrier stops Tilly to compliment her on her "knowledge of history."

After a few minutes, you cross a low bridge onto a wide flat clearing, paved in bricks, and there's the statue. Tilly stops and lets out a little gasp; she loves this moment, when the giant first becomes visible, rising up through the landscape of the ordinary world. She takes your hand and pulls you forward.

The two of you admire the monument, which is not terribly big compared to the others on Tilly's lists, but is quite nice, as these things go. You walk together, slowly, around the plaza, checking out the other components of the memorial: a couple of fountains and four giant slabs of marble containing Roosevelt quotes. They're labeled "Nature," "Youth," "The State," and "Manhood."

"They put those up in the '60s," says Tilly. "I think it was kind of a sexist decade."

You let her wander around on her own, and you head over to one of the low marble benches to unpack your picnic. You can tell that she's going to want to stay here for a while.

Through the trees, you can hear a school group approaching, a small chaos of voices and laughter. When the group arrives, you can see that the kids are around Tilly's age, maybe a year or two younger. You can't tell what school, but they're wearing uniforms: khakis for the boys, plaid skirts for the girls, polos for everyone. A different life, and Tilly could have been among them, maybe. They've all ended up in the same place, for today anyway.

You take a bite of your sandwich. Tilly isn't interested in eating yet; she's still looking around. You're facing the "Nature" monolith, and you read over the quotations. *There is delight in the hard life of the open.* You suppose that's what Scott's trying to get at with his camp.

Tilly comes running up. "Can I borrow your phone?" she asks. "I want to take some pictures of the statue."

"Sure." You hand it to her. You watch her approach the statue, walk around it, capture it from different angles. You rummage through your bag for an apple. Some of the kids near you are playing I Spy.

"I spy with my little eye," says one of the girls, "something that begins with *B*."

"Bench!" says a boy.

"No."

"Bug?" says someone else.

"Eww, where?"

"Nowhere, I just thought maybe she saw one."

"Nope," says the first girl. "Not it."

Sometimes your kids used to play this on long car trips. Tilly would change the wording to include a hint. "I spy with my hungry eye," she'd say as you passed a McDonald's.

"I know," shouts another girl. "Barrette!"

"Yes! Finally!"

You smile. Here in a national park, and they're looking at each other's hair.

You hear sudden laughter from over near the statue, and you glance up, some mechanism of maternal radar pinging.

"Oh my God," says one of the kids near you, peering in the same direction. "What the hell is she doing?"

You don't see Tilly at first, so you stand up so you can see over the crowd of heads. She's lying on her back, taking a picture of the statue from underneath. You grab your bag and head over to . . . well, you're not sure what. To protect her, or rescue her, or do damage control, if necessary.

"I spy with my little eye," says a boy behind you. "Something that begins with R."

"Retard?" asks one of the girls. Gales of laughter.

Little bitch, you think, without meaning to.

"Hey, Tilly," you say. She's sitting up now, looking curiously at the group of kids staring at her.

"What?" she says. She's addressing them, not you. "I wanted to get that shot."

A few kids are laughing, but she doesn't seem to notice.

"Don't worry, though," she says. She pauses to stand up and brush herself off. "It may have looked like it, but I wasn't trying to take a picture of his crotch."

Now they're all laughing. "Come eat your lunch," you say. You take her arm, but she shakes you off. She seems glad to have an audience.

"So this statue's only seventeen feet," she says to the group. "But do any of you know what the tallest statue in the world is?"

"Hey," you say, but she raises her voice to talk over you.

"It's not the Statue of Liberty, if you were thinking that. It's the Spring Temple Buddha in Lushan County, Henan, China."

"Come on," you say, pulling her with you. "We've got to go have our picnic. And these kids probably have to get back to their group."

She lets you pull her this time, but yells back over her shoulder, "It's 420 feet! Not counting the pedestal!" You're really not sure—does she not hear that the kids are laughing, or does she just not realize that they're laughing at her?

Last year, for Christmas, the girls got a Wii, and for a while, they spent all their time playing video games. Their favorite was *Mario Kart*. Iris liked to play as one of the grown-up princesses, but Tilly (for reasons that may or may not have been significant) was drawn to the baby characters. Most often, she'd choose to be Baby Peach, who was admittedly adorable: a little golden-haired cherub, crown on her head, pacifier between her lips. Occasionally, it would strike you as funny, the idea of a baby driving a race car, speeding through factories and shopping malls, barreling into gold mines, soaring down mountains, gliding across rainbow tracks in the depths of space.

One day, you were sitting with the girls but not paying much attention, when you heard Tilly make a joke: "Do you think this would be safe, Mommy? To let a baby drive through a volcano?"

You laughed, surprised that she'd thought of it, too. And then you put down your phone, or whatever stupid thing you'd been focusing on, and you watched your children play their game, rooting silently for Tilly to win. Something about it made you want to cry: brave Baby Peach, poised before the volcano. Baby Peach, starting up her motor and driving right into the fire.

You lead her over to the bench where you've left your things and start repacking the picnic food.

"What are you doing?" she asks. "I thought we were going to eat here."

"I think maybe we can find a nice spot somewhere else," you say.

The group of kids have turned away from the statue to watch you. One of them fake-coughs, loudly. "Loser," he calls, tacking it on to the end of the noise.

"What?" asks Tilly. She turns around to look at the kids, bewildered.

"Sweetie," you say. "Let's go."

"Who's a loser?" she asks the group at large.

For a minute, no one answers. Some of the kids look down or hide their laughing mouths behind their hands. Some are still staring openly, enjoying the show. Where the hell are these kids' teachers?

Then a voice from the back of the crowd—you can't tell who's talking or even if it's a boy or a girl—yells out, "You are, you freak!"

It's like they all have permission to talk, suddenly. "Freak!" yells someone else. "No one cares about stupid statues," calls someone else.

You watch Tilly's face as she begins to understand, finally, that they're making fun of her. You watch her crumble right in front of you. She opens her mouth and lets out a surprised little wail. And then, just before the tears start, she turns around and runs.

She's not a fast runner, but neither are you. You follow as she races back the way you came, out of the clearing, into the trees. You keep her in sight, but you can't quite catch up.

"Tilly," you call. "Wait! Tilly!" You're already out of breath.

She's not stopping. You follow her out across the footbridge and into the parking lot. You don't think she has a plan, exactly; she just wants to get away. But the parking lot isn't very wide, just a pull-off directly from the parkway. If she keeps going, she'll reach a bike path, a narrow strip of grass, and then the road itself.

The only reason she doesn't make it—the metal barriers and the cars flying past—is an uneven patch of asphalt in the parking lot. You thank God for the loose gravel, for her clumsy feet. Thank God for her badly skinned knees, bleeding through her jeans. Thank

God for her wrist, for the tiny bone that snaps when she lands and prevents her from going any farther. Because you weren't going to be able to stop her. Your running and screaming and calling her name . . . it did nothing. You don't know why you thought you'd be able to keep her safe. You don't know how you thought you'd be able to do this alone.

One year, you spent the night before Mother's Day in the emergency room at Children's because Iris was vomiting blood. She was maybe a year and a half old. It turned out not to be as bad as it sounded—she just had a regular old stomach virus, and her esophagus had become irritated from all that puking—but you were there for a good long stretch, maybe from 6 p.m. until three or four in the morning, because that's just how long these things take. Iris had thrown up on your shirt in the elevator on the way up from the parking garage—no big deal, the quantities were pretty small at that point—and when the intake nurse asked what color the vomit was, you just showed her the stain. At 11 p.m., you'd seen a doctor and had been sent to an inner waiting room to try to coax Iris to drink something, anything. (You couldn't, which is why you were there so much longer; eventually, they had to give her IV fluids to rehydrate her.) The local news was on, tossing out a progression of increasingly horrifying stories as you held your squirming girl and wiped away each flavor of juice she drooled back out. Against all this, you became aware of a flurry of activity and looked up to see a stretcher rushing past, a child moaning, a mother chasing behind. The TV news had moved on to something fluffier now, because they wanted to end on a happy note, because it was almost Mother's Day. You were happy to sit there all night, if necessary, happy to be a low priority. You were well aware that there were a lot of mothers in the world who were in worse places than you.

Today's trip to the ER is similar on the surface: another long wait, another injury that's low priority and not life-threatening. But not all trauma can be measured by X-ray. Tilly is uncharacteristically quiet and clingy, and you don't want to take your hands off her. Eventually Josh arrives, having sent Iris to a friend's house, and the three of you sit silently, late into the night, huddled together, watching Disney Channel sitcoms on a screen above your heads.

At some endless moment of night, you search through your purse, desperate for distraction, and your fingers land on one of the flyers you've been mailing out for Scott all week. Josh is sitting on the exam table, holding up Tilly, who's fallen asleep against him, her new purple cast resting heavily on her stomach. He looks as exhausted and frightened as you feel.

You're almost finished here; all you need is to be discharged, and you can go home. But that isn't a particularly reassuring thought.

You hand Josh the pamphlet, and he looks at it without seeming to see it.

"I think," you say, but your voice doesn't come out right, so you clear your throat and start again. "I think this is something we might want to consider."

In another world, you make it work. In another world, you never even hear the name "Scott Bean." Or you do, and you maybe even subscribe to his newsletter, but on the night that he comes to speak at a library not far from your house, Iris is sent home from school with a stomach bug, or Josh is out of town and you don't want to hire a sitter. You figure you'll catch him next time. Later, when you hear his name on the news and it sounds familiar, you shake your head and think, "What a wacko." It doesn't even occur to you to say, "That could have been me." Because you know yourself, and it goes without saying. You would never get mixed up in something like that. End of story.

Instead, though, this is where you are. Right here, in the only

world you've ever known. Sitting with your husband in the last sham-
bles of the day. He's got the Camp Harmony flyer in his hand.

"So," you ask him. "What's life without risk?"

He smiles, just a little. "How bad could it be?"

You finish it up: "You've gotta do *something*."

And just like that, you've decided.

You stand up on your tiptoes and kiss your husband. Rough bris-
tles, soft lips, and the relief of being together in this life. For the first
time in a long time, you feel something very close to hope.

chapter 37

Iris

July 14, 2012: New Hampshire

When the police car pulls up, I'm over by the chicken coop, feeding Henny Penny and her babies. I think I'm the first one to see them; everyone else is busy with cleaning the cabins and doing laundry and all that. I stand and watch while two policemen get out of the car and go up to knock on the office door. But nobody answers because nobody's in there, and that's when one of them looks around and sees me.

The two cops come over and introduce themselves, and ask if I know where they can find Scott. I feel really funny about it, because they're being nice and I know that cops are supposed to help people. But I wonder if Scott's in trouble. And I wonder if I *want* Scott to be in trouble.

Anyway, I go with them to help them find Scott, who's in the dining hall, cleaning up from breakfast. He looks surprised to see them, but not worried, and then the three of them go up to the office and stay in there for a long time, like maybe an hour.

After they come out, the cops leave and Scott stays. That's good, right? They didn't arrest him. But he doesn't look too happy when he comes to lunch. And as soon as everyone's finished eating, he stands up and bangs his spoon against his glass.

"Emergency meeting," he says. "Harmony Circle in five minutes."

And I follow him. I follow him because I'm supposed to. Because those are the rules, and when you're here, every adult is your parent. All of us Core Family, kids and adults, form a loose line and follow him into the woods.

We get out there, into the clearing, and we sit down in a circle. No one bothers to make a campfire. It's still the middle of the day.

Scott stands in front of us, doing that thing where he looks at us for a minute before he talks.

"So," he says, finally. "Help me understand what happened here. Did you guys wake up this morning—or maybe yesterday or sometime last week—and say, 'Huh. Looks like a pretty good day to destroy Camp Harmony'?"

No one answers. At the beginning of the summer, I think people would have been yelling out answers, or arguing with him. But now it's like everyone's a kid, even the adults, and Scott's the parent or the teacher or something. We all know we're in trouble, and we all know we should probably just shut up and let him talk.

"Nobody?" Scott says, after a minute. "Interesting. Because actually, that would have been the best-case scenario. If we've got an evil genius here somewhere, executing a brilliant and villainous plan, then maybe there's hope for us getting back on track. But if not, if you're all a bunch of idiots who just stumbled into this, then God help us all."

"Just tell us, Scott," says my dad. "What's going on? What did the police want?"

Scott smiles, but not in a happy way. "What did the police want? They wanted a whole bunch of things. They wanted to know if I was aware that there's a group of people, led by Candy's father and kidnapper, calling themselves the Families Against Scott Bean. Apparently, they're going around telling people that we're running some sort of cult out here. They've got a Facebook page and everything.

"Second, they wanted to show me a picture that popped up today—also on Facebook—of a child in a cage. Allegedly one of our campers." He looks straight at me. I look down at the grass. "They showed me a picture, and I explained that it was part of a game, but they didn't seem too impressed.

"Finally, they wanted me to know that they got a phone call from Frances Fincher, alerting them that someone at this camp has been searching for underage pornography on her phone."

A lot of the grown-ups start talking now and asking questions all at once. Scott stops them by raising his hand.

"None of it's true," he says. "It can all be explained. And as you can see, I'm not behind bars. But it's out there. People are hearing about it and making up their minds about what to believe. You think we're going to recover from that type of damage? You think we've got Guest Campers lined up to join us? No. Because as soon as a story like that gets printed, it becomes the truth. You understand? We're not ordinary people anymore. As far as the whole wide world is concerned, you're all members of a cult. And me? I'm your leader, I'm your Jim Jones. This is who we *are* now; it's our identity. And if you think we can change it, you're wrong."

He pauses and rubs his hands over his face. Then he looks around at us, all of us in a circle, and smiles at us in a way that's sad and kind of tender. "It's just us here, guys," he says. "So tell me: Where did we go wrong? When did you stop believing we had something good going on here, something worthwhile?"

"Scott," says Tom. "I think you're blowing this out of proportion. I don't think this is as bad as you think."

Scott shrugs. "Well, I don't know. Anyway, it's over."

He reaches a hand behind him, like maybe he's tucking his shirt into the back of his pants. And when he brings it forward again, I can see he's got a gun.

chapter 38

Tilly

Date and Location Unknown

There's an odd detail in the margin of the seventeenth panel of the Hammond Tapestry: nestled among the usual marginalia of fruit and cherubs is a black object, half hidden in the embroidered grass. It's small, almost a smudge, but its shape is distinctive; it appears to be a firearm, most likely a revolver.

Scholars are divided over the significance of this object. Elsewhere in the tapestry, marginal embroidery is used to illuminate some facet of the associated main panel, and Panel 17 is a crucial one, as it depicts the moment when Alexandra Hammond first becomes aware of the charismatic speaker Scott Bean and his teachings on Harmonious Parenting. In a Chinese restaurant—you can see, if you squint, the zodiac place mats on the table—two adults and a young girl watch as a second girl kneels beside their table and presses her face to the floor. The girl's behavior is enigmatic: Is she praying? Expressing submission? Enduring some obscure punishment by humiliation? Posture and body positioning are chosen very deliberately in the design of the tapestry; it's unlikely that the ambiguity is accidental.

What we know for sure is this: Alexandra watches as her daughter bends to kiss the dirty tiles of the floor at Bamboo Garden. And somehow this moment is linked inextricably to an ugly black blotch that may or may not be a gun.

What if we say that the final section of the Hammond Tapestry has been missing for as long as anyone can remember? What if we say that maybe it's better if we never find it?

chapter 39

Iris

July 14, 2012: New Hampshire

Everything that happens now is fast and strange and wrong. Scott
has a gun, and he's holding it up in the air, not pointing it at anyone,
just showing us that he has it.

There's noise and movement. I am screaming; everyone is screaming and pushing and starting to run, but Tilly is staring and silent. I
take her arm and try to pull her away; maybe we can run into the
trees, maybe we can escape through the forest. I can't tell if things
are happening fast or slow.

"Stop," says Scott, and I do. I turn back to hear what he's going
to say. "Seriously?" he asks. "Even now, you think that's where this
is going?"

His eyes meet mine, and he gives me a tiny smile. "Don't any of
you trust me at all?"

My mother is pulling on the back of my shirt, and I'm staggering
back, but I struggle against her, because I need to stay here. I need
to keep watching Scott. He needs to know that I do trust him. I trust
him and I keep on trusting him, right up until he lifts up the gun and
sticks it inside his own mouth.

I scream. Someone yells, "No!" Maybe we all yell no. Maybe we all just stay there forever, all of us in the woods, all of us yelling no.

The gun jerks in the air, and there's noise and smoke. For a while, that's all there is; I am made of that noise, I am made of that smoke. And then someone grabs my shoulders and pulls me away, my heels dragging against the dirt. And I don't understand why we're all leaving. And I don't understand why Scott is lying on the ground.

After that, I don't know what happens exactly. We're back at the camp, we're in our cabin, everyone's crying, and my parents make a circle with their arms to hold me and Tilly inside. But Scott stays, lying where he falls. He stays with the dirt and the pine needles, with the smoke and the noise. He stays and stays, even after the rest of us are gone.

chapter 40

Alexandra

March 2013: New Hampshire

Among the million or more unhappy facts you learn that day—how
the police go about testing a witness's hands for gunpowder residue,
what a human being's brain matter looks like when it's spattered on
the trunk of a tree—one of them is this: his name was not Scott Bean.

The name on his birth certificate and his driver's license (neither
of which has ever been seen by anyone at Camp Harmony, because
why would any of you think to ask?) is Jesse Scott. It means nothing
to you, although Iris seems to find it significant: she bursts out with
a confused story about stickers and fire and Scott being mean to a
brother he didn't really have. But like so many other details you
collect during these days, this one doesn't seem to slot into any particularly useful space.

It's true, at least, that he grew up in Montana. He was born to a
teenage girl (unmarried) and was given up for adoption: not at birth,
but at the age of three. This, at least, seems significant, though exactly
what it signifies remains unclear. He ended up in the foster care system, but never stayed with a single family for more than a year; he
had trouble in school, was branded a difficult child, and managed to

scrape by on the right side of delinquency until he turned eighteen and could be released to take care of himself.

So that explains it, maybe. But which part? His empathy toward children who were different or his grandiose (and sometimes paranoid) belief that he was the only one who could possibly help them? Is it more important that he was fired from a teaching job for striking a kid—another thing that Iris inexplicably knows before you do—or that every child who spent time at Camp Harmony seemed to improve under his care? Which matters more: that for a short time, you were happier than you'd been in years, or that you're not sure you'll ever stop hearing gunshots in your sleep? That he lied to you in order to convince you to give up every piece of the life you knew, or that you're still not sure you were wrong to do it?

All of it; some of it; none of it. Like always. Like everyone.

Time passes and passes. Afterward, of course, life is never the same.

Not that you'd choose to put it so starkly, but it seems to be important to the girls—Tilly especially—to acknowledge and quantify the accumulation of loss. And this "never the same" business is the one that seems to be hardest for them to accept, harder than the sale of the house in Washington, harder even than the memory of the woods, Scott's fallen body, the leaves speckled with red.

They're too young to understand how much of life is shaped by *never the same.* "You know, my life was never the same after you girls were born," you tell them lightly, and you leave them to process it on their own.

In Iris's nightmares, Scott doesn't have a gun; for reasons whose meaning eludes you, he's always holding a knife, drawing it slowly across his own throat. In Tilly's dreams, the gun is front and center, and it's always pointed directly at her. She wakes up when he pulls the trigger.

You spend a lot of time with them in the middle of the night, sitting in the dark, helping them fall back to sleep. You don't mind it so much; it's like when they were babies or when they're sick. Their need for you is sweet in its urgency, its simplicity.

Your life now: well. It's been hard, obviously. What do you do when everything is suddenly over? You cling to each other. You strip away everything that doesn't matter. And sometimes, when your head stops spinning, you find that you've touched down in a land that you never would have discovered otherwise.

It turns out that Scott was right about how the world at large would interpret his legacy. The general consensus (and it doesn't seem to matter what you have to say about it) is that you were taken in by a dangerous man, and you're lucky that the outcome wasn't worse. Maybe. But in your own mind, it's a lot murkier than that. How do you feel about Scott Bean? You are furious at him; you hate him; you miss him terribly. It's going to be a long, long time before you have it all figured out.

Here's one of the details that tends to get overlooked in the news articles: back in the heady days when you were helping Scott plan Camp Harmony, one of the things that everyone agreed on was that the land should be owned equally by all of you. No one coerced you into anything—at least, not financially. You acted like grown-ups: you consulted lawyers, drew up documents, changed your wills. So after Scott's death, one of the many questions left for you and the other Camp Harmony families to answer was what would happen to the site itself.

The Goughs just wanted out, understandably; they asked you to wire them their share. The last you heard, Candy's dad had surrendered custody and turned himself in, though it remains to be seen what kind of consequences he'll face, if any. Like everything else here, it's complicated.

There was never any question of continuing to run the camp. But none of you seemed to want to leave right away: not you and Josh, not Tom and Janelle. At first it was barely even a decision, more of a stunned stasis. But when you were finally able to talk about it, you all believed that there might yet be something you could salvage from all of this. Not all of your ideas had been bad ones. There's something to be said for choosing the company you want to keep; for living more simply; for getting support for the things you don't know how to do on your own.

This winter you've been living in rental housing, homeschooling Tilly and Hayden; Iris is enrolled at the local middle school—her own choice. You've demolished the cabins and are currently drawing up plans for new housing and looking into the process of opening a charter school. It's all very tentative and fragile, far from perfect, and a lot of the time you feel like you don't know what the hell you're doing. You wouldn't say that you wake up every morning filled with joy, but there are days when the sheer lack of dread strikes you as miraculous.

You put it together bit by bit. You go to therapy. Josh takes on some consulting work, long distance. It's not a permanent solution, but he's around more than he used to be, and the cost of living is lower here.

You have time and space and friends. You're thinking about what kind of community you want to be a part of. Josh's mother will be retiring next summer, and you've talked about asking her to come live in New Hampshire. You'll certainly have room for her.

Maybe you actually learned something from those video games you used to play: there's no point in planting crops if you're not going to stick around to tend them.

You've started writing, just a few lines here and there. It's finally occurred to you that you might have something to say. Notes on autism and parenting, conversations overheard from the next room. You're thinking that maybe soon you'll get around to the question of cults and the potent mix of desperation and charisma that helps them thrive. Questions of personal agency and what makes some help dangerous to accept. Right now, the most concise thing you can say about it is this: You know Scott Bean wasn't a villain. Your life will never be the same. And you're grateful every day.

The Hammond Family Monument, you and Tilly decide during one of those middle-of-the-night conversations, is unusual in that it's not fixed in space. Its location—and even its design—is always changing. It hovers in the air outside a house in Washington, DC, and in a forest clearing in New Hampshire where the rain is doing its patient work to wash the rocks clean of blood. It appears for brief moments on the side of a mountain and inside a Chinese restaurant with a slightly grubby floor. You can't always see it, but it's there in the landscape of your dreams and the stories you tell about your life. It's hidden in plain sight, waiting to make its appearance in places you haven't even visited yet.

You've set up a life where your girls have fewer rules; they're allowed to ramble, in their minds and along winding paths lined with pine trees. Iris is adjusting beautifully, all things considered, and that's hardly a surprise. But Tilly. Tilly unconstrained is a magnificent thing to see.

Every day brings something new. She's writing a book; she's designing a video game; she's filling the sky with new constellations. There's a lot that she still needs help with, a lot that will need to happen in a few short years, if she's going to be able to face the world on her own. But these talents she has—imagination and empathy, ambition and eagerness—will carry her a long way.

She's a great kid. And as the days go by, you're beginning to remember where she gets it from.

epilogue

Imagine that your child is born with wings. It's a good thing, right? The freedom to step off the earth, to glide and soar and float. It represents not just flight, but the potential for flight. It works with all the metaphors of child-rearing.

You can see that there might be a downside; it makes things a little more complicated. She's going to get teased; some people will stare. And the onesies you've bought aren't going to fit, not without some alteration. There are plenty of things you could worry about, plenty of things you haven't planned for, but so what? She's your girl.

Her wings are small at first, like the rest of her. Feathered little nubs, lying folded against the skin of her back. They flutter against your arms while you're nursing her; you see them twitching while she sleeps. And even though you wouldn't say it in public, even though you gently remind strangers and friends alike that she's not a supernatural being but an ordinary flesh-and-blood human baby, you can't help but call her your angel once in a while.

When she learns to walk, you buy one of those child leashes. They have nice ones now, not horrible at all: the one you buy is a furry backpack that looks like a monkey, with an extra strap to secure it around her torso. As she zigzags down the street, three feet above the sidewalk, you keep a tight hold of the long tail.

Safety issues are different than they are with other children. She can't sit comfortably in a stroller or car seat without some jury-rigging. When visiting friends, the first thing you do is look around for ceiling fans and open windows. You have to be extra-careful with breakable items and cleaning products and medications. Whenever you see the phrase "Keep out of the reach of children," you feel like calling the company and not hanging up until you find the right person to talk to. You want to explain your situation; you want to talk until you can make someone understand why you're going to need alternate directions.

At the park, reactions are mixed. Other parents are kind and interested, or else they won't meet your eyes. "Watch her, please," one mother says sharply when your daughter flits up and tries to land in the stroller that holds her new baby.

Your daughter wrenches a shovel away from a little boy in the sandbox, carrying it up as far as she can go on her tether. As you're handling the negotiations of sharing and apologizing, tugging gently to pull her back to earth, you see the moment when she realizes the paradox: she can keep the shovel away from the other children, but only if she never settles down in the sand to dig.

Your second child is born without wings. This is something that none of the parenting books cover. You find yourself loving this new child, this ordinary child, almost guiltily. Before you became a parent, this is what you'd imagined it would be like. This baby rolls on a blanket and finds tiny pieces of carpet fluff to put in her mouth. Baby-proofing takes place much lower to the ground. When you put her in her crib, you don't have to zip a mesh tent over her to keep her from gliding over the railings during the night.

Your older daughter is fascinated by the soft, smooth skin of her sister's back. One day, she asks when the baby's wings are going to grow in, and you begin a conversation that you'll probably be having for years. You tell her that the world is rich and varied; you tell her that we're all different, and we're all the same. Your task here is clear, and it isn't really so different from anyone else's. Like every parent, you have to teach your girl to live a contradiction, to be exceptional and ordinary, all at the same time.

You figure out ways to make it work. You enlist her help in dusting high corners and painting over water spots on the ceiling. You divide your grocery list into high shelves and low ones, ripping the paper in half and giving each child a piece to carry around the store. You make up new verses for the Hokey-Pokey.

Eventually, the time comes when there's no way you can justify the leash. You set ground rules for flying: no flying at school, with a babysitter, or at a friend's house. No flying higher than Daddy's head. No flying across or above the street. No lifting anyone else to fly with you.

Clothes are an issue: as she grows, so do her wings. In the summer, in the early years, you generally let her go shirtless—let them *both* go shirtless, since it's hard to make it seem fair to a two-year-old that she has to wear a shirt and her sister doesn't. Your neighbors grow used to the sight of the two of them half naked in your front yard, making up elaborate games and mixing messy concoctions of mud and leaves. Sometimes when they're caught up in playing, you see your older girl begin to flap her wings in excitement, not remembering until she's a few feet off the ground that her sister doesn't like it when she flies away from her. Her wings are remarkably expressive. She folds them up tight when she's sad or hurt; when she's happy, she flutters them softly, without seeming to notice that she's doing it.

You remember being slightly horrified when a well-meaning aunt gave you a sewing machine at your bridal shower, but now you use it regularly. You cut long slits up the backs of your daughter's shirts, then stitch the edges so they won't fray. On cold mornings, it takes a while to work her wings through the different layers, and you're impatient with her when she won't stand still. Occasionally, someone will ask you if you would change things if you could, but it's not a question that makes much sense. Your daughter has wings, and without them, she would not be your daughter. This is not the way you thought things would be, but it doesn't make you wish there were someone else sleeping in her bed.

Her wings are, in many ways, just another part of her body. You pour soapy water over them in the tub; you pat them dry with a bath towel. She asks you to scratch them when she has an itch, and you run your nails gently over the stretches of feathered muscle, the hollow bones jutting at unexpected angles. They seem to get more sensitive for a while when she's going through puberty; she complains that it hurts to lean back against the solid surface of a chair. It occurs to you once—one of those thoughts you wish you hadn't had, but there's not much you can do about it now—that perhaps someday they'll be an erogenous zone for her. That her husband or boyfriend or partner or whatever—well, that's as far as you want to take it, which is just as well, because that's the part that stops you every time. You hope. You hope she'll have everything she needs. Air and sky and, maybe one day, someone to fly beside her.

acknowledgments

My first thank-you, as always, goes to my extraordinary agent, Douglas Stewart, who has continually proven himself to be my best and shrewdest ally. I am also enormously grateful to my editor Pamela Dorman for her enthusiasm, support, and laser-sharp insight.

Thank you to the many wonderful people at Viking Penguin who helped bring this book into the world; I am especially grateful to Madeline McIntosh, Brian Tart, Andrea Schulz, Kate Stark, Lindsay Prevette, Rebecca Lang, Megan Gerrity, Mary Stone, Lydia Hirt, Jeramie Orton, and Emma Mohney. Thank you as well to the many fabulous readers in the sales department and beyond who provided such important early support for the book.

Thank you to Madeleine Clark, Taylor Bacques, Szilvia Molnar, and Danielle Bukowski at Sterling Lord Literistic; to Carole Welch, Nikki Barrow, Caitriona Horne, and Jenny Campbell at Sceptre; to Shari Smiley at the Gotham Group; and to Alison Callahan, who championed the book at its very earliest stages.

Thank you to the MacDowell Colony and the Virginia Center for the Creative Arts, for providing me with much-needed time and space to write. (And a separate thank-you to the mysterious forces of the MacDowell Oracle, which told me in no uncertain terms that it was time to insert a werewolf into my current work.)

I have been extremely lucky to have a number of kind, talented, and hilarious friends who have made every part of this journey easier. Many, many thanks to Leslie Pietrzyk, Amy Stolls, and Paula

Whyman for their ongoing support, advice, and friendship. Thank you to Cathy Alter and Michelle Brafman for reading early drafts and providing invaluable suggestions, and thank you to Caitriona Palmer, Kimberly Stephens, Judith Warner, Alexandra Zapruder, and Mary Kay Zuravleff for lunches, laughter, and helping keep me sane. Thank you to the wonderful community at Writers Room DC, including the father-son super-duo of Charles and Alexander Karelis. And thank you to Tracey von Phul Christensen, who was so helpful in answering my questions about homeschooling.

I owe much love and gratitude to my family—especially my mother, Doreen C. Parkhurst, MD; my father, William Parkhurst; and my grandmother Claire T. Carney, to whom this book is dedicated—for a lifetime of inspiration and encouragement. Many thanks also to Molly Katz, to all of my Carney uncles and aunts and cousins, and to Julie Ross, Matthew and Margaret Rosser, and David and Lynette Rosser.

Thank you to my children Henry and Ellie, who continue to amaze me and to teach me new things every day. And infinite thanks to my husband Evan Rosser, for each year of adventure and comfort, joy, and support.

And finally: Thank you to special-education teachers, every single one. Thank you to occupational therapists, physical therapists, and speech therapists. Thank you to pediatric neurologists and educational consultants, IEP coordinators and psychopharmacologists. Thank you to classroom aides and the National Institutes of Health. Thank you to Temple Grandin and John Elder Robison, Andrew Solomon and Simon Baron-Cohen. Thank you to respite workers and babysitters, camp counselors and leaders of social skills groups. Kind neighbors and helpful strangers, overheard conversations and anecdotal evidence. Thanks to newspapers left on buses and the mysterious forces that dictate chance meetings. Thank you to the solace of the Internet, open all night, and to bright mornings that keep on arriving, no matter what.